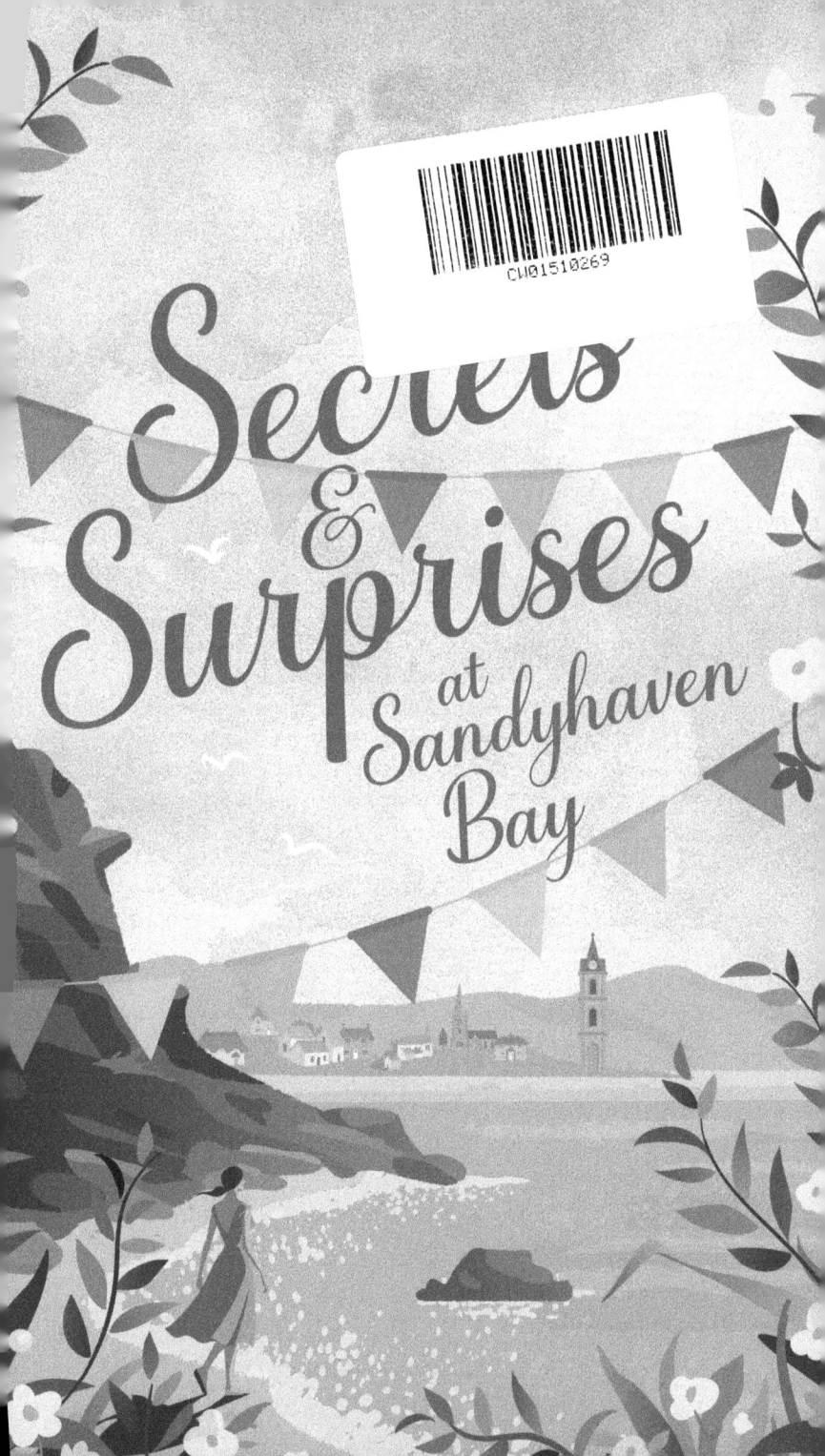

Secrets
&
Surprises
at
Sandyhaven
Bay

Secrets & Surprises at Sandyhaven Bay

Copyright © 2025 Kate Hepplewhite

Cover and Interior Design by We Got You Covered Book Design
WWW.WEGOTYOUCOVEREDBOOKDESIGN.COM

Secrets & Surprises at Sandyhaven Bay

KATE HEPPLEWHITE

Dedicated to past me, who never could have imagined in her wildest dreams that she would be reading this from her own actual book.

You did it! X

One

*L*eaves of golden brown and fire red swirled along the pavement like a vortex. Despite the clear sky and gleaming sun, the early September wind possessed an undeniable chill, causing Millie to swaddle her cardigan further around her body. Escapee hairs fluttered around her face as she meandered slowly down the narrow-cobbled street, heading towards the beach. She was getting closer, she could tell; mainly because she had now walked this path three times, but also because she could feel the wind getting stronger. A sure sign the sea was close. Sure enough, the tiny walkway opened out onto what she imagined was the village square. Instantly, she could tell it was the hub of Sandyhaven; the quaint pub on one corner emanated the soft sound of voices, presumably regulars in for Sunday lunch. Even the faint smells of Yorkshire puddings and roast chicken couldn't tempt Millie away from her trail.

A few metres more, a stony ramp down and she felt sand bouncing underneath her boots.

An immediate wash of familiarity bathed over her, despite having only visited here just a few times. There was something about this tiny village; the pretty brick cottages coated in camellias and crawling ivy, the narrow streets barely wide enough for a single car, and the beach, both pebbly and sandy in different places, accompanying the breaking waves. It felt like she had lived here all her life when, in reality, it had been barely a week.

Finding a quiet spot (which wasn't hard now all the holidaymakers had left in their droves), she perched on the sand, finding a smooth part, not far from the foaming waves. Squinting slightly from the brightness, she carefully removed an errant strand of hair from her eyes. Barely any sounds could be heard, only Mother Nature's beautiful thrum. She *should* feel calm. She *should* feel at peace. In theory, this would be the perfect place to come to escape from everything.

Why then, at this point, did her eyes fill with tears? Why did she bow her head and why did the most pained tears of desperation course down her face?

It had all happened so quickly. One minute she was jumping off the bus, tapping up the steps to the tiny flat in Holborn which she shared with her boyfriend of nearly four years, Sam. An early finish on a Friday was practically unheard of and she was ready to embrace the weekend with open arms. The key turned in the lock, the comforting smell of home washing over her. The house was quiet but she had expected that; Sam was still at work. She was looking forward to having a few hours of quality alone time; a long hot bath, some proper skincare and then making a start on a new painting. As a talented artist, it was a real passion – one day she hoped to do something more proactive with her creative skills but for now, experimenting at home would have to do.

It was only as she reached the halfway landing on the stairs that she realised something was amiss. Noises. Frowning deeply, she continued cautiously, uneasily. They were coming from their bedroom. With a shaking hand, she quickly pushed her bedroom door open. What she saw was sickening and shocking.

"Millie?! Why aren't you at work?!"

Despite her trembling lip and stinging eyes, she'd had to smirk to herself. As if the sight of Sam on top of another woman wasn't shocking enough, she had then reeled from his accusatory question of why she'd left work early! Surely the real interrogations should have come from her? More along the lines of *'what the hell are you doing in our bed with another woman?'* The question was never asked. Millie knew that they'd had problems. She knew their relationship wasn't where it should be at. But she'd sort of hoped he would have communicated his apparent need to move on in a slightly less physical and obvious way, with her alone, rather than letting her find out as explicitly and callously as she had.

She roughly wiped her eyes with the back of her hand. Wearing no mascara made this easier; in fact, she couldn't remember the last time she had worn make-up. It seemed an irrelevant, menial exercise, despite her now having all the time in the world. This sleepy village she'd found herself in seemed to wait for everyone and everything. It was stuck in its own time-warp. She reckoned nothing had changed for years.

"What do you mean, you're moving to *Cornwall?*" Jenny stared at Millie, mouth agape.

"Exactly what I just said. I'm moving to Cornwall." Millie remained monotone, continuing to throw things sporadically into a suitcase. She had to remain stoical. It was the only thing stopping her from breaking down completely. Jenny's mouth remained open, shutting every now and again like a goldfish.

"But…but *why?*"

"I have to get out of here, Jen. Out of this house and out of this area. I can't stay here after what has happened."

"Well yeah, I get that. Everyone needs a fresh start after a breakup, God knows after being cheated on as well. But people usually move in with a friend, move back in with parents…" – she stopped at this point and swallowed hard, realising what she'd said. Millie paused her packing for a moment but didn't break eye contact with her suitcase. Re-composed, she carried on. Jenny continued: "What I'm saying is, yes, they move on. But they don't move 250 *miles* on! I mean, why Cornwall? It's the back-arse of nowhere!"

"Exactly," Millie declared, pushing down heavily on the items in her case, in an attempt to flatten them. "That's exactly why I'm doing it. As far away as possible." Jenny watched her, concern etched on her face. She watched her best friend of many years struggling, becoming frustrated and reached for her wrists, gently stopping them moving. Her tension was palpable.

"But you're going to be on your own. You don't know anyone in Cornwall?" she reasoned gently. Millie turned to her, eyes glistening.

"I know. But I just want to get away. Start afresh. Apart from you, Sam was the only thing binding me to London. And you have your own life here – you're married, you're pregnant. You're going to want to move out of the city soon, you won't stay here forever. Without you, I have nothing. I need to start building a new life for myself, Jen. A life that I've built *myself*."

Jenny's eyes remained on her, searching her face for any signs of uncertainty. But she found none. Ten years of friendship gave you an unlimited pass to the thoughts and emotions of the other person and she could tell Millie's mind was firmly made up. Jenny's thumbs gently grazed her best friend's wrists, and she allowed the tears to spill. Firmly, she threw her arms around her shoulders and squeezed, causing Millie to give a joking exhale. Gently pulling away, Jenny sniffed.

"What about your job? What about money?"

"I still have mum's money," Millie replied, wiping her own nose. "It's about time I put it to some use."

The giggle of some children snapped Millie back to her

present moment on the beach. She seemed to be doing that a lot lately: missing the present moment. Living in the past. The wretched squawking of seagulls, now such a familiar background noise, resonated across the sky. She watched as one of them, larger than a small cat, dived down and aggressively yanked an ice cream from a small child's hand. The girl blinked several times from shock, before bursting into tears. She watched as her family comforted her, checking she was OK, the mother blowing delicately on her hands while the father shooed away the hovering birds. She recognised the family: they lived a few doors down. The girl must have been around six, her brown hair fashioned into pigtails, a ribbon wrapped around both. The mum looked about Millie's own age, she thought, pretty and young. The dad was attractive, she couldn't help thinking, tall and broad. The perfect family. Millie swallowed harshly. Everything she'd wanted to be.

"It's not your fault," Sam had repeated continuously. *"It's just one of those things."*

"One of those things." Just like being cheated on with the hot fitness instructor from next door.

It was just as she managed to get the logs to catch later that day, that the phone rang. Blowing out the match furiously before it burnt her fingers, Millie dropped it into the washing up bowl and answered the phone.

"Millie? Hi it's Alan."

"Oh, hi Alan, how is everything?"

"It's fine thank-you. And with you? I'm sorry I haven't got

around to calling you properly yet." She knelt and prodded the logs with the poker, trying to spread the growing flames. She didn't really have a clue what she was doing, it's just what she'd seen before in films.

"That's OK, I guessed you might be busy," she replied, a guilt tinging her voice.

"Things are a bit manic, but it's all going alright. Your replacement is doing well."

Alan had been Millie's boss. A life-long friend of her mum's, she had worked for him for just over a year. Office work, assistant, general dogsbody; that sort of thing. When the news of her breakup struck, happening only months after the death of her mother, Alan had suggested she take some extended leave. However, he'd then taken it one step further with his next suggestion. He owned Rosemary Cottage in the idyllic village of Sandyhaven in Cornwall. The cottage had been in his family for many years and he'd kept it on so he'd have somewhere to stay when on extended visits to his son, who also lived in the village (though they hadn't happened for quite some time, instead frequented by tourists). After all, London to Cornwall wasn't exactly a fly-by visit. Alan, feeling an overwhelming sense of sympathy for Millie and after hearing her pleas for a fresh start, had offered out the cottage for her exclusive rent. He'd rather it be occupied all year round than just sitting there getting damp.

Alan had taken Millie under his wing since her mother's passing and, whilst it was a scary prospect, the glinting of hope in her eyes made it clear he'd offered a good suggestion.

"I meant to say, it'll probably start to get a bit chilly down there now, especially at night. You'll have to use the card to get your electric topped up for the heaters. It's in the drawer in the sideboard. Sorry I haven't told you already, you must be freezing."

"No problem, I've got the fire going," she explained, a faux brightness to her voice whilst simultaneously pulling a face at the pathetic flickers behind her. Standing up and moving over to the sideboard, she rummaged and found that, indeed, a top-up card lay in the drawer.

"Excellent. I do prefer a real fire, I have to say," he said. "Has my son popped round yet?"

"Not yet," Millie answered, relieved to see the flames finally begin to spread, offering wonderful warmth.

"Ah, typical Alfie. He's probably locked in his house, staring out that window of his."

"Oh, is he a birdwatcher?" she asked in confusion. Alan let out a small chuckle.

"No no, not a birdwatcher. He's an artist. Spends most of his life conjuring up paintings, drawings, sketches. All forms of art, all different tools – it doesn't really matter what he uses, so long as he can make marks with it." The admiration in Alan's voice was clear. Millie smiled and felt a tinge of excitement that there was someone else close by whom had a passion for art, even though she'd never met him. "Well, I'll give him another call, remind him to pop over sometime and check you're all OK. You know you can call me if you need anything."

"Thanks Alan. I'm fine really." There was a pause on the other end. She bit her thumbnail agitatedly – she hated these silences. She never knew what to say. "I'd better get going then. Few things to sort out, you know."

"Of course!" he said abruptly then. "Speak soon, Millie. Take care of yourself."

She hung up the call and placed the phone back in her pocket. Glancing around the room, she wondered what those "things" were she needed to sort out. As far as she was aware, tonight would be spent doing the same as every other since moving here. Staring into space. Wondering what on Earth she was doing with her life.

"There's nothing that can be done. It's purely a case of this being the hand you've been dealt. I'm sorry Miss Jones." Millie swallowed back tears, trying to focus on the doctor's face but watching it swirl and ripple before her eyes.

"But…but there must be something…" Sam's voice was stuttering, disbelieving. She turned her head to glance at him, her blink allowing tears to fall violently from her eyes. She could feel the wetness of her eyelashes, the dewy droplets gathering like raindrops in a puddle. A puddle felt like the perfect metaphor for her life right now. A cold, muddy puddle.

"I'm afraid not Mr Ashton. Sometimes there are things we can do but there is nothing. There are of course other avenues, but for your partner, there is little that can be done." The doctor's

voice was clipped and to the point, yet Millie knew they were just doing their job. Once she and Sam had left the room, they would gather up their notes, file them away somewhere dark and dusty and move onto the next patient. All in a day's work.

Nodding in defeat, Millie stood up, patting Sam on the arm as if to signal her need to exit. She thanked the doctor, who handed her a pile of leaflets. Crumpling them in her fist, Millie exited the room, her legs leaden, as though she were weighed down with half a tonne of bricks. The floor felt strange beneath her, like it wasn't there. She wasn't sure if gravity was present anymore. She'd held it together all the way to the car but as soon as Sam's passenger door slammed shut, she slumped forward and broke down. Sam was trying to say words of comfort, but she couldn't hear them over the howls of her own breaking heart.

Two

She woke with a start. Where was she? Fumbling frantically, she located her glasses next to her on the pillow, where they'd stayed when she'd dropped into a sleeping pill induced coma the night before. Everything moved into focus. Gradually, her heart rate slowed, and her breathing returned to normal as she took in her new bedroom, small but cosy. She was here, of course. In her new home.

It wasn't the deafening sound of her cries in her dream that had awoken her though. It was a banging on the door. Panicking, Millie flung the covers back and peeked out the window, which looked directly down to the front door. A man was standing there. A rather handsome man, she couldn't help but think. He was tall with dark hair and reasonably large shoulders. She couldn't see much else from up here. Who on Earth was this man and what was he doing at her door?

He knocked loudly again, and she saw him glance at his watch. Oh God. She flapped around, yanking her dressing gown on and very quickly scanning her face in the mirror. Why did she care? She wasn't trying to impress anyone. Just as well, really. Unless the visitor had a penchant for puffy eyes, chapped lips and messy hair, she was going nowhere fast. The door rapped again, two quick ones this time, as though he were growing more impatient. She dashed down the stairs, every creak showing the cottage's age. By the time she'd scrabbled with the lock and got the door open, there was no-one there. She leant her head out the door and saw the back of the man, striding away.

"Excuse me!" she shouted, causing an old lady walking past with her dog to jump. Millie smiled apologetically, her cheeks reddening at the woman's scowl. The mystery man turned around and studied her, an eyebrow raised. "Sorry I…I was in bed." The eyebrow moved up a little further. Was that thing on a string?

"At half ten?" he countered, walking back towards her. She blushed further. She hadn't realised it was so late. To be honest, she hadn't got into a routine here yet. She was just grateful to have slept at all. She studied his face, not liking his judgemental stare. *Who was this man?*

"Um, what did you want?" she asked as kindly as she could, wrapping her dressing gown further around her, aware her pyjama top was a little revealing for a first-time meeting someone.

"I'm Alan's son, Alfie? Dad asked me to drop round and

check how you are. But if it's too early for you, I can always pop back later…?" She didn't like his tone. Who was he to judge her and her time of rising? He didn't know her story?! Besides, it was half ten on a Tuesday. If *he* was so important, why was he able to wander freely round the village, knocking on strange women's doors instead of being in some important job?

"Oh. Well, yeah, I'm fine," she replied, unsure what to say. She was still acutely aware of being stood in the street in her unicorn pyjamas and fluffy dressing gown. She noticed the elderly man across the road watering his plant in the bedroom window, staring down at her. She nodded her head awkwardly in acknowledgement. Alfie glanced upwards and then stared back at her closer and she could feel her face flushing again. Despite the sheer awkwardness of this three-way exchange, she noticed herself eyeing him up now she could see him better from down here. He was tall and his dark hair extended to the stubble on his chin and jawline. He had dark eyes, and his skin was much more tanned than hers, she guessed as a result from the Cornish summer just gone by.

He continued to stare at her, giving nothing away. "Great. Then I guess I needn't have bothered coming round," he said shortly. "If you need anything, here's my number." He reached into his back pocket and pulled out a small card, which he held out between them. Taking it, she saw from a quick glimpse *"Alfie Drew. Artist. Ring for commissions."* And then a phone number.

"But it seems like you have it all sussed," he finished.

And with a cursory glance up and down, he turned and walked away! Millie stood in shock. How could a man be so *rude?* Particularly being Alan's son; her lovely, laid back, down to Earth boss who would do anything for anyone? It wasn't possible. Clearly, Alan's gentle nature hadn't rubbed off on his son.

Closing the door gently, she leant against it and exhaled. One thing was for sure: she wouldn't be ringing Alfie Drew for anything, even if he was the last rude, arrogant, exceptionally good-looking man on earth.

Alfie heard the cottage door click shut as he strode off down the lane. Yet another person from the city with too much money taking up space in his Mum's cottage. He was fed up with being his dad's runaround, constantly coming up to "help" when most of the time the issues were so minor they were laughable.

He thought back to the young couple who had stayed a few months ago, who had contacted his dad in a panic when they "couldn't locate the air con switch." It had been a spell of unseasonably hot weather in April, yet when Alfie had been sent up and told them that Cornish air conditioning was opening a window, they had looked at him with a most bemused expression.

Then there was the elderly couple last year – they'd complained in their review that there were too many "mod cons" in the cottage, referring specifically to the kettle, stating it wasn't authentic enough. The urge for Alfie to go round, unplug their kettle and chuck it out the back door had been tremendous. It seemed all people wanted to do was complain about the cottage, either about things it did or didn't have and it infuriated him. That cottage was his Mum's. It belonged to her. He could still picture her in there, with him and to have people in the space at all, let alone complaining about it and not appreciating it for the amazing space it was, was very difficult for him.

His phone buzzed twice in quick succession in his pocket. He cursed, yanking it out and checking the screen. One message from dad – **thanks for popping round, appreciate it**. He considered not replying but knew it would be easier to just type out a brief **no probs** and be done with it. Another message appeared from Dana: **I've just arrived and you're not in – where are you!?** He sighed in frustration, shoving the phone back in his pocket. He really didn't need this stress right now. Why was it he could never do the right thing? It wasn't like he had four commissions to complete before the end of the month, aside from having to babysit some random woman who clearly had no desire to even get out of bed and do something with her day. And then to have Dana on his case as well – it was too much.

Alfie couldn't keep up with Dana and her temperamental attitude towards their relationship. She had started as a mutually casual "situationship" after meeting on a night out (not his usual style at all, but a *lot* of Guiness had been consumed.) He hadn't been looking for a relationship; he never was. He couldn't deny that she was completely gorgeous. In a nutshell she was petite, drove a zippy Mini Cooper, had long blonde hair and worked as a representative for an affluent PR firm up in Manchester. Her wealthy parents lived just outside of Truro, the nearest city to Sandyhaven, which is where they'd met. She visited her parents a couple of times a month and would always come to see him too. She'd insisted she was serious about him and constantly nagged him to move to Manchester with her, but his instinct told him he was just a convenient relationship and several times he'd suspected she was seeing other people up in Manchester.

He genuinely liked her when they were alone together – she could be much more down-to-earth and low maintenance this way and whilst they didn't share all the same interests, they could make each other laugh. She just seemed like a completely different person when she was out in public, and he found it hard to manage. And in comparison, her personality online was like that of a stranger. To look at her social media, it was as though she were a single woman. It was all very confusing.

Plus, Alfie was incredibly busy now that his business had grown and, to be honest, he liked time and space to himself. He found the times she was away were the most peaceful. Alfie going to check on this new woman in the village and leaving Dana alone at his front door had not gone down well, as her text message had clearly implied.

With a yawn and a vicious ruffle of his hair, Alfie picked up the pace to get back quickly. He wanted to avoid an argument today if possible; Dana's arguments were usually long-winded, and he had the finishing touches to add to one piece of work, as well as completing the underpainting of another large canvas. Yes, this Millie woman had really messed up his morning.

Three

It had taken Millie several minutes to manoeuvre precariously out of her tiny space: say what you like about how lovely tiny villages are; they were a bugger for parking. Still, at least she had her own allotted space, which was more than most people in the village had, even if it was wedged in the smallest lane round the back of the cottage. Most residents had to park right at the top in the large car park and walk all the way down. Sometimes this was OK, but she imagined it a pain if you'd just done the weekly shop or had children to carry. Millie's stomach sank at the brief thought of children as she drove carefully out of the village.

Before her arrival, she had vowed to buy all her food locally in Sandyhaven itself in a bid to support local businesses and embrace the country lifestyle. But after a week and learning the only place to purchase food in the village was from one solitary tiny shop, it had become rather limiting and she found herself craving more choice. You can take the girl out of the city and all that. Twenty minutes down the nearest winding A-road, the sight of a well-known supermarket excited Millie more than she dared to let on. She shopped slowly, taking in the wide variety of items on offer and bought some trashy magazines in a pathetic attempt to make her feel better about her life. If Katie Price had just split with another man but was still "happy and independent" then to hell, she could be too!

Her shop must have screamed "single woman" because the assistant on the checkout said "looks like my kind of night" whilst nodding to the conveyor belt of items. Millie smiled feebly.

"Well, one has to have something to keep them entertained in such a small place."

"You on holiday?" the woman asked. Millie glanced at her name badge. *Amy.*

"No, I live in Sandyhaven," she said, unsure as to why she'd just given away where she lived. She felt like throwing in her bank card and National Insurance number for good measure.

"No way? Me too!" Amy declared excitedly. "Well, sort of. I'm in the house just past the car park. It's several flats in one." She narrowed her eyes. "I've never seen you before though. I seem to know most people similar to my age in the village?"

"I only moved in about a fortnight ago," Millie explained, packing the last few items. Amy nodded.

"That would explain it then," she said, tapping the screen

and pushing the "next customer" barrier along the conveyer belt in one swift move. Millie couldn't help but notice her thick Cornish accent.

"You move here with parents then?" Millie swallowed hard and focused on counting through her change. After a few moments she looked up and forced a smile.

"Nope. Just me. Needed a change of scenery so here I am." Keep it vague. Don't incite any questions, she thought.

"Lush! Well, me and some others meet at the pub in the square of a Saturday night. It's not your "bright lights of the city" and fancy cocktails but a strong pint and good company. Feel free to come join us, if you like?" she offered, her smile genuine and warm. Millie smiled back.

"Thanks. Maybe I will." Awkwardly, she gathered up her shopping and made her way back to the car. Had she just made her first friend in the village? She liked to think so.

"I'm pregnant." The earth stopped. The blood beat in her ears. Jenny's face blurred and then came back into focus again, a mixture of emotions etched on her face.

"That's amazing!" Millie exclaimed eventually, exhaling heavily and placing her arms tightly around her friend. "Congratulations." Jenny hugged her back hard.

"Thanks Mils. I want you to be Godmother. I'm not even asking, more just telling you." She let out a strangled giggle and pulled away, looking at her friend. She looked so concerned and it

broke her heart. She should be feeling happiness and nothing else.

"Of course I'll be their Godmother. It would be an absolute honour," she whispered, pulling her friend back in.

Four

The week ticked by. Millie filled her time sorting out her new home. While all the essential furniture was already there, she'd been given Alan's blessing to move things around and change things as much as she wanted. She'd moved some pieces and added in lots of new things which gave it a more personal touch. It was starting to feel a little more like home, although she wasn't sure she'd ever get used to the contrast of the quaint, rustic cottage against the poky, functional flat she used to rent in London. The main reason being, here she was living alone. Still, she was grateful to have the sorting to do. It helped keep her mind from wandering too much.

Saturday had somehow rolled around, and she remembered Amy's invitation from earlier in the week. Should she go? Did she *want* to go? Anxious butterflies fluttered in her stomach. She wouldn't know anyone. Well, that was a lie, she knew Amy. Sort of. Plus, after all she *had* been invited. And how else would she meet new people? She'd spoken to Jenny every day since she'd moved but even Facetime wasn't a substitute for actual human contact. She needed to start making an effort.

Trying desperately to ignore this internal monologue, she pulled open the wardrobe door, then paused. What did people even wear to the pub down here? Up in London, going out for a drink was either fancy wine bars or upmarket Gastropubs, overlooking glorious St Katharine's Docks, off a quirky side-street in Soho or a trendy venue in Shoreditch. Your choice of outfit would match the location and even if you went straight from the office, you still looked smart and would have touched up your hair and make-up in the work toilets before leaving. On the contrary, she had a feeling pubs down in Cornwall wouldn't be quite the same. Most people she'd come across down here in the village wore woollen fleeces and walking boots. OK, maybe that was a little exaggerated and pompous but the stark contrasts with the Londoners she'd surrounded herself with for years were hugely obvious. She didn't want to look a mess, but also didn't want to stand out.

After *much* deliberation, she decided on a pair of black jeans and a pewter grey vest. A chunky knit cardigan and boots accompanied the ensemble, mainly for warmth, and a little make-up finished off the look. She felt she looked OK, considering she had pretty much forgotten how to use make-up after not wearing it in a long while. A little tinted moisturiser, strokes of concealer on the dark grooves under her eyes, some daubs of blusher and a swish of mascara was her effort. Her hair hung loose, naturally wavy.

The pub – The Sandy Anchor - was a five-minute walk from her cottage, just like almost everything in this tiny place. Aside from a few streetlamps straining out some watery rays of light, the lane was pretty much pitch black. Millie trod carefully on the cobbles through habit, her mother's voice echoing in her head from when she was around five years old *"don't step on cobbles, they're ankle twisters!"*

She realised then that she hadn't thought about her mum for a while and felt a rush of guilt, despite their relationship being mostly fragmented for years prior to her death. She knew the fact she was even able to be here in Cornwall, having spontaneously left her old life behind, was due to the money her mum had left her in her will. Most people wouldn't even think twice at this: of course, parents left their children money in their wills, right? But for years, her mum had told her repeatedly that there would be nothing for her, threatening that if Millie didn't support her life choices, then she wouldn't support her. As much as she had wanted to be there for her mum through her problems, she'd never been able to entertain her alcoholism and narcissistic tendencies, choosing instead to step back for the benefit of her own mental health. It was no secret that her mum had had a tough life and with never really knowing who Millie's father was, she'd brought her up mostly alone. Whilst Millie was grateful to her, she'd learned over time that this didn't give her an automatic pass to treat her however she chose. Following all the arguments, it had been a total shock to discover she had received the entirety of her mother's estate after she'd died from liver cancer.

Millie passed three people on her way down, all of whom nodded or smiled and said hello. This was a stark contrast to London, where people practically went out of their way to avoid eye contact or polite conversation. She quite enjoyed it. It made her feel she belonged. Gradually, the pub came into view. Standing quaintly metres from the sea wall and beach beyond, it radiated warmth and cosiness. Hanging baskets overflowing with hydrangeas adorned the front wall and a large chalkboard claiming *"dogs and their well-behaved owners welcome"* added a witty charm. Reaching the door, Millie contemplated turning around, anxiety getting the better of her, but as soon as she pushed open the door, warm chatter greeted her, and she spied Amy almost immediately. Amy's face broke into a smile, and displayed a look of surprise, as though she hadn't expected Millie to come. To be honest, she was still a little surprised herself.

"You made it!" she said warmly, giving Millie a hug. "Great! Come and meet the crew." She was relieved to see Amy was also dressed casually, yet even more so than her: jeans, a cable-knit jumper and Hunter wellies adorned her feet. Her hair, which had been so intricately plaited in the supermarket, now hung in messy waves around her freckled face. Not a scrap of make-up lay on her face, yet she looked fresh and youthful. Millie couldn't help but instantly like her. A group of four other people sat around a circular table, pints in front of all of them. Her heart immediately dropped when she recognised one of the men at the table from their encounter earlier that week, but she managed to keep her face neutral.

Banging the table to get their attention, Amy announced: "So everyone, this is Millie! She's just moved here. I served her at work this week, isn't that weird?! Millie, let me introduce you to everyone. This is Ryan," she indicated to a brown-haired boy with quirky glasses and a checked shirt. He gave a little wave, and she smiled in response. "This is Daisy." A tall girl with incredibly long, thick hair and large eyes grinned at her. "This is Evan, he's with Daisy," Amy added, and Evan nodded his blonde head. "And this is Alfie. Or Alfredo if he's being a knob head, which, let's face it, is quite a regular occurrence."

"Screw you, Collins," Alfie said, flipping her off, but his voice was light. Millie couldn't help but frown. So he could joke around with Amy but with her, he was rude? He didn't acknowledge they'd already met, or attempt to say hello now, so she decided to keep her mouth shut too. Perhaps if she blocked it out, she could pretend their rude encounter had never happened.

"Come and sit down then!" Amy ushered. "What're you drinking?" Millie glanced around at the table. Pint. Pint. Pint. She wasn't overly keen on lager but didn't want to make the wrong impression straight away.

"Just a pint will be fine," she replied coyly, and Alfie

smirked. She shot him a look. "Why's that funny?"

"Nothing…you just don't look like a "pint" sort of girl," he replied, eyebrow raised. That was really starting to annoy her now. Was he trying to offend her? Catch her out, even? She firmly held his gaze.

"Well, typically it's a "pint" of *wine* but I don't want to go too crazy now," she shot back, and the others erupted into laughter.

"I like this girl!" Daisy chuckled and Millie felt a little glow as she settled onto a spare stool. So, she'd have to pretend to like foul lager for the rest of her life? It seemed a small price to pay if it meant she could, maybe, belong.

"Are you crazy?! I can't accept all this!?" Millie's hands shook as she stared at the papers before her. She glanced up at the man sat in-front of her. His forehead wrinkled like a Shar-Pei's; thick-rimmed glasses perched on the end of his nose. He studied her over the rim, eyes narrowed.

"This is what your mother requested you have in her will, Miss Jones. As an only child and with no next of kin herself, she chose to leave her entire estate to you." She skim-read the document again, not really taking in the words. They danced around on the page like confetti, merging and then separating like flour through a sieve.

"But…but she told me there was no way I'd be receiving her money? I was strictly under the impression there'd be nothing at

all left for me. I completely wasn't expecting this?!" The solicitor clasped his hands in-front of him, and a hint of a smile played at the corner of his lips.

"Miss Jones, sometimes we feel like we know our loved ones inside out. Like they couldn't ever possibly surprise us That the way they acted towards us was final and absolute. But ultimately, there are always secrets to behold. Sometimes, they shock us in the most incredible ways. I suggest you read this and see if it has any answers." He pushed an envelope across the table which bore Millie's name in the unmistakable and familiar scrawl of her mother's hand. Swallowing hard, hands shaking, she carefully sliced open the envelope. It didn't take long to read.

I never did well by you, Melissa. I wish I could turn back time and do things differently. For that, I am sorry x

The words shocked her – they were maybe the kindest words she had spoken to her in years. Immense guilt flooded through her, and she had a sudden desire to go back in time and try harder to help her mum. But of course, it was now far too late.

But this money…this was life changing. She didn't know what to do.

So, she just cried.

Five

The following morning, Millie awoke with the most horrendous headache. The previous evening, four pints of lager down, she had drunkenly and theatrically revealed to her new friends (and coincidentally the entirety of the pub) that she, in fact, *detested* lager and it was the worst thing she'd ever drunk. Despite the potential of this seriously offending the locals, they ploughed her with wine instead, insisting she drink that pint she had mentioned earlier in the evening. A local band played until midnight, and she could remember laughing and dancing and, generally, having a wonderful time.

The only thing she could remember clearly was the look of general dismay on the face of Alfie Drew. She really couldn't figure out what his issue was? He was the only one of Amy's group of friends who hadn't really spoken to her all evening. She'd chatted to the others, learning that Ryan worked as a healthcare assistant at a local care home, still living with his parents at the top of the village. Ewan worked on a nearby farm, staying in one of the small outbuildings as part of his wage. Here, he lived with Daisy, with whom she had exchanged numbers. Daisy was a room leader at Sandyhaven Preschool and shared an undying love of prawn cocktail Wotsits with Millie. So, with all the others seemingly accepting her, she had to wonder why Alfie hadn't.

She lay in bed, staring at the bumpy ceiling, replaying every word she'd ever said to Alfie, of which there hadn't been many. Maybe that was his problem? Had she been *too* distant the first time they'd met? Maybe he just *really* hated being kept waiting at the door? The thing which confused her pounding head the most though, was why did she even care so much? It's not like she had anything to prove. He was practically a stranger after all.

The sudden and desperate need for water overtook her and she crawled out of bed in search of fluids. Autumn was clearly setting in for good, as the rain battered the rickety windows and wind howled in blanketing draughts across the kitchen tiles. Damn, she still hadn't topped up that key card for the electric heaters. The village shop wouldn't be open on a Sunday, and she certainly couldn't drive anywhere, what with all the alcohol pulsing through her system. With central heating merely a pipe dream, the fire would have to do.

Stumbling pathetically over to the hearth, she noticed there were no logs left and no logs meant no heat. She whimpered, feeling tears well in her eyes as it suddenly hit her like a ten-tonne truck: *what was she doing here?* Why was she down in, as Jen had so eloquently described it, the *"back-arse of nowhere"?* How come, only a few weeks ago, she had shared a flat, complete with central heating, with her boyfriend, close to the bustle of London city and all the things she loved? Why was she pretending to play "country girl" in a tiny village where she barely knew anyone, had no job prospects and basically had no plans whatsoever? She didn't belong here. She certainly didn't belong here alone. It was as though all the emotion she had held inside over the past week, month, even *years* spilled out in one volcanic eruption of tears and howls. She sank down onto the sofa, the tartan throw falling over her body, and cried. Cried for herself and her unlit fire.

Time must have passed because, when Millie awoke, she was pretty much bathed in darkness. Her head no longer pounded but she was completely parched. She never had made it to get that water! Completely unaware of the time of day, she felt her way over to the wall, fumbling for the light switch. It was hopeless though as, upon finding it, no lights appeared. She flicked it back and forth several times, but to no avail. Hang on, why was the room *this* dark? Normally, the streetlights would be flooding the room with an orange, hazy glow, especially with the curtains pulled back. Making her way over to the window, she could see there were no streetlights, but the wind and rain remained, battering the windows and roof. Terrific. A power cut.

Trying her hardest to remain calm, Millie scrabbled back upstairs and found her phone, relieved it still had a decent amount of charge. She flicked the phone's torch on and stood in the middle of the room. Now what? It was pitch black, she was starving and, oh God, how had she just noticed how cold it was? She cursed herself, wishing she'd checked where candles and other items were before now. She had absolutely no idea what to do.

"Call me if you have any problems," Alan's voice echoed in her head. Without hesitation, she pressed his name.

"Oh bugger, I had a feeling that might happen. Follow the weather there on my phone. Sounds like you've had a pretty hefty storm?" Alan said after she'd explained. Millie felt her cheeks heat up – she'd slept all day so didn't actually have a clue what the weather had been doing. A tsunami could have raged through the streets, and she would be none the wiser.

"Well, I'm afraid there won't be a lot of supplies there. The last time I was down it was spring, and I wasn't prepared for anything like this. I'll give Alfie a call, get him to pop round." Millie's heart sank.

"Oh no, no. There's no need for that. I'll be fine. I'll just go to bed. No light needed there anyway!"

"No, but you need warmth, and food surely?" he questioned, concern in his voice. Ah, food, she thought. It would be nice. But no. Nothing was worth an encounter with that ignorant man again.

"Honestly Alan, I'm fine…" But he cut her off.

"I won't take no for an answer. I wouldn't sleep tonight knowing you're down there with no heat or light. I'll ring Alfie right away. He'll be with you in no time." And with that, the line switched off and she was left alone in darkness, waiting for the knock at the door.

"You could have said something, Sam. We could have attempted to work through things before you got under someone else." She paused. "Or should I say, on top of?" Anger emanated from her body, her words spitting venom.

"You know I never wanted things to work out like this, Mils. It was always you." The use of her nickname stung as she continued to pull her clothes from the wardrobe. Only the people who knew and cared for her the most used that nickname and it certainly didn't seem relevant right now.

"Yeah, well. We all know why you're banging someone else. We all know you have a desire to "sow your seed" shall we say. You know you can't get that from me."

"That's not true! You know I've been nothing but supportive to you from the start." She paused. He'd acted the part of supportive boyfriend, true. He'd said all the right words, in all the right ways at all the right times. And yet she knew, deep down, that he was never OK with it. It was forever casting a shadow over their relationship.

"Sometimes that's not enough though, is it?" she answered quietly, not able to look him in the eye. A pause.

"No. I was never enough, was I Millie?" He snapped out the words and her eyes met his. She shook her head slowly. This would never work out now. Things were too different. There had been a seismic shift, and they couldn't go back.

Six

"So I said we would go and stay over the night. That's alright, yeah?" Dana stated, teasing the curlers out of her hair. Alfie turned onto his back and stared at the ceiling, a frown playing on his brow. The candlelight flickered on the ceiling, creating dancing shadows. Power cuts were common in this part of the county, especially on the coast, so candlelight was not an unusual occurrence.

"I dunno, Dan. I'm not sure I'd feel overly comfortable?" Dana paused, hands in hair and turned to look at him.

"What? Why not?" He turned towards her, taking in the smoothness of her back, the curve of her lacy bra strap moulding into her shoulder. Her attractiveness was undeniable and often made him agree to things he didn't want to, much to his own disgust of himself.

"Well, it's your best friend's wedding. You're the bridesmaid. And me going along with you, staying the night – I don't know. It seems very "serious boyfriend and girlfriend." Have you even told your friends about me?" He regretted the words before he'd even finished saying them. The way Dana stayed silent for a moment, her gaze fixed on him before turning back to the mirror and now furiously yanking the curlers out. He closed his eyes. Oh God.

"Look, Dana, I'm struggling to know what you want from me? This time last week you were posting pictures of you out dancing at a club with random guys. Which, in our current circumstance, I'm fine with. But now you're saying you want us to go to a wedding as a couple? With people I've never even met and don't even really know about me. I'm struggling to know what you want." She stayed quiet for a few seconds, and it was difficult to gauge her response in the dim light.

"It's fine, Alfie. It's just the way it is, clearly," she snapped. She hauled the final curler out, running her fingers through her hair with what Alfie could only see as pent-up frustration. He sighed. He'd always been unsure about what their relationship was and deep down he felt the reason why he didn't pursue the answer is because he knew he wasn't wholeheartedly in it. But that would mean making her very upset, which he didn't want to do. It was such a predicament.

"Dana," he spoke softly, watching as she pulled her cashmere sweater over her head, ignoring him. "*Dana?*" he spoke again, more firmly this time. She paused and fixed him with a stare. "If it means that much to you, I'll go to the wedding with you," he said and he watched a small smile pass over her face.

"Really?" He hesitated.

"If that's what you want? But maybe we need to have a conversation soon about exactly where we see this going. What with you up in Manchester and me down here…I'm not sure I'm down for a long-distance relationship…" Her face clouded over.

"If you *really* wanted to be with me, you'd do anything. You'd move up to Manchester with me," she declared angrily, and he closed his eyes, pausing to take a breath. This was always her default argument.

"And do you *really* want to be with me? Only me? *Really?*" he asked. She faltered, her mouth opening and then closing again. She grabbed her bag off the bed and turned towards the door.

"I'm off out to Truro with the girls. I'll be staying at Mum and Dad's and then heading back up to Manchester on Sunday." With no more time spared, she leaned over him and kissed him with so much passion, he almost fell backwards. She pulled away and flounced out of the flat.

With a huge sigh, he covered his face with his hands. Only that afternoon, after a long, intimate session together, had she expressed how happy she was with where they were at currently: keeping it casual, no official titles. The next minute she's wanting to go to a wedding as a couple, then move to Manchester with her, then she's kissing him like he's the only man on the planet and finally she'd left, with no indication as to when he'd see her again! He couldn't keep up. He needed to break it off for good, whatever "*it*" was, but didn't want to hurt her. He wasn't great with his words. And whilst she had, in the past, been a bit of a nightmare, she wasn't an inherently bad person. Just someone who had maybe a little too much freedom and money, not really knowing what she wanted.

Alfie's phone beeped. A glance caused him to sigh out loud. Just what he didn't need.

> **Heard you've had a blackout?**
> **Millie's on her own and**
> **struggling – could you pop in?**
> **Dad x**

Ten minutes passed. Twenty. Millie sat huddled on the sofa, the blanket wrapped tightly around her, but still she shivered, and goosebumps invaded her skin. Although she'd felt safe in the cottage since the day she'd arrived, the void of darkness around her, coupled with the menacing sounds of the storm were making her feel on edge.

This was ridiculous. There was no way he was going to come round, not at this time of night. He wouldn't put himself out for *her*. Besides, he was an artist. Wouldn't he be sat up in his apartment, candlelight flickering whilst drawing some moody landscape of the storm out to sea, all dark colours and swishy lines? She knew the feeling well, although she spent her creative time producing bright, oil paintings as a contrast. Not that she'd done any creating lately. All her mental efforts were being poured into basic survival and even that wasn't exactly working out.

She pictured him, working by the flicker of a candle, the warm glow casting shadows on his face, highlighting his jawline, the flecks of amber in his eyes, the curve of his bottom lip…A hammering at the door caused her to jump out of her surprising daydream. Within seconds, she was threading the chain off and staring at the outline of Alfie. Thankfully, the darkness hid the pink hue to her cheeks after the thoughts she'd just been having. She had to clutch the door handle to stop the wind flinging it back.

"Ah, you're awake," he said, clearly referring to their last encounter at her door, a hint of a smile playing on his lips. She narrowed her eyes at his rudeness. Didn't take him long.

"Why the hammering? Don't you know how to use a doorbell?" She realised he hadn't used the bell last time either yet shocked herself with her clipped tone.

"I thought you might be asleep and wanted to make sure you'd get up. Four pints of lager and copious amounts of wine seemed to make you a little – a little drowsy, shall we say?" She blushed. People fell asleep in pubs all the time down here, right? A pause.

"Well, can I come in? Or do you just want me to stand out here all night?" Millie bit the inside of her cheek to resist a sarcastic comment but stood back to let him in. He *had* come over here to help her, after all and the wind was whistling around the cottage now.

After shutting the door on the violent weather, she eyed him in the torchlight. It was strange having him here, filling the room, having to stoop to avoid smacking his head on the low beams. She watched him potter around, striking matches and placing candles he'd readily located in a high cupboard around the room. She stood awkwardly, arms crossed, not really knowing what to do.

"You seem to know your way around here well," she said, more of a statement than a question. She noticed him pause his movements, even with his back to her.

"I know the cottage well," he said, but offered nothing more and continued his jobs. Millie sensed the tension but was unsure why it was there.

"Uh…would you like a cup of tea?" she offered pathetically. He paused from placing logs he'd brought round in the hearth to stare at her.

"And how do you propose doing that? Going to breathe fire onto the stove to make it light?" His rude comment annoyed her, but she thought she witnessed the tug of a smile at the corner of his mouth again. She bit her tongue.

"No, but I know someone here who happens to have some matches available." She raised an eyebrow and grabbed the box off the sideboard, heading into the kitchen, blanket still trailing round her shoulders like a cape. He followed behind her, carrying a few candles and set them down near the stove. Soft light coated the surfaces and the shadow of the flame danced against the tiles. She filled a saucepan with water and, acutely aware of his presence in the small kitchen, struck the match several times, to no avail.

"This is painful," she heard him say dryly and he took the match and box from her, his fingers brushing against hers. She felt herself redden and was thankful once again for the low lighting.

Minutes later the water was starting to heat up and Millie was huddled next to the now roaring fire, allowing the warmth to spread deliciously through her body. She felt herself thawing from head to toe and couldn't remember the last time she'd felt this cosy.

To her surprise, a mug was suddenly hovering in front of her face. She glanced up and took in his face, mouth pressed into a straight line. After a few seconds of staring, he raised his eyebrow, and she took the mug from him.

"Thanks," she said softly, turning so her back was to the fire, soaking up the heat. "Not just for the tea," she continued, "for coming over and sorting me out."

"Got to do what dad says," Alfie replied, perching on the edge of the sofa and taking a sip from his own mug. She felt a pang of annoyance – it was clear he was only here because he'd been told to, not because he genuinely wanted to help. He reminded her of a schoolboy – defiant and stubborn. She felt an urge to kick him out but reminded herself that, without him, she'd still be in complete darkness and shivering her skin off.

"So, Alan says you're an artist?" Millie said, trying to strike up a conversation to break the awkward quiet.

"Did he now? I guess my old man's never been shy to share what I do. Although I'm sure he'd have preferred me to go into something a little more corporate."

"What sort of stuff do you do?" she asked. He screwed his face up.

"This and that."

"What style do you use?"

He paused, contemplatively. "Mine."

Millie stared at him intently. Why was he being so reserved? All she was trying to do was make polite conversation and yet, he couldn't even answer some simple questions. She decided not to try anymore, and they sat in an uncomfortable silence for a few more minutes before Alfie finally stirred to leave.

"Well, I'm finished so I better go. I would say thanks for the tea, but I made it so…" Millie stared in disbelief of his impoliteness, watching as he placed the mug in the kitchen and made for the door. Yet despite his sheer ignorance, she felt compelled to thank him.

"Thanks again for coming over. You don't have to rush off so quickly." *You do.*

"No, it's fine. I've finished my tea and it's late." He opened the door, and the crazy weather flew through the house. He stepped outside and before walking away, turned and said, "don't forget to blow the candles out before you go to sleep." There was a hint of care to his voice, she noted curiously. Was the ice man starting to thaw? "Oh, and look after the cottage," he said softly, indicating the building behind her. After that, he was walking away down the street, hands shoved in pockets and collar up round his neck to fight off the cold.

The door slammed shut out of her grip and she sighed. What a fascinating man. She couldn't figure him out. And yet, there was just something about him that intrigued her. Why was he so concerned about the cottage? She knew it was his dad's, but still. There was something niggling her that she couldn't quite work out.

She retrieved both the mugs and when she reached the sink, couldn't help noticing that, despite him saying he had finished it, his was still three quarters full.

Sam drummed his fingers nervously on the worktop, maintaining a steady beat. It made Millie cringe. Nothing could make this time pass quicker. Tick tock, tick tock. Her eyes met his and he stared into hers, unblinking. Unspoken words charged between them, but never once did their mouths actually open. The harsh interruption of the timer made them jump. After two minutes of unbearable waiting, it was ready. And yet, it was the last thing she wanted to do.

"Go on," Sam urged, his voice quiet. Millie swallowed hard and with trembling hands, lifted the pregnancy test. With a deep sigh and eyes squeezed tightly shut, she flipped it over in her hands.

"I can't look. What does it say?" she whispered. There was a

pause. A longer pause.

"I…I'm sorry Mils. It's OK, we can try again." She slowly opened one eye and with a shaky sigh viewed the screen. Not Pregnant.

"Try again?" she said, tears clouding her vision. "How many more 'agains' are we going to have?" She dropped the pregnancy test and felt Sam's arms go around her, strong and solid. When would she be able to give him what they really wanted? She feared the answer was 'never'.

Seven

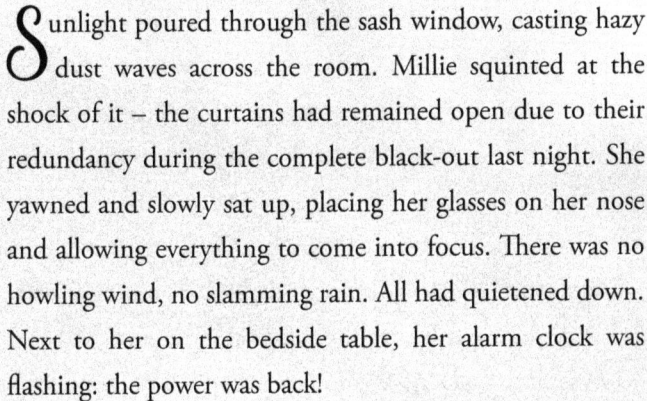

Sunlight poured through the sash window, casting hazy dust waves across the room. Millie squinted at the shock of it – the curtains had remained open due to their redundancy during the complete black-out last night. She yawned and slowly sat up, placing her glasses on her nose and allowing everything to come into focus. There was no howling wind, no slamming rain. All had quietened down. Next to her on the bedside table, her alarm clock was flashing: the power was back!

Like an excited child at Christmas, she flew downstairs and flicked the kettle on, a large grin on her face. She had only been without power for a few hours and was half asleep and hungover anyway, but it made her realise how much she'd taken it for granted. To be able to just flick a switch and get instant light and noise – it was quite remarkable!

The half-burnt candles placed sporadically around the

cottage gave her flashbacks to the night before: as she studied the hardened wax, now congealed mid-way down the candle's wick, she remembered how strange it had felt having Alfie in there. How arrogant and sarcastic he had been, again, for no apparent reason. She couldn't decide if it was just his personality or whether she had done something wrong. Racking her brains, she tried to think of every single encounter they'd had: his first visit to the cottage where she'd kept him waiting, the infamous night in the pub and then last night during the blackout. That was it. Nothing untoward had happened. He'd just seemed to take an instant dislike to her. Maybe she'd ask Alan. Or Amy? She seemed to know Alfie quite well. Yes, that's what she would do. Now she had Amy's phone number, she'd give her a call. Ask to meet up. Then, she'd casually drop in conversation about him and see what she could find out about Alfie Drew. The kettle clicked and she smiled to herself, feeling content with her plan.

The weather was an infinite improvement on the previous day and night – it was as though Mother Nature had had her rage, then had a good nap and gotten over it, stretching and yawning lazily, bringing in a new day. The village smelt fresh, the aftermath of several hours of continuous rain, and the cobbled streets glowed with the dew. Pale pink and lemon-yellow painted cottages passed on either side as she walked, with bright coloured doors fit for, it seemed, only a hobbit to pass through. Each had a cute name like *"Sunseeker"* or *"Gull's Reach"*. No ordinary *"Number 28"* here. It was miles away from where she had lived the last few years but she strangely felt like, in time, she'd feel more at home here than anywhere else. It was crazy what a bit of good weather could do.

She thought of her old flat often – did it still look the same? She'd left with scarcely any possessions, not wanting to take memories with her, nor waste the time packing things up. She certainly hadn't entertained hiring a removals van, choosing instead to stuff her car with as many items as possible. Every inch was used; the foot-wells, the glove box, even the space for the spare tyre had become home to some possession or another.

More pointedly, she'd wondered if the woman she'd caught Sam with had been there. Was she cuddled in her old bed, on her side? Had she discovered the rogue spring on the mattress that every so often would prod you in the back if you turned the wrong way? Or the creak on the second step down into the bathroom, which would give you away in the night. Had she messed up Millie's Tupperware system in the kitchen cupboards, where she'd painstakingly labelled every grain, pasta and cereal they owned using her trusty label maker. Sam had bought it for her for her birthday, insisting it was a "rubbish present" despite it being all Millie had asked for and had beamed with delight when she'd torn the paper off.

As she made her way down the lane to the local shop, Millie pulled her mustard cardigan tighter around her, folding her arms to keep it closed, all of these thoughts causing her to shiver more than was necessary. Her tartan scarf peppered with hues of brown and beige was thick and enveloped her neck, keeping out the unmistakable chill the damp air also brought. Several people said hello to her as she walked the few hundred yards, and she liked that she was starting to recognise faces – and more so that they were starting to recognise hers.

"Mornin' maid!," Mr Slee the shop owner called cheerily as she stepped in, the bell above the door signalling her arrival.

"Good morning," she smiled back.

"Heckova' storm last night, weren' it?! Did yer' power go off?"

"Yes, in the middle of the night! Did yours?" She felt intensely aware of how "BBC English" her accent must sound alongside the heavy Cornish lilt of Mr Slee's, even though hers was no posher than anyone else's. Everyone just seemed to have such a twang to their voices down here. She found it incredibly heart-warming.

"Course! If one house goes out, you can be sure the whole village will! Bleddy nightmare it is. Still, hope you were alright?"

"Yes, Alan Drew's son came round and leant me some candles and things," she explained nonchalantly, placing milk, bread and her electric card on the counter. She knew the moment it slipped her lips that this information would cause a stirring in the village.

"Ah, dear ov' 'im. He's a good lad. Quiet, but good." She watched the large man as he scanned her few items and topped up her card, as requested.

She frowned slightly. "Do you know him well, Alfie?"

"Reasonably," he began, leaning both his huge hands on the counter. "I've known Alan for, ooh, around forty years all told and knew his wife too, before she died. Lovely couple. Very sad, all that. Alfie's a lovely lad an' all but keeps 'imself very much to 'imself. Still, means 'e gets a lot of paintings done. They're right good they are, proper job!" Mr Slee continued to talk about Alfie but Millie's mind had gone blank. Alfie's mum had *died*? But that couldn't be true – Alan had a wife, she knew that. Eleanor? She'd met her several times when she'd worked for him back at the office and he talked about her a lot…

"Sorry Mr Slee, did you say Alan's wife had died?" she pressed.

"Oh yes. Three year ago. Terrible, terrible business. Nasty illness, very sudden. Rosemary was a dear, dear woman." *Rosemary. Rosemary Cottage!* "The cottage yer' in now was hers, actually. Alan bought it for her and she spent many a summer in it with Alfie, whilst he worked away back in London. Shame he let it out though. I think Alfie would've wanted it but his dad is letting out his current flat to him instead. Bit of an awkward business I think." She swallowed, the mist beginning to clear on why Alfie had maybe been so aggrieved with her. She was staying in his mum's cottage. He continued, "I knew Alan married again, although haven't met her. Think she's called Emily, Elodie…?"

"Eleanor," Millie corrected softly, the face of the woman

she'd met at the office flashing in her mind and she realised her mistake. That was Alfie's step-mum. "Thanks for the shopping, Mr Slee."

"See ye dreckly, maid," he saluted.

She left the shop quietly, carrying her few items. Instead of turning left and walking back up the lane to her cottage, she found herself heading for the beach, feeling pensive as she went. It was halfway across the road to the beach when she stopped and looked up. She'd known where Alfie lived from Saturday night, when she'd watched him walk away and go home – it was about all she *had* remembered clearly. He had a loft flat right on the beach. So that belonged to Alan too. He had quite the empire, she mused. She imagined the views must be tremendous with his panoramic window – the village back and up to the right, acres of pretty woodland stretching up behind it – and extending out for miles in front of him, beautiful sea complemented by an endless horizon. Perfect for an artist. She felt a pang of jealousy. It still wasn't hard to see why he'd have wanted to stay in Rosemary Cottage instead though. As wonderful as his current flat probably was, there was likely no connection to his mum there. Her heart sank for the sadness he must feel every time he'd seen someone else in there. In the space he had stayed so many times before. If only she'd known.

She glanced up at the top window and felt her heart skip a beat as she saw him sat there, easel in-front of him, working away. She could have stopped and stared for hours, but the fear of being caught forced her to snap out of it and she hurried away back up the lane.

Another week passed in the sleepy village and by the weekend, Millie found herself pretty much sorted, house-wise. She had made several trips to the local discount chain store, stocking up on accessories and nick-nacks which complemented her taste and the rustic, cosy feel of the cottage, but which could easily be removed if she had to leave. The whole time she was browsing, she felt wracked with guilt at the thought of transforming Rosemary Cottage, feeling like instead she should be leaving it exactly how it was when Alfie was a boy. But it was hers now, for all intents and purposes, so she should make it her own, right? It was likely she'd rarely see Alfie now, certainly not in the cottage, so he'd never know.

A few of her own paintings adorned the walls – she'd deliberated for hours about hanging them. Sam had never been keen on putting her artwork through the house *("it seems a bit egotistical?"* he'd explained) but in the end she thought, stuff it. Sam wasn't here anymore, and, after all, she was proud of her work. Overall, she felt like it was the closest she was going to get it to feeling like her home.

There were still several areas of her life which felt seriously *un*-homely, though. The fact that she still had barely any actual friends here, although she was now starting to recognise many more faces. Also, people tended to treat her as just a regular local, rather than some random girl down from the capital. She hadn't had the chance to meet with Amy again, although several texts had pinged back and forth, and she'd accepted social media friend requests from all the group in the pub - this was progress? The only person she hadn't received such an invite from was Alfie, but she discovered after some covert stalking that he rarely used his profile. This didn't surprise her. It matched his mysterious, secretive personality.

She also hadn't had the pleasure of crossing paths with Alfie again in the village. She had very much kept herself to herself, but this was beginning to wear thin. The lack of routine, which was a stark contrast to her old life in London, was missing and Millie couldn't help but grieve for its loss. It really shocked her that the monotonous rat-race which she one day hoped so much to be free from was missed: get up at 6am, fight Sam for the shower, dab on some make-up half asleep, grab pre-made smoothie and slurp on the way to the tube, jostle with half of London on the Central and Bakerloo Lines…the same thing every single day. Of course, weekends were different. They'd enjoyed trips up town, or taking walks around one of the many incredible parks, theatre trips, day excursions to the seaside towns of Margate and Brighton… When she and Sam had been in a good place, her life couldn't have been any better. Apart from that one thing she couldn't have or achieve, which constantly hung over her like a sodden towel, weighing her down, suffocating her…

Millie blinked hard, trying to eliminate the thoughts

from her brain. It didn't even matter now, right? She was in no position to be aiming for such a thing anyway, so it was irrelevant. Shaking off her feelings of self-pity, she flicked on her laptop for a few hours of dedicated job hunting. She had no idea what she wanted to do and, to be honest, she wasn't really qualified for anything. The one and only real passion in her life was art and that was an impossible thing to make a living out of unless you had friends in high places, or you had an extremely rich father who could fund it. Seeing as she barely had any friends at all and she had never had a "dad" for all intents and purposes, it was a completely unachievable and unrealistic goal.

Forty minutes later, she was grateful to be distracted from the unsuccessful and increasingly degrading job hunt by a phone call from Jenny.

"So, how's the *"Escape to the Country"* lifestyle treating you?" Jenny spoke down the phone.

Phone balanced between shoulder and ear whilst pegging out washing on the line in her tiny courtyard, Millie was doing what she did best – multitasking.

"I mean, I *love* the village overall. It's tiny but perfectly formed and everyone is so friendly. People actually make eye contact and say hello to you when they pass you!" she replied.

"Jeez, what sort of a weird, 1950s-time warp are you living in?" Jenny answered sarcastically and Millie chuckled.

"You joke, but it can feel a bit stuck in the past sometimes. Still, enough about me. How are you doing? How's baby Brannon?"

"Won't sit still. Can tell they're going to be just like their father, he can never bloody sit still either. Last night in bed he was thrashing around like a beached whale! Felt like knocking him one." Millie smiled at the familiarity of her friend's feeble moans. She'd always adored the relationship Jenny had with her husband, Paul. They were so playful, but you could see how much they adored one another. This baby was the beginning of a new chapter for them and Mille couldn't be happier for them both.

"How long have you got now?"

"About another hundred years, I expect," Jenny replied with a groan and exaggerated sigh. "No, ten days, if they play their cards right." Millie's stomach flipped. In ten days, her best friend could have a *baby*. Like, an actual *baby*.

"You will call me as soon as you go into labour, won't you?" she asked, swallowing hard. She felt so guilty that she wasn't there to support her best friend.

"Of course I will, you muppet. When I get the very first twinges."

"Even if you're not sure it's that?"

"Even if I think it could be some dodgy wind from the many curries I am going to consume, yes." They both giggled.

"Oh and, Mils, before you go…I have something to ask you." Millie paused, pegging a pair of jeans on the line and frowned. This sounded ominous.

"Go on…"

"Where did you get that dodgy West-Country accent from?!"

It had taken several days for Millie to get out of bed. A bad case of the flu had wiped her out and she'd spent her time in bed, hallucinating, drifting in and out of consciousness, sweating like a pig and generally moving only to go to the toilet and fill up her water. She'd never really gotten ill back in London; strange considering the air was so much more polluted, she spent hours on a packed, disease-ridden tube and in an office with unfiltered air con. It was only since moving down here, getting more exercise, eating better and generally slowing down that she had gotten ill.

"That's what happens," Amy had told her the day before, when she'd come to check up on her. "You keep going and going and going and you manage but then as soon as you stop BAM! You get ill. It's a fact of life." Millie watched Amy explain whilst simultaneously stuffing brownie bites into her mouth (reduced stock, a perk of working in a supermarket, apparently). She hadn't eaten in several days and the smell of the brownies made her feel queasy.

"Is that so?"

"Yeah! You'll feel better once you start getting more acquainted with everything. How's the job hunting going?" Millie looked down and picked at a stray thread on her blanket.

"Um…not great."

"Does that mean you haven't been offered an interview yet?"

"It's a bit difficult to be offered an interview when you haven't applied for anything…"

"You haven't applied for *anything*? You've been looking for weeks!" Millie screwed up her face and rubbed her forehead. She could feel a headache coming on.

"There just isn't anything I've really seen yet…"

"There are jobs going at my work! And like I've always said, it can be a little dull but there are great perks!" She indicated the spread of reduced sweet treats with a flourish of her hand. Millie managed a smirk.

"Thanks, but I'm going to keep looking for a bit. I'll keep it in mind though." Amy shrugged her shoulders and brushed crumbs from her sweater. Millie cringed, trying not to make a face at the dirt making its way onto her carpet.

"So, what sort of jobs have you been looking for? Like, what's the DREAM?" Amy asked, flourishing her arms as she said it. Millie paused.

"The dream? The dream is different from what I could *actually* do."

"Huh? I don't understand. Your dream can become a reality if you want it enough."

Millie let out a snort, with the effort causing her still tender chest and throat to throb. "Alright, didn't realise you were a motivational speaker on the side." Amy pulled a "screw you face."

"All I'm saying is, you don't seem like the sort of person who plays it safe? You lived and survived in *London* – the sort of place that seems like a terrifying, uncharted planet to a country bumpkin like myself. Then, you've upped and moved down to this tiny corner of Cornwall, all by yourself, no job, no real plans – people don't just move down here for no reason. People like that are usually hiding from something…"

Millie hadn't really thought about it like that before. To her, the move had come from a place of desperation and sadness, not from someone searching for adventure. She questioned her move every single day.

"Whilst we're on that…" Amy said in a confused voice, "…what IS your story? I've realised I'm sat here in your house, sprawled across your sofa, drinking copious amounts of your tea, with you sat there looking a snivelling mess in your dressing gown – and yet I don't actually know who you really are?" Amy was looking at her with such interest and questioning, Millie suddenly felt under extreme pressure. She didn't particularly feel up to explaining right now. Maybe not ever. The only person down here who knew anything at all about her was likely to be Alfie. He'd know about her connection to his dad and that her mum had died. That was enough.

"Do you know what? My throat is absolutely killing me, and I think the exertion of sitting here and talking to you has knackered me out," Millie replied, teasingly. "Seriously though, I think I may need to go to bed." Amy paused, raising an eyebrow. Millie waited for Amy to take the hint and felt relieved when she did so, standing up with intent.

"Alright then. Call me if you need anything?"

Millie exhaled, relieved. There was only so long she could go on running from the past. At some point, she knew the past and present would have to collide. But not right now.

"She's so poorly," Amy explained about Millie to the rest of the group later that day, placing the full, frothy pints down on the wooden table.

"Gosh, I hope it's nothing serious," Daisy replied, pulling an anxious face, before sipping the head off the top of hers.

"She's always in bed, it'll be nothing," Alfie cut in, picking the edges off an already-worn beer mat. The girls stopped and stared at him, confusion on their faces.

"And, how would you know, Alfredo?" Amy enquired, eyebrow raised.

"Yeah. Anything you'd like to share with the group?" Ryan teased. Alfie looked at their faces, realising what they were all implying.

"Oh, grow up. Dad sent me round the cottage a few times to check up on her, that's all." He took a lengthy gulp of beer. The others waggled eyebrows and made little nudges with their elbows.

"That old chestnut, eh?" Ryan smirked. "You're a sly fox, Alfie. She's barely been here two minutes!"

"That's all it takes," Evan bantered back, mouth full of the pasty he was scoffing.

"Yeah, and don't I know it!" Daisy responded, causing

Evan to mock laugh whilst the rest of them burst out into peals of laughter. Amy glanced over to the bar, where Dana was perched on a stool, laughing loudly with a group of men nursing glasses of Jack Daniels.

"Also, I bet *someone* would have something to say about that," she murmured, tipping her glass towards her. Everyone grew quiet and gradually returned to their conversations, while Alfie cast Dana a glance. She sure would. Even though *her* latest Instagram post had featured her with a very good-looking guy she insisted was just a colleague. Despite his innermost feelings telling him he needed to leave the toxicity of their relationship behind, he couldn't help feeling a pang of jealousy. He found it surprising that his mind started wandering back to Millie, and how it maybe would be easier to be with someone like her.

He shook the thoughts away as quickly as they had arrived.

Eight

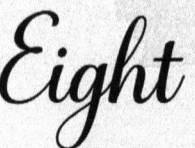

"*I*magine pushing out a bowling ball...that's been covered in hot chilli sauce."

"I'm not sure I want to, to be honest Jen," Millie screwed her face up. The video in front of her – slightly blurry due to dodgy hospital Wi-Fi – showed her oldest and best friend Jen with the most gorgeous bundle of newborn baby. Leo had come into the world only a few hours prior and Millie had listened to the exact play-by-play of his dramatic entrance from Jenny.

"She wasn't a diva at all though Millie," she heard Jenny's husband Paul call from off-screen. He appeared in shot, much to Jenny's dismay. "I only had to hand-feed her ice chips and imitate calming whale noises." Jenny stuck her tongue out at him as he grinned, and Millie couldn't help but smile.

"She did a great job really," he said softly, and I could see the look of adoration on his face and the way Jenny's arms tightened around baby Leo. She felt tears spring to her eyes and a feeling of overwhelming pain course through her body at the unwanted envy she suddenly felt.

"It's great to see you guys and I'm so happy for you but I need to go." Millie gave a little wave and pressed "End" before they could reply. She felt terrible but there was no other way she could deal with it. Slamming the laptop lid shut, she let the tears drain from her eyes.

She wasn't sure if it was the fact she'd cried herself to sleep for the third night in a row, or that the sun was streaming in through her bedroom window for the first time in what felt like years, but Millie woke up a few days later feeling a renewed sense of positivity. She'd lived in Sandyhaven now for almost two months and was gradually becoming used to the slower pace of life. She was, however, going a little stir crazy with the lack of purpose and routine in her new life. She hadn't picked up a paintbrush in months and she missed it terribly. Her wardrobe was looking a little pathetic too, due to the fact she'd dedicated only a suitcase for clothes and shoes when she'd hurriedly left and abandoned the rest. It didn't leave her with many options. Besides, Cornwall fashion was proving to be very different to the formality of her office-wine bar London wardrobe.

"You about today? I could do with some help," Millie asked Amy over the phone, as she popped moisturiser on her face.

"Hmm – "help" - sounds intriguing. You're lucky that it would just so happen that I don't work Sundays. Day of God and all that." Millie frowned.

"You're religious?" she questioned.

"No, but if you say you are, you get Sundays off. Clever, eh?" Millie shook her head in disbelief and gave a little laugh.

"Well, I need to go shopping and as I presume there's no equivalent to Oxford Street round here - I need some guidance on where to go."

"Oh, you have *definitely* asked the right person. Shall I see if Daisy wants to come too? She mainly lives in her wellies and dungarees, but she loves a good trip out," Amy explained.

And so, with that, Millie found herself on a road trip down to the city of Truro, around an hour away, with Amy and Daisy.

It was very small for a city, Millie found herself thinking but it still had a decent selection of shops and lots of quieter alleys with cobbled streets, cafes with seating outside and pretty bunting fluttering in the autumnal breeze. However, after a browse round some of the chain stores, she found her heart sinking.

"Why is it that fashion these days seems to cater for just a certain type of figure?" she sighed, putting another cropped jumper back on the rail.

"I don't know what you mean," Amy replied, absent-mindedly adding another pair of low-rise jeans to her basket from the sale rail. Daisy raised her eyebrows.

"I think you're proving her point Ames," she chuckled. "You're a petite size six and your basket is stacked."

"Exactly. And that's not to say that there shouldn't be fashion available for people of your build. It's just, what about the rest of us? The ones who have a stubborn muffin top or an arse the size of America," Millie continued.

"I wouldn't say that. Canada maybe," Daisy responded with a cursory glance to Millie's backside and cheeky grin. Millie nudged her in mock offense. Amy swung her basket round before it dropped it on the floor.

"It's chain store, mass produced tat. You're hardly missing out. I've just picked up a load of stuff I can't even afford." Millie watched her with amusement as she made for the door.

"Where are you going?" Amy paused and turned around.

"Let's get a coffee. I'm done in."

"I can't get over how lifelike it is," Beryl sobbed, wiping a tear away. "It's just exceptional." Alfie gave a small smile, but inside he was weeping. He'd just handed over a commission to Beryl, an eighty-seven-year-old widow who lived in a cottage on the edge of the village. Her husband had died around four months ago, and she'd asked Alfie to do a painting of the beautiful coastal landscape which adorned Sandyhaven, but with her beloved husband in it. He'd used the view from his apartment window, a stunning seascape looking across the peninsula to the further villages of Trewithen and Carnglaze. It had been particularly grey and stormy the past few weeks and he was going to use a little artistic license to brighten it up, but upon consulting Beryl she'd asked to keep it true to life.

"He'd always commented on the bloody weather, so it wouldn't seem right to mask the truth," she'd said, warmth in her voice despite cursing. Alfie had painted in her husband, sat with his back to the onlooker, perched on a bench which was now dedicated to him. He always fussed over commissions because he wanted the customer to be happy, but this one seemed particularly poignant.

With a final squeezing hug from Beryl and some homemade cookies from her tucked in his pocket (he'd politely refused several times, but she had insisted), he left her door and headed back down the hill towards the beach, towards his apartment. The rustle of the cookie bag was just too tempting and with one swift motion he found himself crunching into the oatmeal and raisin treat, the moist, buttery taste spreading over his tongue. As he progressed further through the village, he noticed a commotion down by the village hall. Situated right on the beach front, it featured the old hall – home to several clubs and social events throughout the year – and the historic, 200-year-old clock tower. It was a key feature of Sandyhaven, standing proud before the surrounding cottages were even built. If you bought a postcard from Sandyhaven, it would one hundred percent feature the clock tower. As Alfie drew closer, his inquisitiveness grew.

"It's madness! It's just crazy!" he heard Mr Slee from the shop prevaricating. There was a rumble of agreement.

"What's all this?" Alfie asked, scrunching the cookie bag between his hands. In his head, he expected it to be due to a shortage of pasties or a one-time only cancellation of the local W.I. meeting. This is the sort of "drama" the villagers were used to.

"It's the village hall! It's going to be knocked down!" a lady called Ethel, hand clutching a lead belonging to Dennis the enormous Great Dane, exclaimed. Alfie blinked.

"Knocked down?" he repeated, not sure if he'd heard correctly. "But that's ridiculous. Who would let that happen?"

"The bloody council, that's who!" Mr Slee raged, growing redder by the second. "These lot who want to sell the land to build luxury flats!" He stabbed furiously at the Perspex covering the noticeboard on the outside of the hall. Alfie squinted and saw a blueprint: *"Seascape Towers – coming 2026."*

"But...the village hall...?" Alfie began.

"Village hall, village schmall! The money grabbing thieves at the council don't care about that. All they can see are the bloody pound signs! A "desirable plot" they say!" Ray the local locksmith who wore an eye patch, growled. The tension was palatable.

"But what about all the events that go on at the hall? Surely if it's so well used, they can't possibly knock it down?" Alfie continued, clinging at straws. The truth is, he hadn't utilised the village hall for years, not since he'd come down for summer holidays with his parents and attended all the children's activities. He'd remembered going on bouncy castles and getting his face painted there by his mum, who was a fantastic artist. His lovely mum…

"That's the trouble Alfie. It's being used less and less these days. People are choosing to venture further afield over to Trewithen for their Slimming World or Pilates. There's very little uptake for new ventures. The council have been heard as describing it as "dead wood"," Ethel explained sadly, still a hint of anger in her voice. Alfie glanced upwards at the clock tower, stood gloriously in the autumn air. If the village hall went, so would the clock tower, taking a huge piece of Sandyhaven heritage with it.

He turned on his heel, leaving the gaggle to grunt and despair. This was most certainly horrible news. He hadn't lived in Sandyhaven all his life like the others, but it had been a staple in his life from birth – he'd visited every summer holiday without fail. In B&Bs at first, then progressing to self-catering cottages and eventually Rosemary Cottage, which his dad purchased when he got a promotion. When his mum died, his dad had considered living there but it required so much work and he could barely breathe when he was there, the grief sticking to his lungs like molten tar. Instead, Rosemary Cottage had become a holiday home – at least his dad had named it after his darling mum.

There was so much history and nostalgia wrapped up in this village. He felt more connected to this place than anywhere else he'd ever been. He *couldn't* let anything happen to the village hall and the clock tower. He'd already lost so much from his life. He couldn't let the village he loved lose their landmark either.

"They look fantastic!" Amy declared loudly, as Millie dramatically *swooshed* through the changing room curtain and stood in front of them. "And there you were moaning about your figure." After a lunch of paninis and cake, the girls had made their way to *SeaSpray*, a small, independent boutique shop down a cobbled lane. The clothes here were much more to Millie's taste; properly fitting, with high-quality fabrics and designed with a variety of body types in mind. The type of bodies that sometimes do exercise but also very much enjoy pasta and chocolate.

With hands on hips, she twisted left and right to get a full view of the outfit she'd tried on. She'd gone for jeans and a jumper – quite standard casualwear you might think – but instead of the usual faded jeans and baggy jumper she'd opt for, Amy had chosen. This time, she wore fitted, dark wash jeans, with a figure-hugging, cashmere jumper. Daisy had insisted on "function over fashion" so had handed a simple black gilet into the changing room as well but added to Amy's accessories of a long, silver necklace and knee-high boots, the overall effect was casual chic.

"I guess it's OK," Millie relented, her lips curving into a smile. The jumper clung to her, accentuating her shape.

Her glance strayed to Daisy, who was sat on a lounge chair in the changing room, chewing on a strawberry lace. "What do you think?"

"It's very nice. The boots are a bit extravagant for Sandyhaven, though."

"Oh please. Coming from the woman who wears muddy wellies and fleeces every day of the week? And yet, somehow still looks a stunner…" Amy retorted. Daisy snorted.

"I'm practically perfect in every way, I'll have you know," she said in a mock-posh voice. "In all honesty though Millie, you look great. What's brought all this on though? The need to change?"

Before she could fashion a reply, the store assistant reappeared with some different sizes they had asked for.

"So here's the grey wrap dress in the next size down and then the jacket as well," she said, setting them up on the rack in the changing room. "You look wonderful!" she beamed, taking in Millie's current ensemble.

"I told you you'd find better stuff here, compared to that mass produced tat," Amy announced, looking pleased with herself. "Try the dress on next!"

Millie peeled off the jeans and slipped into the grey wrap dress. It pulled her in at the waist and, teamed with the boots and necklace, looked like a winning outfit for a night at the pub. Amy whistled as she walked out the changing room. Daisy's mass of dark hair bounced as she nodded her head in appreciation.

"That's cracking," she agreed, sucking on a lollipop now.

"I like how the boots go with the jeans *and* the dress," Millie thought out loud.

"It's called a capsule wardrobe, honey! It's the way forwards. I still think you need to buy the skirt though. And the jacket. Oh, and those tops here…" Millie rolled her eyes. But a quick glance back at the mirror confirmed an increase in self-confidence. She looked OK: for her.

"I love that painting," Millie mused as she waited patiently for the shop assistant to scan and fold all her items. It was one of those shops where they delicately fold each garment, wrap it in tissue paper and slide it intricately into a pretty striped bag (as opposed to her usual choice of clothes store where it was bundled aggressively into a ball and practically chucked at you).

"Hmm? Oh, yeah, it's alright innit'?" Amy agreed half-heartedly, barely looking up from her Instagram.

"It's pretty isn't it?" the sales assistant agreed, smiling at her.

"Yeah, it's by Lauren Shilton, isn't it?" Millie asked, easing her credit card out of the tight slot in her purse.

"Yeah…how do you know that?" the sales assistant paused, looking bemused.

"Oh, Millie is an art geek," Amy said, waving her hand. Millie rolled her eyes.

"I'm just a fan of her stuff. Since moving down to Cornwall, I've seen a lot of it around."

"Ah, I see. That's because she lives around here," the sales assistant replied, gently tearing the card receipt off the machine and handing it, along with the card, back to her. "Well, I'm sure Lauren would be very pleased to know that," she smiled. "Thank you for shopping with us, enjoy the rest of your day."

Nine

The air was noticeably crisper this evening, Millie thought, as she gently pulled her door shut and wrapped her new jacket around her. With the clocks going back last weekend, the evenings had drawn right in, and the weather had turned. The week had flown since her shopping trip with the girls last weekend. Most of her time had been taken up with painting and it made her realise just how much having a full-time job had hindered her creativity.

She'd cleaned the cottage thoroughly from top to bottom, not quite believing just how much dust could exist in one place. And, after much convincing from Amy, she had gotten a haircut and colour. Her dull, mousey brown hair which she had lived with all her life (apart from the phase of dying it red to look like Cheryl Cole circa 2010 – never again) had gone and been replaced with freshly cut chestnut brown locks and a sweeping fringe cut in to frame her heart shaped face. It had taken some getting used to, but she was now starting to really like it.

There had been no further developments on the job-hunting front, but she just felt a sense of achievement that she had made it through another week unscathed, she had a cleaner home with art drying on her makeshift drying rack (precariously balanced cooling trays were a satisfactory dupe, she'd learned). Now, it was Friday night and even though she hadn't been slaving it away at a 9-5 all week, she felt content that she was on her way down the lane to the pub to meet her new group of friends, almost as an "end-of-the-week" celebration. Things almost felt…happy?

"Oww!" she shrieked, staggering slightly from the impact she'd just received. Something or someone had just come round the corner, right before the pub and smacked right into her.

"I'm so sorry, I…" A frown. A widening of the eyes. "Is that…Millie?"

"Yeah, it's me! I'm barely standing now though!" she grumbled.

"Well, maybe you should look where you're going?" Alfie countered back, his face clouding over. She brushed her new jeans down.

"I mean, I'm struggling to even stand in these new boots, let alone survive a collision," she said. She glanced up the long, darkened lane she had just come down, towards her house.

"Look, I'm sorry, I genuinely didn't see you…" he began, his voice softer now but he was interrupted by a *click clack* echoing towards them. Out of the dim light of the streetlamp, a girl emerged. It was Dana; she recognised her instantly. Millie couldn't help but notice how striking she was, with beautifully long and styled blonde hair, a perfect face of make-up and a figure-hugging outfit. She leaned in and wound her arm around Alfie's waist and Millie couldn't help thinking how great they looked together. She held her hand out, indicating that they should go into the pub first.

Heat hit her face as she walked through the heavy, wooden door. Chattering filled her ears, and the odd outburst of raucous laughter mingled with the clinking of glasses. A cursory glance around and she spotted the group sat at a round table. Millie had to allow a small smile. She felt very fortunate to have met a group of friends like them and for them to have just taken her under their wing. Things might be very different now had that not happened.

"You're late," Daisy stated, watching Millie with concern. "You're never late."

"I had an altercation with Alfie Drew," she said discreetly whilst shrugging off her jacket, her eyes wandering to the door as she noticed him and Dana come in together. "He was somewhat distracted by his *girlfriend*." She spoke the last word very obviously but quietly and Daisy's eyes flashed over to Alfie, who offered a wave over at their group, before heading to the bar with Dana.

"And it bothers you, why?" she asked, looking back at Millie.

"It doesn't," Millie insisted firmly, feeling herself turn red.

"Just drop it, yeah?" Daisy pulled a face but turned to Evan, who was gesticulating so wildly, his beer was nearly spilling. Something about the latest football match all the boys had played together. Millie rolled her eyes. Her gaze roamed around The Sandy Anchor: it really was a sweet pub. Cosy but not too cramped, huge open fireplace and plenty of choice in drinks.

She noticed Dana at the bar, arm draped around Alfie, her hand grazing his cheek. He looked a bit uncomfortable; she couldn't help noticing. It did feel very much like he was being paraded in front of everyone. His eyes flickered over to hers and she looked away quickly. Football. Yes. Focus on the football chat. No need to stare, nothing to see and…. she was looking again.

Oops. Dana was looking back at her now. She truly was startlingly beautiful and really didn't look like she belonged in a small village like this one. She wouldn't have looked out of place in a Michelin starred restaurant back in London, sipping Cosmopolitans at The Shard. As a matter of fact, she wouldn't look out of place on the *front cover* of *Cosmopolitan!* Yet, she hadn't seemed approachable at all. She wasn't a *warm* person. The look she was giving her was completely frosty and she wasn't sure what she'd done to deserve it. Millie's gaze snapped away quickly when she noticed Dana had clutched onto Alfie's hand and was making her way over to their table. Eeek.

"Room for a little one?" she announced, dragging a stool noisily into the smallest gap around the table. Daisy was slumped to the side by the movement and made a face. It was clear that none of these guys were that keen on her. They'd never said explicitly but she got that impression. She guided Alfie to the stool and pushed him onto it, perching sideways on his lap and arms draped around his shoulders. Millie took a long sip of her wine, feeling uncomfortable at this obviously outward display of affection. Dana's tight, leather trousers puckered up around the thigh as she wriggled in his lap.

"I don't believe we've properly met," she directed towards Millie. It was an announcement rather than a friendly ice breaker.

"No, I don't believe we have," Millie replied, lowering her wine glass.

"So, where have you sprung from?" she asked, in a condescending tone.

"Errr, I've moved here from London," she explained, trying not to look at Amy's amused face. One look and that would be it. The giggles would ascend.

"Oh my god, no way?! You moved from *London*, to come *here*?" A pause. "*Why?!*"

Despite the rude, intrusive tone of Dana's voice she suddenly felt six pairs of eyes boring into her, wanting to know the answer to a question they hadn't yet asked (apart from Amy's minor intrusion.) It's something she still hadn't really shared and was an obvious elephant in the room. She felt herself flush and started to stutter a little, frantically thinking up a garbled explanation that didn't involve her cheating scumbag of an ex, her fertility struggles or her dead mother. She felt somehow that it might dampen the spirits a little.

"Um, Dana, isn't Arthur calling you from behind the bar?" Alfie suddenly piped up, glancing to the landlord who didn't look like he'd called her at all.

"What? No, I don't think so…"

"Oh, but he is. We better go and see what the old bugger wants." Hurriedly, he gently shoved her off his lap and led her over to the bar. With that, the moment was shattered, and the group had gone back to discussing the Halloween do at the pub the following weekend. Millie exhaled discreetly and glanced over at Alfie. He peered across and gave her a small, knowing smile. He'd saved her on purpose. Why, she wasn't yet sure, but she was extremely grateful for it. And a little surprised.

Ten

It was one of those autumn mornings you read about in books: crisp, clear and fresh. Millie moseyed along the shoreline of Sandyhaven beach, her gaze following the winding coastline. When the tide was out, you could walk across to neighbouring beaches, exploring the many rocky coves and inlets. When the tide was in, the beach was tiny, barely room to fit more than a few families squeezed up against the rocks. The sea came right up close to the wall, almost brushing it with each ebb and flow of the tide.

There was magic in both circumstances, she had realised. She enjoyed times like now, where she could wander for what felt like miles, lost in thoughts tainted with sea spray and wet firm sand before she'd lose her nerve and have to start heading back before the tide cut her off. But there was also great comfort sought in sitting, back against the crumbling sea wall, legs outstretched, and toes being teased by the waves as they broke.

Did she prefer living here to London? On paper, living in a quaint cottage in a charming Cornish seaside village was a dream. Having a group of people who had taken her in and looked after her was also incredibly fortunate. It's not like she was *alone.* But there was still so much missing. She had no purpose. It wasn't even the absence of a job that was causing her discomfort: she'd only ever worked in menial jobs that anyone could have done. They didn't require any real skill, and she didn't feel like she'd contributed anything as a person or was even greatly missed once she'd left. It was just convenience, something to get up for in the morning and feel like she was participating in society's expectation of 9 to 5, paying taxes and being an adult. What she was really missing was *purpose,* feeling inspired and productive. Not once had she woken up in Sandyhaven and thought *"I've got a real plan for today."* She'd spend her days drifting through, no real direction or aim and it was starting to really affect what was left of her positive mental health. She needed a direction and a motive.

Almost right on cue, she felt her phone vibrate in her pocket. She felt immediately twitchy as she always did now when her phone went off. She kept having these horrible visions of it either being Alan telling her he was sorry, but there had been a change of plan and she'd have to leave the cottage. Or even worse, that it would be Sam contacting her out the blue, either to yell at her or to plead for her to come back. She wasn't sure which one would be worse.

She was relieved to see Jenny's name requesting a FaceTime. There wasn't great signal on the beach, but she was closer to the Sandyhaven end which usually offered at least 3G, so she swiped. Jenny appeared, with baby Leo swaddled somewhere within a large, patterned wrap around her body. Millie recognised it as the one she had bought and sent her shortly after he was born, and it made her heart do a little flip.

"Hello gorgeous lady," Jenny announced, swaying noticeably from side to side. "How are you doing?"

"I'm OK! Are you? You look drunk," she replied, mimicking the rocking and giving a little chuckle.

"Oh, I bloody wish. I can't remember the last time I was tottering around due to the effects of a sexy gin and tonic! This is the only way I can get him to sleep!" She sounded tired and annoyed but the way she had one hand resting gently under his tiny bottom and the other delicately stroking his head suggested otherwise. Millie glanced downwards and brushed a strand of wavy hair out of her face as a means of distraction. Jenny's face broke into a frown.

"You look thin. Are you eating?" She had never been one to mince her words.

"How are you deducing that, you can't even see me properly?!" Millie answered in mock outrage. Deep down, she knew Jenny was miraculously correct. She hadn't been eating properly. It was either a major pizza and chocolate binge washed down with a bottle of wine or picking at pieces of bread and fruit. She had to remind herself to even drink water some days. It was likely that she may have lost weight, and it was now that her best friend had abruptly pointed it out that she realised it was true.

"I can see it in your face Mils. You're all gaunt."

"Gee, thanks," she responded, rolling her eyes.

"I'm just worried. I can't keep an eye on you from all the way up here. By the way, where are you? It sounds like you're in a washing machine."

"I'm down on the beach." Millie flipped the camera and panned around the shoreline, pausing at points to allow the beauty of it to sink in. She flipped the camera back.

"Looks beaut. You lucky bugger. I bet you've got loads of inspiration for painting down there!"

A little switch went off in Millie's brain.

"I haven't done a huge amount with a brush, to be honest, considering the time I've had."

"I can tell, your hair's a state," Jenny countered but with a smile playing on her lips. "Seriously though, why haven't you been painting? I thought now would be the perfect time to crack on with something like that?" Millie picked a piece of stray fluff from her tartan scarf whilst contemplating an answer.

"I don't know really. I don't have many supplies here. Just random bits I'd managed to grab when I left."

"Then go to a shop. They do have shops down there, right? Come on Mils, you can't use that as an excuse! Use this time wisely. Enjoy the freedom to just *create!* You've got such a talent and you're letting it go completely to waste."

Millie felt a tweak of a smile pulling at her mouth – she wasn't used to being complimented.

A little gurgle sound was heard, followed by a full-blown wail coming from deep within the bulge of cloth.

"Oh, all systems go again," Jenny sighed, before planting a gentle kiss on the shock of dark hair peeping out from the swaddle. "I'd better go. But I mean it, Millie, get off your arse and get creating. And EAT SOMETHING. That's an order." She blew a kiss before disconnecting the call.

Despite the demanding nature of her friend's words, they had stirred something in her brain. Would it be as easy as buying up some resources and really throwing herself into painting? What would it achieve? Where would it lead to? As she picked up the pace across the sand, she realised she didn't really care. She had a mission and that was to "get off her arse" as Jenny had so eloquently put it and get creating. *Properly,* this time.

"What is it?" Sam stared at the canvas in front of him, a frown etched on his forehead. Millie's face fell.

"You mean you really can't tell?" He tilted his head from side to side, like a dog hearing numerous high-pitched noises, or the crackling of a food wrapper.

"Uh…no not really," he replied. She exhaled loudly and let out a huge shrug.

"It's the white cliffs of Dover!" she declared, storming closer

to the canvas. "See?!" she pointed. His face slowly de-wrinkled.

"Ohhhhh...of course," he announced, still not looking convinced. "I think I was looking a bit too deep into it. I was expecting it to be something all abstract." He said the last thing like it was a dirty cuss word. She rolled her eyes.

"You know my style isn't really abstract," she explained, knowing full well he probably didn't know that despite how much she'd talked about her art. It was something Sam had never really "got". And she didn't mean that in a snobbish way. It was more that he didn't really have a desire to try to get it. He viewed art as the manufactured pieces you'd buy ready framed in Ikea or The Range. Not that there was anything wrong with those, but she just appreciated how long it took to create original pieces, and she wished Sam would give her the credit for that.

Still, they couldn't match on everything. There would always be differences in interests and intrigue. He liked his numbers; she liked art. Opposites attract and all that.

Eleven

Millie stepped back and took a sip of warm tea. Her neck and shoulders ached, and her vision was starting to blur. Her right hand was tender with cramp and there were smudges all over her. She was pretty sure she even had some paint on her cheek, judging by the weird texture. And yet, despite these discomforts, she felt more alive than she had done for a very long time. Probably ever since she'd moved to Sandyhaven. Even well before that. She'd spent the whole day just creating. She'd woken up at 7am without the aid of an alarm clock and felt motivated and driven. A trip to the craft store the previous day had been glorious – it was over an hour by car to get to Truro, where she could find a shop that would supply what she'd need, but she'd enjoyed the drive. First on the narrow, winding B roads and then opening out onto wider, faster dual carriageway that allowed her to put her foot down and enjoy the feeling of zipping through unspoilt countryside. She also felt this tremendous sense of privilege, swanning around on a weekday with no miserable job or demeaning boss to answer to. She knew this couldn't last forever but for now she was determined to enjoy it.

The store had been quiet, as expected for a rainy Thursday at the end of October. Being an independent shop as well meant completely individual products, which was a plus. Upon walking in, she had been struck with familiar and comforting sights and smells: reams of paper of all different thicknesses and textures were ordered satisfyingly on one wall, some loose and some bound into thick sketchpads with faux leather covers. The smell of thick wax crayons and powdery chalks hung in the air as she moved around the shop, her boots making the scuffed wooden floor creak underneath her. Acrylic paints every colour of the spectrum had been sorted into individual cubbyholes and delicately wrapped paintbrushes adorned shelves beside them. Further back in the shop was the haberdashery section, something which she had never really toyed in, but which intrigued her all the same with the large balls of chunky wool and various sized knitting needles amongst other treasures.

"Hi, can I help you?" A female voice came from behind her and when Millie turned around, she was face to face with a dark-haired woman. Older than her, about 45 to her 50, she guessed, wearing a long skirt and bright coloured pashmina over a vest top. She had stunning amber coloured eyes and wore a chunk of amber around her neck to match.

"Yes, I'm looking to get some art equipment," Millie replied, instantly feeling a little silly because what else would she be doing in a specialist art shop?

"Well, you've come to the right place!" the lady replied, indicating around the shop with a warm smile. "What sort of things are you after?"

"Well, I want to get back into painting. It's something I used to do a lot of but since moving I just haven't had the drive, bar a couple of dabbles."

"Ah, the dreaded 'painter's block'. Much less known about than the popular 'writer's block'," she smiled, knowingly.

"Indeed. So, I know what I'd usually go for but anything you can recommend would be great!"

"I can certainly do that," the lady replied. "What would you say your level of experience is?" Millie's mind strayed back to 'white-cliffs-of-Dover-gate'.

"I've been doing it a while…" she stuttered out, not really sure what else to say. The lady smiled knowingly.

"Ah, so that means you've got some talent, clearly," she said warmly. "Only a true artist would be so humble." Millie gave a shy smile. She wasn't so sure about that.

"What medium do you use, may I ask?"

"I'm an oil painter mainly but I'm starting to branch out into other styles. I've been experimenting a lot with gouache paints, so think I may purchase some of both," she explained. Lauren nodded thoughtfully.

"Well, I can pull a few pieces together and give you a bundle price, if that's ok?"

"Absolutely," Millie smiled, grateful for the decision making to be taken out her hands. It had been so long since she'd purchased art materials, she almost didn't trust herself to make such decisions.

The lady started busying herself around the shop, returning to the counter every now and again to place items down. Millie felt uncomfortable just watching her so instead turned her attention to the framed artwork on the wall. The pastel, nautical colours and cartoon-sequence style looked familiar and when she stepped closer and saw the scribbled signature she realised why.

"Ah, these are Lauren Shilton's paintings! I adore her work," she spoke out loud, mostly to herself.

"Well, thank you very much. It's always nice to feel appreciated," the lady replied with a chuckle, still fussing about extracting an easel from its selected spot in the store. Millie turned around to face her. Had she just said what she thought she had?

"I'm sorry. Did you say you are Lauren Shilton?" She turned and smiled.

"I am indeed!" she replied, and Millie felt a little flutter of butterflies. She couldn't believe this was the artist whose work she had admired for a long time, not just for the pure talent but because she had stepped outside the box and created things which obviously *she* liked, not just what sold for big money in galleries.

"Wow. It's so great to meet you. I absolutely adore your work!" Millie said, aware she was gushing but not feeling in the slightest bit embarrassed for it.

"Well, that's so lovely to hear! It's always nice to hear lovely things about your own creations." She finished collecting bits and pieces together and came back behind the counter, taking out thick paper bags to contain it all. "Where do you know my work from?"

"Back in London where I used to live there was a café I used to stop at on my way to work in the morning. I first saw one of your paintings in there and I remember looking at it every day and thinking how amazing it was. It was the one with all of the cats and dogs sat around in a café," she recalled. Lauren burst out laughing.

"Oh yes, I know the one. I think that's the most stress a painting has ever cost me. The original version ended up with muddy prints all over it when my delightful cat Margot decided to tread on it. After a good cry, I pulled myself together and ended up creating something twice as good, so I guess it wasn't all lost." Millie listened with amusement and almost pure disbelief that she was hearing this story straight from the artist's mouth, as Lauren added the last few bits into the bag and pushed them gently towards her, as an invitation to take them. "Here you go. That should be everything you need to get you back into the swing of things."

"Thank you. I do hope so," Millie replied, fumbling in her bag for some cash.

"And do keep in touch and let me know what you create," Lauren said, popping a business card into the bags with everything else. "I have social media and I love being tagged in pieces, especially when it's my shop's products that have helped to create them!"

"Oh, I definitely will," she replied. This little rendezvous may have seemed completely coincidental to others but to Millie, it definitely felt like fate that she had met one of her favourite artists, pretty much on her doorstep, right at the beginning of her revived creative journey.

Gazing at her new work of art in the fading light the following day, she contemplated sending it to Lauren, but nerves got the better of her. Besides, it wasn't completely finished yet. She always liked to leave a piece for a couple of days before going back to it to add and change bits. Sam had referred to it as the "faffing period." She'd never been quite sure what to make of that.

Her mobile buzzed and her heart gave its automatic expectant flip. Luckily, the screen flashed up as an incoming call from Amy and relief washed over her.

"Hey," Millie answered, walking over to the fire and prodding it. With the fading light came the chillier temperatures.

"Hey girl. I hope you're getting ready?" Her eyes flickered immediately to the clock on the wall, and she did a little gasp. Where had the day gone?

"I take it from that exhalation that you're most certainly

not getting ready," she replied drily. Millie caught a glimpse of herself in the mirror and began to rub furiously at the cracked paint stain on her cheek.

"Uh, got a bit side-tracked, to be honest. It's OK, I've got ages," she protested, taking the stairs two at a time and rushing into her bedroom. God, it was cold in here.

"Ages? We're meeting at Alfie's in just over an hour!"

"Yeah well, how long does it take to make yourself look like a zombie anyway?" Millie replied. It was the night of the Halloween party at the pub and the whole village was abuzz. She would be meeting Amy and the gang at Alfie's at eight for some drinks, before heading to the pub where there would be food, more drinks, dancing and "scares" (as promised on the chalkboard outside the pub). There had been family events during the day: a little Halloween disco for the kiddies, pumpkin carving and apple bobbing. But this evening's celebrations looked to be a little more raucous for the adults. Millie wasn't entirely looking forward to it in all honesty– both dressing up in costume and Halloween weren't really her favourite things. Back in London, Sam had complained about trick or treaters, calling them "little mercenaries" and declaring that "when we have kids, I shan't be facilitating such thievery." That comment made her stomach drop now, knowing what she knew.

"Well, just don't be late. I'm knocking on your door at five to eight, zombie-fied or not." And with that she hung the phone up.

Twelve

"*I* can't believe how late I am," Dana complained, flouncing about Alfie's bedroom whilst getting ready. Alfie felt this had turned into her favourite pastime – making him feel like crap. Her train down from Manchester had been severely delayed, meaning she'd arrived at his two hours later than planned. She'd said numerous times how dire the transport was to Cornwall and how much easier things would be if he was up there with her. Her usual argument, but this insistence on developing their relationship didn't match up with the fact she hadn't messaged him for nearly a week whilst she was up there.

He lay back on his bed and closed his eyes. Prior to her arriving today, he'd rehearsed words to say to her to break things off but from the minute she'd arrived, she'd been a whirlwind of stress and frustration and panic, and it just hadn't felt like the right time. Much like all the other "wrong times" before.

He watched her as she struggled to pull her corset tight around herself, wriggling around.

"A little help would be appreciated," she muttered with annoyance, and he took a deep breath, moving to help her. Her hair tumbled down her back in intricate curls, brushing his fingertips and with each yank he gave on the corset ties, her waist became tinier. He glanced up to the mirror in-front of them both, taking in her outfit. She would certainly impress in this, yet it made him realise their differences even more – she was happy to stand out from the crowd and be recognised. But for him, he was quite happy keeping a low profile in this little village, selling his paintings and living slowly. Which was another on his long list of reasons he didn't want to move to Manchester with her and why she had this constant, underlying annoyance towards him.

"What do you think?!" she pronounced, turning around, hands on hips and giving a little bob. She was wearing a tight, black corset, black hot pants and fishnet tights. Teamed with rabbit ears and drawn on whiskers.

"Very cute," he offered. Her face dropped.

"*Cute?!* Is that all you can say?" Alfie stayed quiet for fear of saying anything else that may annoy her. She rolled her eyes.

"Fine, whatever. Come on, I need a BIG drink." She tottered into his kitchen, where numerous drinks were laid out ready for the guests. A small gathering at his flat for a few hours max, then onto the pub. He could get through this night. He could.

"Gosh, you look…hot!" Millie declared in shock when she opened the door to Amy just before eight. She was a "zombie Dorothy" and, despite the scary make-up and neon contact lenses, she looked seriously attractive. She'd let her hair hang straight and loose and the gingham dress and apron clung to her body. She was going to get some serious attention tonight.

"Thanks doll. You don't look so bad yourself, considering you got ready in less than an hour." She winked and Millie rolled her eyes. She'd gone for a last-minute homemade zombie look: she'd torn an old grey shirt dress and smeared it with red food colouring, ripped some holes in an old pair of tights and added her battered old Doc Martens. Teamed with wildly backcombed hair, some seriously smoky eye make-up and a red lip she thought it was a pretty good effort!

There was a serious chill in the air as they made their way, arms linked, down the cobbled lane towards Alfie's beachside apartment. The turn of the season was clearly visible; where pots of charming flowers once sat on doorsteps, there were now glowing pumpkins, carved with a variety of designs and faces. Frilly bunting in windows had been replaced by cobweb netting and fake, oversized spiders. These cottages were primed and ready for trick or treaters tonight. Millie had made sure to leave a little bucket of sweets outside on her step for any late arrivals.

She felt a flutter of nerves as his house came into view: she had never actually been inside, and she'd only seen him in passing once since the incident in the pub when he'd saved her skin from Dana's insistent inquisition. It was in the village shop: she'd been buying a few standard essentials (mainly wine) and they'd met in front of the alcohol fridge.

"Buying a pint of wine?" he'd asked drily, giving her a sideways glance. She reddened, surprised he'd even remembered her first night in the pub when she'd got inexplicably slaughtered and used the same expression.

"Maybe," she'd replied, trying to sound mystical and aloof, but just sounding pathetic. A smile tugged at his lips (his full lips, she noticed without thinking).

"I'd better get a few more bottles of this for the party then," he said, reaching for two more bottles of Merlot. He brushed her arm as he reached across, and she felt a little fizzle. No, just static. It must be static. Back in the present, they'd reached his door, which she'd seen from the outside many times on her way to the beach. She could hear laughter from inside and the thrum of music. She felt herself take a large exhale. *Pull yourself together Millie.*

The door opened and the music became instantly louder, a surge of warm air hitting her. It was Ryan, dressed as a mummy, thick bandages around every part of his body. On the rare gaps between bandages, there were flashes of skin.

"Not naked under there are you Ry?" Amy cooed suggestively.

"Wouldn't you like to know," he winked, leaning in for a hug. "Wow, Millie you look great!" he said, reaching in and putting his arms around her too. She could feel flesh beneath her fingers. He was definitely naked under there.

"Thanks Ryan. I look better as a zombie than anything else."

He ushered them inside, shutting the door. They headed up the narrow stairs to the first floor and into the living room which was surprisingly spacious. There was a definite buzz in the air, and you could tell people were up for a party tonight. She went straight into the kitchen to pop her bottle of wine into the fridge but also to pour herself a large glass. She suddenly felt like she'd need it. She couldn't help admiring Alfie's kitchen whilst in there: small but spotless and minimalist, everything following a black and white colour scheme. Interestingly, his fridge door was the only thing in the room that was in any way cluttered. On closer inspection, she could see an array of paper tagged to the fridge with magnets, an old shopping list, a football ticket stub for the local team, a business card for a plumber. All mundane things. It was the slightly blurred photograph which caught her eye. It featured a beautiful lady with a beaming smile, wearing a pretty tea dress. In her arms, she held a gorgeous little boy, all dark hair and eyes and a cheeky grin. Behind them was a building in a very familiar pastel colour. Squinting even further, she could see a wooden, carved sign on it. *Rosemary Cottage.*

"His mum," she breathed, somehow recognising her instantly, remembering the conversation with Mr Slee the shopkeeper about Alfie's mum. She felt compelled to touch the photograph gently, subconsciously drawing comparisons with her own situation with her mother.

"It's a shame I couldn't stay that cute," a voice behind her said and she jumped out her skin, snatching her hand back from the photograph. Turning round, she came face to face with Alfie. He was really rather close due to the small proximity of the kitchen, and she could feel his presence. The delicious, woody smell of his aftershave was prominent. He was dressed as Count Dracula and the dark liner he'd put under his eyes looked surprisingly striking.

"I'm so sorry, I was just looking..."

"It's OK," he frowned, and he sounded like he really meant it. "It's there to be looked at."

"I didn't realise you'd lost your mum," she continued, unsure if she was overstepping the mark but carrying on anyway. "I met Eleanor when I worked for your dad and I just presumed..." she trailed off, realising she may be acting disrespectfully, talking so personally about his family when she barely knew him.

"That Eleanor may be my real mum? No. She's OK as a person, she's nice enough. I guess I'm just a bit old now for all that 'step-mum' stuff. I don't need another mother figure." Their eyes stayed interlocked, and a moment passed before she blurted out:

"I lost my mum too. About nine months ago." His face instantly changed, registering shock mixed with sadness. He learned against the counter, placing his can on the worktop.

"I'm really sorry to hear that," he replied quietly. "From

experience, I know there's nothing else I can really say to you except that it really fucking sucks." She let out a sharp laugh, not expecting those words to come from his mouth and he smiled back. It was like she could sense him defrosting from his usual icy manner.

"That's definitely one way of putting it," she replied finally. "Although our relationship wasn't the rosiest, so…"

"I'm not trying to brag but I can't relate that time. My mum was just the best," he said quietly, warmth radiating through his voice, edged with vulnerability. She watched him stare at the photograph.

"My cottage is named after her, isn't it?" she asked. He nodded and swallowed.

"It is. Please look after it."

Unspoken words hung in the air like a thick fog. She swallowed hard, not able to take her eyes off the photograph. A weird cocktail of emotions writhed through her: sadness, empathy, jealousy. She had no photos of her and her mother. Any that may have existed were clearly lost or misplaced because when she'd had the gut-wrenching job of clearing out her mother's flat after she'd died, there were no albums, photo frames or loose photos to be found. It was as though no-one else existed in her mum's life. Certainly, there was no trace of anyone. Alfie speaking snapped her back to the present.

"Did you want some of your wine or some of this?" he asked, producing a bottle of champagne from the fridge with a flourish, acting as though the sincerely intimate and sensitive conversation hadn't just happened between them.

"Ooh, some of that definitely," Millie replied, pointing to the latter, the intensity gone. But it felt like something had shifted between them, a wall broken down possibly.

He started to pour and then paused: "I warn you; it's strong stuff."

"I can handle it!" she declared confidently, chin jutting out.

Famous last words.

The rain hammered deafeningly on Millie's car windscreen. It was the type of day where you couldn't go outside, even for a moment, without getting soaked through. The clouds were an ominous blanket across the sky and the humidity almost unbearable. She drummed her fingers against the steering wheel and her leg jigged up and down in a nervous twitch. Staring out the window, she could see the soulless tower block where her mother lived, where she used to live. Since she could remember, this had been her childhood home. Back then, it hadn't seemed as scary or threatening as it did now. It was just home. When she was tiny, she'd actually found it quite cool that she lived in an "extra tall house", with a lift that whizzed you right up to the top and where you could see right out over everyone else from the windows. It was much more interesting than the three-bed semis her friends lived in anyway.

The outside space was still exactly the same from back then; multiple signs stating: "no ball games allowed" (which she noted with a snort had numerous footballs next to them now), a fenced off park which looked like it hadn't received a lick of paint in years and many walkways leading off to the rabbit warren of tower blocks. Back then, she'd remembered spending hours in the park, either alone or with friends, and loved pointing up at her bedroom window, right up on the sixteenth floor.

Until she turned around ten years old and started going round to friends' houses more often. It wasn't the difference in the physical buildings in which they lived, that still didn't bother her, but she started to notice stark contrasts between her home and theirs. There were no empty drinks cans and bottles piled up on the draining board or overflowing from bins in their houses. There was no lingering smell of stale alcohol in the living room and kitchen. There was no "Do not Disturb" sign on their parent's bedroom doors. The whole atmosphere seemed lighter, less on edge.

She'd found herself wanting to visit her friends' houses more and more, mainly Jenny's who was now her best friend. A couple of hours of playing would turn into a whole afternoon. Afternoons turned into staying for dinner, until eventually, she found herself staying the night most weekends. She didn't know why Jenny's parents were so welcoming of her being round all the time. She knew now it was because they knew what her mum was like and wanted to protect her.

The rain continued to hammer down and it was clear there would be no pause in it for a while so, with all the courage and energy she could muster, pushed open the car door and made a dash for the entrance. It had been years since she'd been there, choosing now to only meet her mum in neutral spaces. Not there had been many meetings. She'd seen her dentist more times than her mum in the last five years.

The lift to her floor seemed to take forever (why had it felt so quick as a child?) and her nervous jig continued as she waited. What sort of headspace would mum be in today? She'd left a message on her landline to say she was coming as it was the only way to contact her, so it wouldn't be totally unexpected. But maybe that was worse. Knowing her mum, she'd have purposely gone out.

Finally, the number sixteen flashed in digital red on the screen and the doors opened. The familiarity of the hallway to her flat was almost frightening. To think, she'd walked up and down here thousands of times in her life. The last time was many years ago, when she'd made the decision to move out for the sake of saving any shreds of relationship which still remained between them. She'd vowed never to go back; yet here she was.

She'd recently found out her mum was very ill. Exactly how ill, she wasn't sure but Sam's sister Tasha, who worked at the hospital, had contacted Millie a week previously, stating that she knew she was breaking all confidentiality protocol by telling her, but her mum had been in for several visits because she had liver cancer, and the prognosis wasn't looking good at all. Mum had stated she didn't want Millie to know but something in Tasha had compelled her to tell Millie, as her gut feeling was that she didn't have long left at all. Despite their differences and the heartbreak her mum had put her through, she knew she needed to see her. She'd regret it eternally if she didn't. Besides, maybe her mum had changed...

Nervously, she knocked, feeling uneasy at the quietness around her. It had never been particularly noisy in the corridors, but now it felt like everyone had moved out. She knocked again, feeling impatient now. Her mum had obviously gone out. It was so infuriating. It was always her putting the effort in, always her making the first moves...

Footsteps sounded the other side of the door and a scratching noise, like a chain being slid off a catch sounded. Slowly, the door opened a crack and Millie peered closely.

"Who is it?" came a weak voice.

"It's Millie," she replied, shocked at the voice. Surely that couldn't be her mum. The door opened wider to reveal a gaunt woman stood there, in a grey, washed-out tracksuit. Her hair was lank and balding in places and her face was so sunken in it looked almost skeletal. The tracksuit was far too big for her, making it clear she'd either been gravely ill for a long time, or she'd purposely bought one five sizes too big.

"Mum?!" Millie breathed, unable to comprehend what she was seeing.

"Yes, it's me. And yes, I know I look like shit. You don't have to look so shocked," she snapped.

"I'm sorry, it's just..." Her mum waved her hand in annoyance, as though flapping at an irritating fly.

"Spare me. Just come in and say what you need to say." Millie swallowed hard. Every inch of her logical brain was screaming at her to run away as it was clear this was going to end in hurt. But still, she followed her shell of a mother inside

and closed the door.

"So, who told you then?" her mum called snidely from the living room. As she walked down the narrow hallway of her childhood home, Millie's curiosity got the better of her and she peeked into her mum's room as she walked. A bed with a single sheet covering it was in the middle of the room. The ceiling was stained brown from cigarette smoke and the air was thick with it. This was a new thing; she had never smoked when Millie lived here. She wouldn't have been able to tolerate it. Her old bedroom door was closed.

"I just found out through the grapevine," Millie replied vaguely, not wanting to get Tasha in trouble.

"Hmm, sure. Someone sticking their nose in where it's not wanted, more like it." Her mum was moving unbearably slowly and when she lowered herself into an armchair, she winced. Millie perched on the edge of the sofa. Looking around, not much had changed. If anything, there was less furniture and less evidence that this had once housed two people. There were no photo frames on the walls anymore, only an armchair and a small sofa filled the space, with a tiny television in the corner. It looked bleak, uninviting, stagnant. The only familiar sight from her childhood was the empty spirit bottles lined up on the fireplace. Her mum must have spotted her looking because she snapped.

"Going to tell me off, are you? Tell me you 'told me so' about my drinking?" Millie swallowed. She was spitting her words like venom.

"I only came here to see how you are mum," she replied, honestly.

"See how I am? Well, I'm wonderful, as you can see." She

indicated her appearance. Furiously, she scrabbled in her pockets and pulled out a packet of cigarettes and a lighter, lighting it up then inhaling rapidly on it.

"How long have you smoked?"

"Not long enough for it to kill me. The liver cancer is doing that. So I thought I might as well do it now." She continued to suck on the cigarette like a lollipop.

"And the drinking…"

"Still going. What's the point in stopping now?" There was a minute or so of silence, as her mum finished the cigarette and immediately lit up another. The smell was overpowering but she couldn't leave yet.

"How's that boss of yours?" her mum asked, and Millie felt her heart leap a little. As Millie's previous boss and a friend of her mum's, it felt touching she was asking after him. They had met at an Alcoholics Anonymous group – Alan was a recovered alcoholic of fifteen years who now ran sessions for others and her mum was attending.

"He's good! He asks after you all the time." She snorted.

"Never comes to see me though, does he."

"He has offered you counselling many times though, mum. You can't forget that." She rolled her eyes.

"Counselling doesn't work. Talking to someone for half an hour about why you desperately need a drink makes you just think about drinking more. Pointless." She desperately wanted to point out that Alan had successfully stopped his alcohol abuse with the help of counselling, but she bit her tongue. There was no point. Her mum was clearly past the point of helping and

the effects of years of drinking were irreversible.

Another few awkward minutes of silence passed, her mum finishing the second cigarette and, much to Millie's relief, not lighting up a third. She was already having to fight back spluttering.

"Sam's doing well," Millie spoke suddenly, wanting to break the uncomfortable silence.

"Is he?" her mum answered, her voice sounding uninterested. She'd only met him once and hadn't been hugely welcoming then. Millie had decided afterwards there was no value in them meeting again after that. Another few pauses.

"I know why you're really here, Melissa," her mum croaked finally. Millie's eyes looked into her mum's. She frowned, not knowing what she meant. "You're just here because you've heard I'm about to snuff it and you want my inheritance. Well, I'm telling you now, it won't be yours. You think you can just rock up after years of lecturing me, making me feel like the worst mum in the world and then practically ignoring me, and then get everything I own? I know I've never been exactly rolling in money, but I have this flat and a little tucked away from when I worked. And I feel like you know that and you're wanting to take it!"

"Mum, that's completely untrue. I've come round just to see how you are!" Her mum snorted.

"That's rubbish. You need to at least admit to being a sneak if you're going to be one! Everyone thinks you're so perfect and well behaved but I know the real you, Melissa Jones, and you can be crafty when you want to be!" Millie blinked back tears, unable to

process what her own mother was saying to her. She'd said some hurtful things in the past, but this had to top it. She opened her mouth to reply but her mum started screeching at her.

"Just leave Millie. I know what you want and you're not getting it!" She started to splutter and cough, either due to the strain of shouting or the cigarettes she had just chain-smoked but Millie found herself standing abruptly and pacing quickly down the hallway. She heard her mum's coughs continue, hoarse and rough but getting fainter as she passed her childhood room. She wanted to go in but was afraid of what she'd find so left it. She needed to get out. Now.

What she didn't realise at the time, was that was the last time she would ever see her mother alive.

Thirteen

The pain. Oh, the head pain. The…the…light? That wasn't *normal* light. This was surely the searing light you experienced when you stood just metres from the sun?! Her mouth was as dry as the satsuma you forget about in the bottom of the fruit bowl: shrivelled and crusty. Her body felt clammy and there was a horrendous grunting noise coming from behind her.

Cautiously – mainly due to her fragile state but also because she had no idea what it was – Millie rolled over and was met with a sight that made her eyes widen. It was Amy, flung out on her back, one arm above her head. Her costume make-up from the night before was smeared over her face and her hair a remarkable bird's nest. Her mouth was wide open, contributing to the horrendous, guttural snoring rumbling in her throat. Despite the annoyance and her pounding head, Millie let out an exhalation of air, smiled and shook her head. There hadn't been many times she'd woken up with an unexpected person next to her, but this one would definitely be the most memorable.

Knowing Amy would be feeling like utter crap when she woke up (she'd never seen someone mix so many drinks before), she decided to let her sleep. Ignoring the screaming voice in her head telling her to down a pint of water and go back to sleep, Millie couldn't ignore the pull of the beautiful sunlight and the temptation of some fresh air. After two huge glasses of water, a gorgeously warm shower and a slice of toast, she headed out for a walk around the village. It was deathly quiet, even for an early Sunday morning and she knew this was likely down to last night's antics. Only the odd seasoned dog walker passed her, but she was grateful for the peace.

She turned the key in the lock extra quietly so as not to wake Amy – she would need her sleep today. Pushing the latch shut gently, she unwound her scarf from her neck and padded through to the tiny kitchen to pop the kettle on.

"Morning!" a voice came, making Millie yelp and jump out of her skin. There, leaning against the cooker and munching an enormous bowl of cereal, was Amy. Her face was completely flawless, every scrap of crazy make-up removed, her hair was pulled up into a casual bun, glistening wet from an apparent shower, and she was wearing an ordinary pair of joggers and a hoodie, which Millie recognised as hers after a longer look. Amy frowned slightly, pausing with the cereal spoon halfway to her mouth and looked downwards.

"Ohh, don't tell me...you're one of these people that get freaked out by other people taking your clothes without asking?" she asked.

"No, it's not that! I'm just...how are you...you were fast asleep?!" she pointed to the ceiling, indicating the bed she'd inhabited a mere hour before.

"Aaaand then I woke up. It's something I will strive to keep doing for quite a few years to come yet," Amy replied, placing the bowl in the sink and chugging back a glass of water. "Plus, I'm glad you don't get funny about sharing clothes. I just used your face wipes and your toothbrush," she continued, tapping her teeth. Millie rolled her eyes and reached past Amy to flick the kettle on.

"I take it you wouldn't be too hungover for a cuppa?" she asked, waggling a mug. Amy glanced at her watch.

"Better make it a quick one. I'm at work in an hour." Millie widened her eyes at her again in dismay. This girl would never cease to amaze her.

"So," Amy began and the word felt loaded, "what happened to you last night?" Millie slowed the unscrewing of the milk cap at the words.

"Uhh, I don't know, what did happen to me last night?"

"You mean you don't remember?" Amy replied, her voice shrill. Millie's heart dipped.

"No... should I?" These weren't words she wanted to hear. Amy's face of disbelief cracked into laughter, and she pressed her face into her hands.

"Oh wow...oh NO!" Millie groaned, shaking her head.

Fear flashed through her head as she desperately tried to remember something – anything – from the night before. Images flashed like an old-fashioned silent movie, flickering and fuzzy. She remembered being in Alfie's kitchen, looking at his fridge. Sharing an emotional moment. Drinking champagne straight from the bottle. Some unsavoury dancing with Amy and Daisy. Vague visions of the pub... She lifted her gaze to meet Amy's, who was staring at her with intent. Millie shook her head.

"Oh my gosh. You really DON'T remember! Let's just say *Dana* isn't your biggest fan right now," she half-explained.

"Dana? Dana, as in Alfie's girlfriend Dana?" she pressed. Amy's eyebrows shot up.

"Do you know any other Danas?" Millie ignored her sarcasm.

"Well, what did I do to upset her?" she asked, her voice shaking slightly. *Please* don't say she'd kissed Alfie. Surely she would have remembered that?!

"Well, Dana was dressed as some sort of naked-bunny hybrid. And you can't have a bunny without ears and a tail. Well, not that you seemed to think so..." her voice tailed off.

Like a light being switched on, Millie suddenly remembered something. Dropping the teaspoon into the mug with a loud clink, she rushed over to her bag from the previous night which had been discarded on the floor. A quick rummage and her hands felt on something fluffy. With trepidation, she extracted the not-so-mystery object from the bag, to reveal one, jet black, fluffy pom-pom tail and a pair of furry rabbit ears. She stared from the objects up into Amy's face. After a few seconds, they simultaneously burst out laughing and Millie flung a hand to her mouth.

"Did I *take* these?" she asked in disbelief.

"Took. Stole. Yanked from her very own head and arse." Millie's eyes widened.

"Nooooo!" Why?!"

Amy had explained the whole sorry story. It had happened in the pub, with Millie being approximately three bottles of wine under. Apparently, everyone had drunk a fair amount and the atmosphere was charged. They had been sat around a table together: Dana had perched on Alfie's lap, as had become compulsory in any social situation where other women were involved and her dominance had to be asserted. She'd been questioning the other girls on their choices of outfits, which were more "scary" than "sexy" in comparison to her own efforts. Millie had taken a drunken offence to Dana's interrogation, not pleased that her homemade effort had been mocked. So, the next time Dana had stood up to go to the bar, she had leapt out her chair and, in a swift movement not commonly associated with a person as intoxicated as her, had whipped the ears off Dana's head and ripped the tail from her behind. Absolute hilarity ensued, with the majority of the pub falling about laughing and jeering, some staring on in disbelief and Millie there in the midst of it all, holding the items aloft like some sort of trophy. Dana had stared daggers, practically expelling steam; had Millie not then fallen backwards over her own feet, she would likely have been on the receiving end of a wicked slap.

She peered out from behind the cushion she had pressed against her burning face. Her pounding headache had returned two-fold, and she couldn't believe what she was hearing.

"And what happened then?"

"Dana stormed out. She'd protested to Alfie to do something, but he was aware you were flat-out on the floor so he kind of just stood there like a shocked lemon. She ended up pushing him in the chest and leaving in a haze of distastefulness and fishnet tights."

"And Alfie..." she continued. Amy shook her head slightly and made a face.

"We got you out of there before we could chat to him. He looked pretty pissed though."

Millie couldn't quite believe what she had heard. She had never been the type of person to do something like this when drunk. She was the person *relaying* the drunken story, or laughing about one she had just been told, feeling second-hand embarrassment alongside a secretive smugness, relieved that it wasn't about her. She'd even been known to question how anyone could get in such a state to act out like that. Oh, how the tables had turned.

Amy had left shortly after finishing her explanation to go to work, leaving Millie alone with her shame. Her face was still burning red – she'd even considered sticking it in the freezer for a while in an attempt to cool down. How had her life come to this? She had come to Cornwall and the quiet, unassuming town of Sandyhaven to live a peaceful life away from drama. She wouldn't even have been bothered if she'd never gone out to a pub again. She wasn't interested in scandal. She wanted to live simply, try to find some inner peace, and hide out. And yet here she was, no doubt the talk of the village, behaving raucously, making enemies with powerful women and seriously pissing off the brooding village heartthrob. Her mother's words of *"you can be crafty when you want to be!"* and *"I know you think you're so perfect but you're not"* echoed in her head, as they regularly did and any shreds of positivity she'd developed about her new life and ability to move on were now decimated before her. How wonderful. She could and would *never* show her face again.

Fourteen

The village shop queue always snaked out the door, which usually didn't bother Millie. In all honesty, it wasn't often she came here as she preferred the larger variety available from the supermarket in the larger town nearby. Today though, she had wanted to keep a low profile, despite a few days passing since "the incident." However, those plans had been scuppered when she'd spilt a whole palette of paint after a misjudged step at the backdoor. She desperately needed some supplies to get the splattered mixture out of the carpet. Millie wasn't holding out much hope, especially as with each passing minute, she envisaged it spreading itself deeper into each individual cream thread. Maybe it would have been quicker to race to the bigger supermarket after all.

She watched the lovely Ivy, who lived a few doors down, come out clutching a wooden basket and dressed in her finest, like someone from the 1940s after exchanging their ration book for their weekly allowance of bread, milk and eggs. She gave Millie a curt smile and she returned it, shuffling forwards another few steps. One more customer and it was her turn. *Come on.*

"This bloody building business," she heard Ivy shriek, just over the square. Millie couldn't help but turn and see what this declaration was all about. She saw Ivy and a couple of others congregate around the village hall. She had never been inside but had often admired the outside of the building; a spectacular structure likely steeped in history, built to form part of the clock tower which stood proudly above the village square.

"There a date now, ees' there, maid?" Mr Slee hollered from inside the shop.

"Damn well is!" Ivy shouted back. "There's a final hearing in the New Year about whether they're knockin' the bleddy lot down! We need to make sure we're all there. Turn up in our droves!"

"Our droves of…ooh, couple a hundred?" Ethel replied sarcastically, her enormous dog appearing with her.

"Well, it's better than nowt'! We gotta do somethin'!" she retorted. "Else there'll be brand new flats 'ere blockin' up our square, our village heirloom will be crumbled in bits and we'll be overrun with them second home owners from bleddy LONDON!" she shrieked. Millie cringed awkwardly – is that what they thought of her?

"They don't mean you Millie love, take no notice," Mr

Slee said, making her jump. She realised she was next and stepped up and into the tiny shop, where the kindly shopkeeper served from behind a counter. It was *that* tiny.

"I hope not," she replied, pulling a face. "I mean, I know I'm from London but the cottage was offered to me. It's not like I just pop down on weekends and leave my penthouse up in the capital."

"We all know that, love. We love Alan and his family. And of course Alfie, e's a good lad. Stubborn but his 'eart's made of gold." She considered his comment – whilst he seemed very much a closed book she couldn't really blame him for that, knowing what she knew about him. And especially not moving forwards, after the spectacle she'd put on the other night…

"So, what can I get yer today m'lover? Drop of alcohol?" Mr Slee asked with a cheeky wink and Millie snapped back to the present, her cheeks pinkening.

"I need cleaning supplies please," she asked, deciding to avoid the jibe altogether (gosh, everyone really *did* know everyone's business around here), instead explaining the unfortunate incident from around half an hour before. It was probably dried in by now, creating an abstract mural on the floor. Mr Slee furrowed his brow and moved to the end of the shelves where all the cleaning products were kept.

"Hmm, I dunno if I've got anything of that strength in 'ere," he replied sorrowfully. "You'd have been better off going over the way to the big one." Back when she'd first arrived, she would have struggled to decipher that phrase, but she could now translate that as "you should have gone further afield to the bigger supermarket." *Hindsight is a wonderful thing, she thought.*

"I tell you who can help yer though!" he declared, his eyes lighting up and arms opening, as if gesturing to something behind her. She turned and saw Alfie coming up the steps behind her. He had on a charcoal grey winter coat and dark jeans, complimenting his dark hair and eyes. And matching the dark expression on his face.

"What am I helping who with and how?" Alfie asked, a confused tone to his voice.

"This beautiful young maid needs a hand getting some paint out 'er carpet," he explained. "And as our local artist, I think you'd have just the ticket!?" She swallowed, looking downwards. If the silence hung any longer, she'd just curl into a ball and wait for it to all go away. But suddenly Alfie, spoke.

"You'd better come with me then."

She faltered awkwardly in the doorway of his kitchen, not knowing whether to move or speak. Thankfully, his house was just across the square from the shop, so the walk there hadn't been long. Yet, they'd still walked in an uncomfortable silence and Millie couldn't help feeling eyes on them both as they made the trip. She was surprised he'd even let her in his house at all. The sight of his kitchen sparked some memories from the previous weekend, though still blurry and alcohol-tinged, particularly the arrangement on the fridge. The old photograph was still there – had it been her imagination or had the photograph been moved, as though he had taken it off and put it back on? Strange how she could remember that, yet couldn't remember practically *assaulting* his girlfriend...

He rummaged underneath the kitchen sink, bottles and spray cans taken out and lined up on the worktop. She stood and swayed from foot to foot, not sure where to look or what to say. After what felt like an impossibly long time, he selected three products and nodded to her, which she interpreted as a "let's go." He couldn't have looked any less interested if he tried.

"Thanks for doing this," Millie said quietly, watching Alfie apply product after product and expertly dabbing and wiping at the intimidating stain. Each time he scrubbed back and forth, she couldn't help but notice the muscles in his arm move along with it, visible even through his thin jumper. Despite the clear thawing in his frosty attitude towards her at his Halloween party, he certainly had his guard up again, but she couldn't blame him. Truth be told, she had half expected him to fling the cleaning products at her and push her out his home, yet here he was, grafting at it himself. He didn't pause his efforts, nor did he acknowledge her comment. She perched awkwardly on the sofa, wishing the ground would open and swallow her. Or better still, that she hadn't split an inordinate amount of paint all over the carpet in the first place.

"You look like you've done this before," she tried again weakly. She saw his hand slow down and if she wasn't mistaken, a small exhale left his lips.

"Not really. Most of my paint tends to end up *on* my canvas," he responded, and she would've been offended if it wasn't for the light, teasing tone to his voice.

"What exactly *were* you creating?" he asked. He imagined she'd tried repainting the walls and made a total hash, although there was no evidence of any amateur home decorating going on. She shifted. She hadn't expected him to ask anything which remotely indicated he was interested.

"Just... experimenting. I've been working on a few different things lately but just had a mishap with my palette." He paused and his eyes locked with hers, a look of faint curiosity on his face.

"Palette? You paint?" Millie realised that despite having brief discussions about *his* artwork, they had never broached the subject of her own passion. She shrugged.

"I try. I work on things for a while that don't always come to fruition. My ex called it my *"faffing period."* Alfie frowned lightly. That was a bizarre expression, he thought. It was weird hearing her mention an ex as well. Had she mentioned him before? He couldn't recall. He carried on dabbing, realising he didn't really know anything about her, apart from the fact she'd also lost her mum and then rocked up here thanks to her dad offering her the cottage. He wondered what her backstory was until, after a few minutes, realised the stain was lifting quite satisfyingly and his thoughts were cast aside.

"If you leave this last product in to soak and then give it one final dabbing in a few hours, you should be safe," he explained and he watched the worry drain from her face. He stood up, wiping his hands on his jeans. He had large hands, she realised. Alfie looked around.

"Do you have any artwork here?" he asked, a hint of inquisitiveness in his voice. Surprise registered on Millie's face.

"Are you suggesting you want to see some?" she asked, an edge of teasing to her voice. She may have been mistaken but she could have sworn she caught a lopsided grin playing on his lips.

"Maybe." She gave a small smile and against all the voices in her head telling her not to share it, she opened the cupboard under the stairs where she'd stowed away the easel and carefully manoeuvred it out.

"I used to hide in there as a kid, when we used to stay down here," he said, indicating the same cupboard she was battling the easel out of. She let out a small laugh at the image of Alfie curled up in the tiny space.

"A real *Harry Potter* in the making," she teased, gently placing it down, rotating it so Alfie could see.

She dared not look at his face initially, fearing a smirk or even a laugh but after a few moments of silence, couldn't resist. His face was registering shock, eyebrows raised and eyes slightly wide. Was that good or bad, she wondered?

"Say something, Alfie, please," she stammered out with a

nervous laugh. He broke into a smile himself and her heart flipped – it wasn't an expression she was used to seeing on his face. He ran his hand round the back of his neck and then through his hair.

"It's…good. Amazing, even. When did you learn to paint like this?" he asked. She could feel heat rushing to her cheeks and knew she was turning pink, so turned her face slightly, as though studying the canvas.

"Uh, well, never really! It's something I just started doing as a hobby one day. I'd always enjoyed being creative so decided to give it a go. I bought a cheap canvas and some even cheaper supplies and just kept trying. Oh, and I watched a lot of Bob Ross." He raised an eyebrow.

"Funny you say that, but I can see a lot of his "wet-on-wet" technique in here," he replied. "Oil paints, right?" Millie nodded.

"It's all I've ever really used. I've recently purchased some gouache though. I want to try and broaden my skillset a bit." He leaned in even closer to examine and she felt a rush a pride flow through her – how amazing was this? She was actually having a conversation with someone about her artwork, and someone who clearly was incredibly talented with a paintbrush. She felt some of the insecurities she had about her own ability- mostly drummed into her by Sam's petty comments – draining away.

She noticed a frown on his face all of a sudden.

"What is it? Is there something wrong?" she asked hastily, rushing to his side and swivelling her eyes over the canvas.

"No, no, not at all. Nothing wrong. Like I said, it's amazing. I'm just intrigued how someone as clumsy as you could create *any* art form," he responded, drily with a side-eye.

She looked up into his eyes and exhaled loudly. "I am *not* clumsy?! What makes you say I'm clumsy? Just because I've spilt one bit of paint?" She indicated to the now drying patch on the carpet.

"I'm referring more to your display in the pub back on Halloween. I don't think I've ever seen anyone *trip backwards* before..." he replied. There was no denying it, his eyes were twinkling as he said it. She suddenly had the feeling she was off the hook. She paused and started to stammer over her words, although somewhat pleased the elephant in the room had been realised.

"I'm *really* sorry about that, Alfie. I know it must have been *so* embarrassing for you. And even more so for Dana! I don't really know how it happened..." she stumbled. He let out a small chuckle, stopping her in her tracks, and shrugged.

"Forget about it. The sooner you forget it yourself, the sooner everyone else will."

"But I need to apologise to Dana. No matter how outrageous her outfit was, she didn't deserve what I did."

"She's out of the village for a few weeks now. It'll have blown over by the time you come back. If you really want to, I'll pass on your apology." He paused, holding her gaze a moment longer before turning to pack his products away in a bag. She watched him intently, wondering exactly what his relationship with Dana was all about. Was it purely for convenience? Was it because there were very few other young women in this village? Maybe they genuinely were in love. Hmm. Her instincts told her that wasn't the case.

Why did she even care? It was no business of hers who Alfie Drew associated himself with, which is why she was even more surprised when she found the following words leaving her mouth before she could stop them:

"Do you want to stay for a coffee?" He hesitated and she noticed a flicker of something across his face. Surprise?

"Thanks for the offer but I can't," he replied, and she felt her heart sink. Damn. She'd taken it too far. How awkward... "I need to get back, I have a commission to finish," he continued, making a beeline for the door. Pulling it open, Millie felt the November chill swirl into the cottage and watched Alfie pull his coat on. "I *am* interested in this artwork of yours though," he continued, doing up the buttons one by one. "I'd love to see more of it sometime. There are very few people around here I can "talk shop" with." He finished and his eyes met hers. Her stomach gave a flip. "How about you come over one evening and we can share pieces?" She was so shocked by his proposition, she just nodded, and he gave a small smile.

"What about Dana?" she asked. He paused and let out a small shrug.

"She doesn't like art. She won't want to be involved," he answered. That's not quite what Millie had meant but she just nodded, and a smile tugged at her lips.

"How about Friday evening. Seven, at mine?" he said,

moving down the two tiny, stone steps at the front of her house.

"Ok," she replied, still feeling slightly confused. He gave a brazen smile.

"You can even bring some wine if you like." She blushed intensely and he smirked, raised a hand and started to walk down the lane towards the main village and his apartment.

She turned and closed the door, staring around the room. What had just happened? Had she just accepted a date with Alfie Drew? The man who had seemingly detested her when she'd moved here.

Her head pounded and she was pretty sure there would be at least three permanent frown lines etched into her head from now on. It just wasn't coming together this time. Colours didn't make sense anymore – was this even a shade of blue?! It looked green?! Maybe it was. Her eyes were tired and her back aching. But this was a once-in-a-lifetime opportunity to provide a piece of art for a local showcase. So many incredible people were going to be there, and it could be her chance to get her work taken seriously. All her previous chances had failed but you never knew when luck could change... Must. Keep. Going. It would transform into something. It would.

Arms snaking round her waist caused her to jump and resulted in a smear of blue (or was it green) paint to spread across the canvas, right over an already painted section of creams and greys.

"Fuck's sake, Sam!" Millie yelled in frustration, quickly diving for her wet cloth and carefully dabbing at the messy gloop.

"God, sorry. I was only trying to show you some affection!" he declared, arms retreating. She felt her heart sink at the annoyance in his voice and exhaled loudly.

"I know, it's just I've been working away at this for hours and I'd really like to finish it."

"I know," he replied huffily. "I've barely seen you this weekend." She glanced across to where he was stood, hands stuffed in pockets, lip pouting like a four-year-old. She resisted the urge to roll her eyes.

"You know how much this means to me, Sam and I've been working flat out this week in the office. This weekend has been my only chance to get this done. The exhibition is only two days away." The fresh paint that had been splodged in error was mostly removed and the painting was saved.

"There. No harm done," Sam said lightly, as she put down the cloth and paintbrush and wiped across her face with the back of her arm. He came towards her again, his arms grabbing her waist again and pulling her close into him. He started to run kisses lightly down her neck, his hands tightening and untightening in rhythm. She sighed internally. It wasn't that it wasn't nice, but she just wasn't in that place right now. Regardless of the fatigue from her ten hour straight painting session and the aches and pains that had been inflicted mentally and physically, Millie was still feeling very fragile from the devastating news she had received weeks earlier. Learning she *couldn't conceive had drained all her needs, desires and wants for physical connection. She wasn't sure if this was going to be a temporary sensation or something more serious. She didn't want to think about it.*

What she did know, is that Sam clearly didn't share her feelings. If anything, his desires had increased two-fold. He could barely keep his hands off her. She hadn't really communicated her feelings with him, and she had no idea herself, let alone how she would explain it to someone else. Instead, she'd just made continuous excuses as to why she couldn't. She could tell his patience was wearing thin.

After a third attempt to subtly move away, Sam let go a little too roughly.

"What is the problem? I'm trying to show some affection to my fiancé and yet all I'm getting is constant rejection?" She paused, a little shocked at his outburst. He'd always had a short fuse, but she put it down to work stress and passion rather than a genuine intolerance of her.

"I'm sorry Sam. I'm just not in the right headspace," she stammered, tucking strands of escapee hair behind her ears nervously.

"But you never are," he responded, anger in his voice. "I know you're dealing with some stuff right now, but we can't let it affect our relationship." Millie tried to process his words, feeling a simmering mixture of annoyance, anger and hurt, yet struggling to process them. "Some stuff" completely demeaned what she was going through. He stared directly into her eyes whilst she tried to formulate a response. This conversation

shouldn't be happening whilst she was covered in paint and fighting off eye strain. He remained quiet but looking at her intensely, as though anticipating a response.

"You've still got energy for all this though, haven't you," he said venomously, indicating the almost-finished canvas. She glanced at the artwork, feeling a sense of pride overcome her despite the intense situation she was in.

"It's different Sam. This helps me. It gives me time to process..." He cut her off abruptly.

"I'm your FIANCE Millie. Do I not matter to you at all? You've completed neglected me the last few weeks and for what? This will destroy us if you let it, Mils!" She felt anger bubbling up inside her. She couldn't believe how ruthless he was being, how uncaring. He'd never have won awards for his compassion, but this was next level. Muscles tightened in her face, and she felt her teeth begin to grind.

"You don't get it Sam. I've been told I'm not able to have children. NOT ABLE. Does that register in any way with you? That you do not understand how I'm feeling? That I may need time before I'm able to just jump into bed with you to do the act that – oh yes – for so many people, creates children?! I need time and you just don't understand. You're too concerned with your own needs and desires that you don't consider my feelings! You can be such a selfish bastard!" The word lava that erupted from her mouth ceased and she found herself out of breath. His face remained red and focused on her face for what felt like hours but could only have been about two seconds. Without saying a word, he turned and stormed out the room. She heard *his heavy footsteps on the wooden stairs, the clatter of keys being retrieved from the pot and finally the slam of the front door. Intense silence ensued.*

Millie felt a sickening feeling course through her, and hot, angry tears simmered in her eyes. She glanced across at the canvas she had spent the last two days poring over intently. Each brushstroke became so clear, evidence of hours of concentration and hope. Hope for what, she asked herself. It had allowed her to smother her feelings of desperation and focus on something else but, she realised, as soon as the painting was finished and there was nothing else to concentrate on, these would come flooding back in a river of pain and loneliness.

In one swift movement, she picked up the open tin of white paint she had been using to mix and without hesitation, launched it. The thick liquid smacked spectacularly against the canvas, splattering on the floor and up the wall behind. Some seeped down the painting, leaving spatters of white, other places were so thick they covered the painting, causing irrevocable damage. She stood back, realising she was exhaling heavily and stared at her now destroyed painting. Hot tears leaked from her eyes and down her cheeks and she found herself sobbing out loud, dropping the paint tin to the floor and sitting down in its contents. Nothing mattered. Nothing mattered anymore and never would again.

Fifteen

The watery winter sun kept hiding behind the clouds and then emerging again, causing a constant changing rhythm of shade and light in Alfie's flat. All on the first floor, set above the tiny village Post Office, it was a moderately sized place: one main living area which housed a squishy, corduroy corner sofa, coffee table, a large spotlight lamp and a farmhouse style dining table, complete with benches. The main feature was the huge picture window, providing a glorious, unspoilt view across the bay. A small kitchen dog-legged off, containing everything one could need but not much free worktop space after that. The only other room was the bedroom, which amazingly also sat on the scenic side of the building, so he could wake up in his bed and literally see the sea stretched out in front of him. His small en-suite completed the apartment. He knew how lucky he was to have this place; he could remember looking at it every time they used to visit in the summer and thinking how fun it would be to live there. It felt like fate. Whilst it was hugely tainted by the fact he'd had to lose his mum in order to live here, he knew in other ways he was extremely fortunate: there were clear benefits to having no mortgage and no rent; it meant he had the freedom to follow his passions for art and creating rather than scraping through in a job he hated. He'd swap it all in a heartbeat, though, if it meant having mum back.

He'd been shocked to learn about Millie's mum at the party – his dad had never mentioned anything but then I guess he'd never had a cause to. She'd said something about their relationship *'not being rosy'* and he wondered what that meant. He couldn't fathom ever having a big fall-out with his mum – aside from the usual gripes and bickers during his teenage years, they'd never argued. He couldn't imagine saying a harsh word to her, ever.

He pondered on this whilst trying to work on a commission. However pretty, the changing light in the living room was giving him some issues with his artwork this morning. The shade caused his colours to dim, appearing dull and lifeless and yet when the sun decided to make an appearance, he found the shadows cast made it impossible to focus on shape and line. He sighed, placing his paintbrush into the water pot and conceding defeat. He had really wanted to finish this by tomorrow when Millie would be coming round. For some reason, he felt incredibly apprehensive about her looking at his work, even though he had invited her himself. Why had he done that? He wasn't entirely sure; it was something about being in close proximity to her, acting the hero by cleaning her stained carpets, seeing her eyes up close for what felt like the first time. The deep green with honey flecks...

Jeez. This felt strange. She was just some girl from London who had moved here on a whim and who he suddenly discovered liked art. He hadn't warmed to her when she first moved here – he suspected it was something to do with the fact he was staying in mum's cottage. Well, not *her* cottage but the once which held so many memories of her. It felt deeply personal, even though that hadn't been Millie's fault. Yet the fact he knew very little about her intrigued him. Plus, there were very few people around here who shared his passion for art and that had piqued his curiosity.

He hadn't mentioned it to Dana. To be honest, he hadn't spoken to her much at all lately. There was little to say: she had been away for a few weeks up in Manchester. He had seen a few social media posts, mainly selfies of her with a perfectly made-up face and signature pose (which he knew would have taken about twenty attempts until she was satisfied to post). There were some of her friends and others he didn't recognise in a trendy looking wine bar; several of them were young men but Alfie didn't feel too jealous – he almost hoped she was with one of them so there was a solid reason to break it off with her for good, which spoke volumes really. Their connection had never been one to rival that of Jack and Rose. In fact, the more he reflected on it, the more he just felt like a convenience to her when she decided to come back. But still, it remained that it would be simpler to keep quiet about his plans with Millie – she was only coming over to look at some art, after all…

The light had waned considerably, despite it only just turning three in the afternoon. This was winter starting to show itself and he conceded defeat for the day, packing his art things over to the side of the room and settling down instead with a book, on his sofa overlooking the beach. The art would have to remain unfinished.

No matter how many times she had taken this walk down the lane towards the village square, it never once grew tiresome. Even now, in rapidly fading light and with fat drops of rain beginning to fall; it held a wholesome and homely feeling which Millie had never felt in her London neighbourhood. She'd spent months on end, hours on Pinterest and what probably ended up an inexcusable amount of money revamping the rented flat she and Sam had shared together, desperately trying to make it feel like home. And yet, with only two mere months and a small injection of cash, Rosemary Cottage felt more like home than ever. She hadn't dared to think about whether she would stay, or if this would just be another chapter in her dramatically changing story. I guess it depended on whether she ended up having something to stay for. Or, she pondered, as Alfie's flat came into view in the distance, if there was some*one* worth staying for. It wasn't something that had even been remotely on her radar, but the last few days had got her thinking…

Her stomach was churning as she edged closer, quickening her pace now that the rain had started coming down sideways. A wind whipped up through the lane like a mini hurricane, blasting her hood back down and she cursed. What a waste of time doing her hair had been. One swift flare of wind off the beach and the gentle waves she had teased into it were blown out and starting to frizz. No doubt the minimal make up she'd put on would also be worse for wear. She grumbled to herself. At least her carefully chosen outfit of bottle green jumper dress and thick, cosy tights would be safe underneath her enormous coat. She hadn't wanted to look like she'd tried too hard. She was only going to look at some paintings, for God's sake. Yet, she didn't want to look a total mess either. It had been so long since she'd done this whole dating thing, she had no idea what she was doing. Especially when it hadn't even been confirmed whether this was actually a date or not?

Another two hundred metres or so and she'd be there. The watery glow of the streetlights in the square were becoming more visible but, through the rain, it was difficult to see anything at all. That was, except, for a moving figure further in the distance, right down on the beach. Millie narrowed her eyes; there was definitely something there, just discernible through the gap which sloped down to the sand. Surely no-one would be foolish enough to be on the beach now, in high tide and such stormy conditions! There was barely any daylight left either. A faint yet urgent sound caused Millie's feet to automatically pick up speed. Something didn't seem right. As she grew closer, it became apparent something was, in fact, very wrong. Around five metres into the choppy, dull grey water was a child. Millie couldn't make out exactly how old but at a vague guess she'd think about ten. Once she'd reached the slope, she could clearly see the child was bobbing frantically in the water, her screams being carried on the wind.

"Please help me!" her guttural cries came and the petrified look on her face caused Millie to find herself unzipping her boots and throwing off her coat before another thought could enter her head.

"Just keep trying to stay afloat, I'm coming in!" she yelled back, entering the water already.

The severe cold was a shock, but Millie kept ploughing onwards. She hadn't yet swum here properly herself, but she knew from conversations with locals that the sand shelved down dangerously at high tide, with only around a metre of level ground before your feet would give way beneath you, succumbing to the depth of the water. The water lashed and thrashed around her, smacking her in the face and causing her eyes to brutally sting. The noise was deafening and for a brief moment, she felt at the mercy of this powerful machine. But the sight of the child's ashen, terrified face ahead caused her to keep cutting through the water. She was quite a proficient swimmer, having gone to the local pool three evenings a week after work back in London. But the Cornish waters presented a whole different challenge, especially as she was fully clothed, and the shock of the cold was beginning to seep through her.

She reached the child who immediately flung their arms around her neck, gripping on for dear life. The sudden weight dragged Millie under but then she found a wave shoot her back up to the surface and she gasped in the air. It felt like they were in a washing machine, being thrown around.

"Try…not…to…. push down…on…me," Millie tried to communicate with the girl between gulps of air, but the girl wasn't listening, pure panic etched on her face and her nails digging into Millie's neck. Millie tried frantically to look for the shore but to her horror, it seemed further than it had before. *Just kick your legs Millie* she thought. *You can do this…*

Gosh, the weather was really lashing down out there, Alfie thought to himself, hearing it violently pepper the picture window looking down onto the beach. It had come on so quickly too. He cranked the thermostat up a notch, to ensure it was super cosy. He couldn't help but notice that Millie was ten minutes late – was she not coming? He wouldn't really blame her if she wasn't, to be honest – he realised he hadn't exactly been the friendliest of people since she had moved here. Maybe she'd decided to keep a wide berth. But the last time they'd talked, in the cottage, things had seemed lighter, friendlier. He'd even sensed a little spark of something...

He pondered over his thoughts as he sipped one of the two glasses of wine he had poured in anticipation of her arrival. There would be no jokes about wine tonight, he'd vowed, although once a bottle or two had gone down, who knew what they may be saying to each other. He took another large glug and stood in-front of the picture window, hoping to maybe catch sight of her heading down the lane to his right.

Instead, movement in the sea to the left caught his eye. The light was all but gone now, yet a small shaft of light from the lamppost closest to the beach cast a ray across. He squinted. It looked like a buoy. Yet the buoy looked like it was in two parts? Two parts which were moving. He focused even harder and to his sheer horror, he realised it was two people, there in the sea. Without hesitation, he placed the wine down and raced down the stairs, not even pausing to close his front door. The storminess of the night hit him immediately, the deafening roar of the waves echoing through his brain. The tide was so high and so ferocious that water was starting to spill out up onto the pavement at the top of the slope and spraying over the wall. He gulped, looking around as he ran. There was no-one else around but him.

Reaching the top of the slope he could see these two figures now – they couldn't have been more than five metres from land, but the violent waves and the depth of the water was stopping them from coming in.

"Help!" he heard a voice call and something in him dropped. Grabbing his phone out his pocket and switching on the powerful torch, he shone the light onto the water and his stomach twisted when he spotted a young, terrified looking girl clinging onto an equally terrified looking Millie.

Before crashing into the water himself, he hollered "HELP NEEDED ON THE BEACH, PEOPLE IN THE WATER!" at the top of his voice in the direction of the pub, which was only metres from his home and within seconds found himself in the water. His body shrunk at the shock of the cold. He felt himself dip involuntarily under the water. When his head bobbed back up, he was a metre or two from shore and out of his depth, but he was also face to face with Millie.

"Come and hold onto me!" Alfie called to the young girl who tentatively released her grip from an exhausted looking Millie and flung herself onto Alfie. With all his strength, he swam backstroke towards shore, finding his feet and carrying the girl up the slope and onto the safety of the pavement, where a crowd from the pub had now gathered. As soon as he could see the girl was being tended to by several people his head snapped straight back to the water where, to his utter relief, he saw Millie exiting the water at the bottom of the slope, crawling forwards. He raced down and hooked his hand under her arm, aiding her to the top and away from the dangerous waves.

He didn't speak to her, allowing her to catch her breath. She was clearly drained, and her entire body was shivering, hair plastered to her face and mascara trailing down from her eyes. After a few moments, he helped her slowly stand and with one look at her, she collapsed, the full weight of her exhausted body leaning onto his and sobbing into his shoulder. He held her head firmly and assured her everything was OK now. She was safe.

Sixteen

"Thank you," Millie said her voice almost a whisper. She accepted the steaming mug from Alfie and cradled it close, a layer of fluffy blanket over her skin taking the edge off the heat. Her voice was hoarse, her throat still stinging from the influx of salt water she had involuntarily consumed a mere hour before. Had it only been an hour? Time seemed to have moved in slow motion from the moment she had felt her tight-clad feet leave the relative safety of the beach and crash into the waves after the girl.

It hadn't entered her mind who the girl was or why on Earth she'd found herself in that predicament until long after she had left the water. As she slumped at the top of the slope, clinging onto Alfie for dear life and desperately trying to regain her breathing, she could remember seeing a man and a woman with their arms wound around the girl, all three of them sobbing. She had overheard snippets of conversation as Alfie supported her up the bank, saying they were on holiday from Germany, visiting a town further down in Cornwall but had come here for the day for a beach walk gone seriously awry. She struggled to think how the incident could even have happened, or what made them think it was in any way a good idea but decided not to expend too much mental energy on it – it had happened, it was done and thankfully no-one was seriously hurt. The parents had tried to grab her for a thank-you hug but she was just too depleted and continued to stumble in the direction of Alfie's home.

She really had thought that was it: the end. She had never swum in water like that before and had never felt truly at the mercy of such powerful waves. It would take a long time to go back in after that, she knew. Even sitting here in the warm glow of Alfie's apartment, seeing and hearing the still-roaring waves made her feel uneasy. She turned her body slightly, so she was facing away. Alfie had sat next to her but not too close, leaving a gap between them and holding his own mug of tea on his knee.

"Are you sure you don't want something stronger?" he enquired, nodding his head towards the tea. Millie smiled weakly.

"No thank you. My head's swimming enough already, if you mind the pun, without adding alcohol to it," she replied, pulling a face. They both took a contemplative sip.

"Are you sure the clothes are comfy enough?" he asked tentatively again, and Millie smiled inwardly. This was the kindest she had ever known Alfie to be, even topping his assistance cleaning up her paint spillage - it was like a complete one-hundred-and-eighty-degree flip from the man she had first met.

"They're fine, honestly," she answered. It was strange to be sat in his clothes, let alone on his sofa in his flat. After the incident, she had felt so completely drained and exhausted, and her entire body soaked through that walking the half a mile back up to her house in the driving sheets of rain and wind had seemed an inexplicable thought. It just naturally happened that she found herself back at Alfie's. He had immediately handed her a pair of his shorts (which hung halfway down her calves), a t-shirt, a soft, grey hoodie which completely swamped her and thick, welly socks. It had felt downright bizarre padding back into the lounge in the attire - particularly because she was hyper aware she had no underwear on underneath - and getting comfy on his sofa. After a steaming hot shower which had brought warmth back into her body and drying her hair roughly with a towel (the hairdryer seemed too much effort) she felt a little more normal, although still very shaken. This is where the hot mug of tea and fluffy blanket had helped to take the edge off even more.

"It's really howling out there," Alfie observed quietly, and Millie could hear the waves smashing against the sea wall and the buildings along it. She shuddered slightly at the thought.

"How is it that the clock tower stays up? It looks ancient and it must have taken a battering over the years," she enquired.

"Ah, that clock tower has withstood all manner of weather, including the great storm of '88. Made of strong stuff. They don't make them like that anymore," he replied, then raised his eyebrows, "or so they all tell me." They both laughed.

"Besides," he continued, reaching forwards to set his mug on the coffee table, "there's every chance it won't be there for much longer." She frowned.

"What do you mean? You just said it's virtually indestructible?"

"I heard some news down in the square a few weeks back now. Some huge property companies are looking to build luxury flats there. The council are behind it all the way of course because they'll get a hefty sum from the land. Apparently, it's "dead wood" as it's not used for enough events. Not listed, apparently, which surprises me. Unless the village hall gets a new lease of life very soon, it's done for." He sighed heavily. "Don't get me wrong, I know I'm not a lifelong local like Mr Slee or Ethel, but the village just wouldn't be right without it. It's historic."

"Plus, your apartment would lose its view if luxury flats went up," Millie added. Alfie's face darkened.

"Oh yeah! I hadn't thought of that!" he retorted. "There must be something we can do to save it, if not just for my spoiled sea view." She could tell he was joking but agreed with him. They both went quiet, as if musing on the subject until Millie couldn't stifle it any longer and let out an enormous yawn. Alfie turned to her and gave a little laugh.

"Tired?"

She nodded. "Exhausted. But hey, I came here to look at your art," she answered, shuffling up slightly and rubbing her eyes.

"Another time, maybe?" he replied, taking in her tired voice. "It really doesn't matter now. Shall we get you home?" She pulled a face at the thrashing sounds of the sea outside, the wind still whirling and the rain battering the window. "Or…" he continued, noticing her hesitation, "you could stay here? I'd be on the sofa, of course," he clarified quickly, taking in the shock on her face. She didn't say yes, but she didn't say no either and Alfie decided to make the decision for her. "Let me show you where everything is. Hopefully by the morning, after a good sleep and when it's all settled down outside, you can go home safely." Millie smiled gratefully and gave a small nod.

It was weird, Alfie noted to himself whilst taking her through to his bedroom, that it didn't feel weird to do this, despite her still being virtually a stranger. Once he'd shown her where everything was that she might need, adding extra blankets to the bed, they paused by his bedroom door.

"I appreciate this," she said quietly, "thank you." He exhaled and smiled, glancing down at the floor, so to break the intense eye contact.

"Consider it a peace offering for how foul I've been to you," he replied. She moved closer a step and he could feel the heat coming off her body, catching her delicate scent. She reached down and took his hand gently, the touch passing electricity through their hands. Surely it couldn't just be him who felt it? She held his gaze as he held his breath and after another second had passed, she pressed her mug into his hand and let go.

"You haven't been *completely* foul," she murmured, a small smile playing on her lips. "Maybe just a little bit of a twat…" Despite the fact she was outright insulting him, the intensity of the moment was palpable. Should he go in? Or stay where he was. It seemed a fine line decision he hadn't seen himself having to make earlier that evening…

"You did WHAT?!" Jenny's face conveyed total shock on the screen. Millie watched her on the screen, a mass of curls scraped back off her face with a bright headscarf. She was feeding Leo who was making cute little noises which made her heart ache.

"I did what I had to do! You can't tell me you wouldn't have done the same Jen? The girl was *drowning*." Millie continued washing out her paintbrushes in a bowl of warm water, as Jenny pulled a face.

"Yeah but, don't they have lifeguards for that?" she responded, and Millie let out a laugh.

"Not in November, after dark!" Jenny rolled her eyes.

"Sorry. Forgot you're a Cornwall expert now," she said but the teasing in her voice showed she was being light-hearted.

"There's something else as well…" Millie began. Instantly, Jenny sat up.

"Yes…" she encouraged. Millie paused, laying some brushes down on a towel and beginning to pat them dry.

"Afterwards, I stayed in Alfie's bed."

"I'm sorry?! Is this Alfie the artist? You stayed in his *bed*?!"

"Yes, but don't get *too* excited. He was on the sofa." She took in her friend's raised eyebrows and knowing expression. "He *was*," she insisted. Jenny sat back again, looking dejected.

"*THAT* – quite frankly – is poor gossip. How am I supposed to live my boring sex life vicariously through you when you don't jump at obvious chances? Come back to me when you know his shoe size, if you know what I mean," she winked over-exaggeratedly. Millie burst out laughing and Jenny joined.

"I think *everyone* knows what you mean when you're around Jen. I'm sorry to disappoint you, but I was recovering from my near-death experience!" Jenny rolled her eyes.

"Even heroes are allowed their happily-ever-after Millie. You deserve some goodness in your life. And goodness from hot, creative type men is most certainly encouraged!"

Millie rolled her eyes; her friend was way off the mark. The morning after her traumatic ordeal, she'd woken early, the weather now calm and still. She'd wanted to leave before he woke and, after retrieving her clothes from the dryer and putting them on, had quietly padded through his apartment to leave. She paused to watch him asleep on the sofa; he looked uncomfortable, barely fitting with nothing but a small cushion under his head. She'd felt a stab of guilt having just spent the night in an extremely large, comfortable bed which she'd been far too aware smelt exactly of him. His bedroom had matched the rest of his flat – minimalist yet still warm and inviting. Despite the events of the night before, she'd slept more soundly than she had on any other night since arriving in Cornwall.

Quietly, she'd left without him knowing and they hadn't spoken for a few days following. She wasn't sure what to say. Whilst nothing had happened between them, sleeping in his bed had still felt intimate and there was no doubt that they had shared a moment at his bedroom door. Yet, the fact he hadn't messaged or called by spoke volumes to Millie that he clearly wasn't interested, in *that* way. Besides, he was with Dana. God knows what she would say to Millie if she knew she'd slept in his bed. Thank goodness she was away and would never find out.

"Well, you know I know you well Mils and, whilst I believe you, I also think there's more to this story than you're letting on," Jenny said, lifting Leo onto her shoulder and gently patting his back, no doubt encouraging him to burp.

"Whatever you think," Millie replied, airily.

"I *do* think," Jenny answered. "Anyway, have you had any thoughts about coming back to visit us? Leo is desperate to meet his Godmother and I'd love you to meet him before the christening in February." Millie slowed her cleaning as she articulated a response.

"You know I'd love to come and see you all Jen it's just… there's some things I'm still trying to work through. About coming back to London."

"I haven't seen Sam around, if that's what you mean," Jenny replied bluntly.

"It's not just that. It's a whole feeling I have and…I'm working on it," she replied, wanting to close off the conversation as soon as possible.

She couldn't keep putting off a return forever, especially as her Godson was there – she had been so honoured to be asked to be his Godmother and he deserved one who made the effort to come and see him. Once again, she felt like she was the problem, letting people down. It was such a difficult feeling to shake.

Seventeen

Dana strode down the lane leading to Alfie's house with purpose and intention, the rage seeping through every step. It never helped that she had to park her car up the top and walk down – *such* an inconvenience. Despite the fact his flat (or *apartment*, as she preferred to call it) was worth a lot of money, it was purely because it was in this tiny hellhole that other people seemed to go mad for it. All she saw was an apartment that was far too small, only on one level and far too overlooked; it was the goldfish bowl of the village.

Still, that wasn't why she had returned early that week. She hadn't wanted to leave – work was prosperous, and she was making so many connections – some professional, but some personal too. She'd enjoyed sharing pictures of her events on Instagram, garnering plenty of likes and comments. None, however, from Alfie.

And last night, she'd clearly learned why he had been too busy to comment. For she had received an Instagram message in the early hours of yesterday morning with a photo attached of that weird London-deserter, Millie-something, leaving his apartment early in the morning. It had come from someone who worked in the village shop who Dana had barely spoken to – she could only assume they were trying to stir up trouble. Her blood boiled at the notion of someone pitying her, especially when it was over this Millie. Very plain, she had seemed, and clearly not a clue in the world about who she was or where she was going. Leaving London for the back end of Cornwall? What was this woman's story? Not to mention the way she had showed her up in the pub on Halloween. She was still fuming about that and Alfie's pathetic non-reaction to it.

The light had faded by now and she passed a familiar looking door on her right…the light was on up in the bedroom. Of course, this was *Millie's* door! She remembered it faintly from several weeks ago now when she had been with Alfie. Without thinking, she changed course and stormed over to it, fist raised ready to batter the door down but at the last second, thought better of it. She hadn't time to waste on her and she wanted to hear it from Alfie first, if he really had decided to have some sordid affair with this woman. She just couldn't fathom how he'd possibly choose her over herself?!

Instead, she sashayed down the lane towards Alfie's house, deciding to plough her intense fury into his door instead.

BANG BANG BANG. Screw the doorbell, Dana thought. Knocking had much more effect. Hastily, she fluffed her hair and then perfected her scowl. He needed to know just how *angry* she really was about this. Slowly, the door opened, and Amy appeared. What was this? *Another* woman!

"Oh, hey Dana," she said in a monotone voice. "What's up?" Rage seeped through her veins.

"Where is he?" was all she could reply.

"*He?* If you mean Alfie, he's up here with us. We're all watching a film." Dana huffed and moved Amy aside - she didn't have time for this. She clattered up the narrow steps which lead to his apartment and upon entering the living room was met with the sight of a whole group of people sprawled out on various parts of the sofa and laying on the floor, cushions scattered everywhere and numerous empty bottles of wine on the table. She recognised them all from the pub, Alfie's group of friends. She had never felt an urge to get to know them all. They were clearly tight-knit and very different to her.

As soon as he saw her, Alfie's relaxed expression immediately turned to one of confusion.

"Dana? I thought you weren't back for another three days?" he asked, sitting up.

"Hmm, I thought the same until I was sent a picture of that London woman coming out of this apartment early in the morning?!" All the groups' heads collectively turned to face Alfie, some eyes wide in shock, the foreheads of others wrinkled with confusion. Alfie's mouth dropped open as the cogs began to turn and he realised what must have happened.

"Dana, let me explain…" he began but before he could move even a metre off the sofa, she had picked up a full glass of white wine and launched it straight into his face. He blinked in shock (and because his eyes were stinging from the acidity) and could blearily see Dana storm out, shoving the wine glass into Amy's hands, who was standing open mouthed at the door to the living room.

"What. The. Actual. F…" Amy began to stutter. The rest of the group just looked at him in dismay and silence hung in the air, before Evan picked up a half full glass of white wine and launched it at Alfie's middle before mockingly saying "you *bastard*. You mean you cheated on us with Millie and you didn't tell us?!" After a moment of tension, all the friends, minus Alfie, burst out laughing. It was obvious she had somehow learned about Millie staying and come back in a rage. He couldn't blame her, in fairness, and it was clear she felt really betrayed. The rest of the gang had all known about Millie's dramatic lifesaving feat, yet he'd resisted telling them she'd slept in his bed, because he knew even if he'd explained he hadn't been actually *in it* with her, too many questions would still be asked, and he didn't want anything getting back to Dana. A niggling voice in the back of his head told him there was a reason he didn't want it getting back to her. Because as innocent as he wanted to make it out to be, it hadn't felt all that innocent in reality…Yikes. He felt an urge to explain to Dana because, as overdramatic as she could be, he understood her anger this time.

Hurriedly scrambling off the sofa and past Amy, who was still stood chuckling at the door with the others, he raced down the stairway and out onto the square. It was early evening, and a few people milled about but he didn't let that stop him calling out Dana's name, at the sight of her rapidly moving further up the hill. She turned to face him and he ran over to her.

"Hear me out Dana, I promise it's not what you think," Alfie spluttered out. *But it could be, one day,* his head taunted him. She glared at him, hurt flickering over her face. Arms folded, she retorted:

"Why should I give you the chance to explain yourself?" He paused for breath a moment before replying.

"Because you've obviously heard something and taken it the wrong way. Yes, Millie stayed the night here," she exhaled sharply and moved to walk away but he gently grabbed her arm, "BUT…it wasn't like that. I didn't even sleep in the bed with her." *But you wanted to*, the voice in his head teased and he blinked firmly, trying to shake it away. "Please come back to mine and I'll explain?" Her features softened, which wasn't a usual sight, and reluctantly she agreed. They walked more calmly now back to his, where he led her into his bedroom (shutting out the others) and explained the whole tale – well, the whole tale except for the fact that he'd asked Millie to come over that night. He left that bit out – that might have been harder to explain. Even though it was just a friendly meet up to discuss some art, nothing more…

He didn't even need his irritating head voice to remind him that wasn't necessarily true.

Once they'd had a conversation and she had softened, they'd shared several kisses, except Alfie found his mind wandering towards Millie, which increased his guilt. As much as Dana wasn't always the friendliest of girls, she didn't deserve to feel betrayed which was why he had made such an effort to talk things through with her. He still knew he needed to authoritatively end it with her – here she was here in front of him, why couldn't he just do it? But the guilt of his partial lie crept in, and he couldn't face it. He *would* do it. He had to. Just not tonight.

"I promise you, this isn't what it looks like," Sam blurted, although his hand pulling the covers up over himself and the woman next to him seemed to suggest otherwise, Millie thought.

"What is it then Sam? Care to explain? NOW?!" she screamed furiously. She couldn't bring herself to get any closer to the bed – her bed. She locked eyes with the woman who immediately looked away and remained still under the sheets. She was called Amelia, and she lived next door. She trained in the gym all day and taught fitness classes at night.

"It's…we…she…" he began, and Millie couldn't listen to his

pathetic spluttering any longer. She picked up the closest thing within reach – a trainer – and lobbed it straight at him. She'd turned before she could see where it landed but the "ow!" from him suggested to her it had succeeded.

Hot tears sprung in her eyes as she flustered back through the flat and out the front door, the heat from the bright, summer's day smacking her in the face. She felt in a dream, like what she'd just seen hadn't really happened. She'd seen this situation play out many times in films, in the books she had read but never had she envisioned it would be her. There had been no indications that he was having an affair, if that's what it even was? Sure, they had problems, and they had never been the same since the news she had received about her inability to have children. He'd tried to be understanding, yet every so often she couldn't help feeling the frustration pouring out of him. The feeling that he was still waiting for something to happen even though they knew it never could, as though she would just magically "mend" herself. Because that was how she felt; broken. She was damaged goods and whilst she understood his disappointment, the fact the bottom had literally fallen out of her life meant she just couldn't feel sad for him. If she was completely honest with herself, she'd always had an inkling he might do something like this. Because for her, it was her fate and there was no way she could get away from it. But he could. He didn't have to live with it for the rest of his life. He had a choice and he had clearly chosen, even if subconsciously.

She reached the park a mere few minutes away from the flat, filled with happy families, loved up couples and throngs of friends, hanging out with BBQs and drinks as though her world hadn't literally just shattered. It took all her energy to collapse onto a bench, pull out her phone and call the only person she now trusted in this world. It took only two rings.

"Sup Mils," the answer came but all Millie could do was sob hysterically down the phone. She managed to stutter out where she was and within ten minutes Jenny was there, holding her friend as she broke down in her arms.

Eighteen

"Oh, my goodness," Millie shook her head in disbelief. "I can't believe I've technically caused all this!" Amy and Daisy had just been filling her in on the explosive events of the previous night, whilst on the hour drive to Truro. She was in desperate need of more art supplies now her creative spark had reignited and wanted to head back to Lauren Shilton's shop.

"Imagine if *you* had been there Mils, think of the drama then!" Daisy spoke from the back seat and all the girls exclaimed.

"Thank goodness I was so into my current painting. I *was* planning on coming, but I totally lost track of time," she responded. That was a lie; she'd contemplated going and had actually stepped out the door at one point, but the nerves got too much. The thought of seeing Alfie again after what had happened – she knew he'd told their friends what had happened, but did they know she had slept in his bed? She couldn't trust herself not to give the game away that something had occurred, and that would blow it completely out of proportion. Because in reality, nothing had *actually* happened. It had been safer to stay at home, where she had worked on her painting until gone midnight. It was the first time she had felt true pride in her work, without any self-deprecating words or thoughts entering her head and it had felt like a huge milestone. It was this which had inspired today's impromptu trip to the art shop.

Glancing in her side mirror, she checked before pulling out around a truck. She wondered why she didn't do this journey more often. An even combination of winding country roads and dual carriageway through pleasant scenery made for an enjoyable journey and if travelled at off-peak times, it was usually pretty quiet. Even on a dull, late November day like today, the wide fields either side looked lush, and the wind turbines stood proud on the hills in the distance, whizzing round like gigantic fidget spinners in the sky.

"Mils?" She snapped back to the conversation. She'd zoned out there.

"Sorry, what did you say?"

"So what *is* the situ with you and Alf? Something we need to know about?" Millie rolled her eyes.

"You said he'd told you what had happened?!" she responded wearily. Amy and Daisy exchanged a glance.

"*We* didn't say he told us that," Amy answered. Millie paused, realising it was Alfie himself who had explained he'd told the group the events of that night. He'd dropped her a WhatsApp in the early hours of the morning, and they'd carried on messaging that morning, back and forwards, about this and that and everything else. Maybe that explained the giddy feeling in her stomach and why she'd purposely stowed her phone in her bag instead of out on view in the car. She didn't want to risk a message popping up from him and the girls seeing, because then they really *would* be prying further.

"Oh, well, he must've told me then," Millie brushed it off, indicating to come off the dual carriageway and continue the smaller A-road towards the city. A knowing look passed between Daisy and Amy.

"Hmm, alright then," Daisy replied. "But it all sounds a bit secretive and suss to me," she slumped back in her seat. Millie caught her eye in the rear-view mirror; she may have looked innocent enough in her corduroy dungarees, embroidered with large daisies and her hair in plaits but the wicked smile on her face indicated otherwise.

"Shush now children," Millie mock scolded, wanting to divert the attention away from herself and her feelings which she herself couldn't make sense of, "I haven't driven this road many times and I need to focus."

The heady scent of chalk, paper and paints washed over Millie as she pulled open the door to *The Artful Den*. Millie had come alone, after Daisy and Amy had expressed an interest in trying on a full basket of clothes in the previous shop. Plus, Millie preferred to shop alone and take her time, with no disturbances. And it was no secret that the pair of them together could cause a disturbance.

Hints of Christmas were appearing in the shop compared to her last visit; a bountiful wreath on the door and tasteful decorations peppered throughout indicated the season was coming. She'd seldom thought about it this year. She wasn't even sure she wanted to celebrate it as such. Maybe she'd spend this year alone in her cottage, tucked up warm with plenty of rich Yule Log and a large bottle of wine.

"Hi there," she heard a voice call and when she turned round, she saw Lauren standing on a small stool, stocking some calligraphy pens on a higher shelf. On seeing Millie, a smile crossed her face. "We've met before, right?" she asked. Millie beamed, imposter syndrome creeping over her that her favourite artist was right here in this shop, *recognising* her.

"Yes, we have. I came in about a month ago for a bundle of supplies," Millie replied. Lauren got down from the stool, her chunky Doc Martens landing heavily.

"That's right! You were the - "amateur" - artist who needed to remember how good she was," she said, smiling. Millie flushed, remembering the conversation. "How did the creating go?"

"Really well actually! So well, I'm back for more supplies!" she answered, feeling a rush of pride. To say that times had been hard lately would be an understatement, so Millie felt extremely proud of herself that she had managed to pull some energy out and crack on with something productive. So, she didn't have a job yet. She'd realised there was more to life than work and whilst she had the opportunity to survive without a job she would do so for a little longer. Her New Year goal was to start seriously looking but, for now, she loved the chance to be creative and just gather her thoughts. She doubted she'd have the chance again for a long while if she got back into a career.

"That's great!" Lauren said, beaming at her. "Do you have any pictures you can show me of your art?" Millie faltered for a second but then pulled her phone out her pocket; it was rare that she'd share her artwork at all, let alone with a stranger. Alfie seeing it once by chance that time had been mortifying. The only person she'd freely painted in front of was Sam and he'd made many a peculiar – bordering on scathing – remark.

She deftly scrolled with her thumb until she found a group of photos in their own dedicated album showing three separate pieces of work. Two were older pieces using the oil paints she had grown familiar of, the third demonstrating her new style using the heavier, more vibrant gouache paint. She mainly painted landscapes but with a keen focus on people – she believed even the most beautiful, striking of places wouldn't be complete without people there to appreciate it. She was enjoying using the thicker paints and they dried considerably quicker than the oil paints she had become so accustomed to.

Lauren peered at the phone screen whilst Millie stood uncomfortably holding the phone out – gosh this felt awkward. Would Lauren tell her outright that they were absolutely awful and what the hell was she doing in an art shop? Or would she give some pleasant yet clipped response which indicated she wasn't at all impressed but didn't want to offend? After a few moments, when she had scrolled through using her index finger she said:

"Goodness, they're incredible! What did you say your name was again?"

"Millie. Millie Jones," she replied.

"Well Millie Jones, you really do have a gift! All that rubbish about you "not being very good?" Lauren tutted in mock outrage and Millie smiled, blushing outrageously. "Please tell me you share it with others?" Millie glanced downwards.

"You're actually the only person who's ever seen all of those photos together," she admitted and realised then how silly it seemed.

"You need to share those, Millie. I mean, forgive me if I'm being too bossy! But there are so many people who would be inspired by them. Inspired even to pick up a paintbrush and have a go themselves," Lauren said passionately. At her words, something pinged in Millie's brain.

"Do you think so? Are people really keen to learn how to paint these days?"

"Absolutely!" Lauren replied. "I get several people in here a day looking to start a creative new hobby. A surprising amount of younger people too. Seems they're not all just into learning the latest TikTok dance," she laughed, her eyes crinkling.

"Interesting…" Millie began. "I wonder if I could pick your brains on something. And then after that I promise I'll buy something," she laughed.

Nineteen

This was the most positive and downright happy Millie had felt for a *long* time. Her afternoon of shopping had been exciting enough without the unexpected turn of events that happened whilst in Lauren's shop. During her visit to *The Artful Den*, Millie's curiosity had been piqued by their conversation, and thoughts of the village hall and its unseemly demise had popped into her head. Lauren was adamant that crafty hobbies were on the up and there were plenty of people wanting to learn – or in other words, be *taught* – how to do them. From there she'd come up with the idea – art classes for the village hall! And on the journey home, those thoughts had spiralled. Why stop at art? There must be so many hobbies people are interested in pursuing and many talented people in the area who could offer their services to teach them. She hadn't been inside and seen the space, but it looked a good size from the outside – what about hiring it out for birthday parties, home education groups? The possibilities could be endless. They could have the village hall packed out most nights of the week. Let the council say it's no longer used then!

The cherry on top of the already very exciting cake was that when she had verbalised this to Lauren, she herself had agreed to come along and "open" the sessions, almost like a special guest. Her paintings were widely known throughout the county and were sold nationwide so she was the perfect person. After exchanging numbers, and with Millie promising to call her once she had a more solid plan in place, she'd left the shop feeling excited. And what had surprised her more was that the first person she wanted to tell was Alfie. She hadn't mentioned it to Daisy and Amy as it felt like a secret and one she wanted to keep until she had told him first.

She wanted to tell him in person following their discussion previously so had managed to hold off messaging him, despite her excitement. She would tell him tonight at the pub; all the gang were heading there for the Saturday night quiz followed by live music. Now a little more in tune with the fashion culture down here (basically anything on a scale of jeans and nice jumper to dungarees and wellies was deemed acceptable), she had no problem putting an outfit together using some of the purchases from a few weeks back. Her light-wash "mom" style jeans were pulled in with a tan belt and complemented by a plain white vest and adorable cropped, mustard coloured shirt she had found tucked away in a charity shop in Truro. The shirt was adorned with white polka dots, and she wore it open to show off a long necklace she'd had in her jewellery box for ages, silver with a crescent moon on the end. She'd also taken the plunge that afternoon and allowed Amy to cut her hair – when she had first suggested it, Millie had told her in no uncertain terms to "get stuffed" but once Amy had shown her photos of other friends' hair she had cut after a year stint as a hairdresser in the past, Millie had agreed. Besides, it hadn't been cut properly in nearly a year.

Almost 5 inches had fallen to the ground, resembling a small dog, which made them both laugh. Amy had cut in some layers, and it now sat just below her shoulders. Millie styled it with loose waves, trying to give the impression she'd done nothing with it (when in fact it had taken rather a long time and a bit of swearing). She'd treated herself to a brand-new pair of brilliantly white Converse, and they completed the look. She felt comfortable and confident; it was amazing what a new haircut and a wardrobe refresh could do to lift your mood. Along with the incredible idea she'd had about saving the village hall, of course.

The stroll down to the pub was a chilly one but the half a bottle of wine she'd drunk whilst getting ready helped to take the edge off. Soon she could see the warm glow and hear the faint thrum of The Sandy Anchor. The landlord had clearly been busy that day too as the windows were newly decorated for Christmas and more lights than usual twinkled from inside.

It warmed Millie's heart realising the difference in atmosphere from when she'd first visited; back then people had looked at her a little odd, because she was a stranger and one from *London,* at that. Now, the minute she walked in people greeted her by name, smiled at her or raised a glass. She knew people's names and even paused to chat with Ray, the local locksmith whilst waiting for her drink to thank him again for the work he'd done to sort the door out to her garden. Was she becoming part of the community? She dared say it felt like it.

The Christmas decorations had continued inside also, with a large, real tree taking up the space where one of the corner tables had once stood. Above the bar hung several garlands and festive lights adorned many surfaces, giving off a very cosy vibe.

"Millie! Over here!" she heard a call and turning round spotted Ryan sat at a table alone. She smiled and made her way over.

"Hey," she said, taking a seat and sliding her bag off her shoulder. "How's it going?"

"It's good!" he replied. "Just waiting for those other wasters. They should be here soon." She smiled in response, unsure what to say. Ryan seemed like a lovely man; quiet and unassuming, yet she had spoken to him less than any of the others in their friendship group. She often felt paranoid around him and Evan; did they genuinely like her or were they just forced to spend time around her because Amy and Daisy had chosen to? A pause followed, which Millie filled by taking a long sip of wine – she'd need a refill within minutes at this rate.

"Your outfit looks amazing," Ryan spoke suddenly, and Millie blushed.

"Oh thanks. Just something I threw together really," she replied and then felt embarrassed at such a cliché response.

"Me too," he countered, fancily indicating his own standard black jeans and jumper. She giggled, the wine going right to her head. Was he flirting with her? It had been so long since someone had seriously flirted with her – sure, she and Alfie seemed to have *something* happening between them but no real, blatant flirting. The flippant comment from Ryan seemed very 'playground' but there was a small buzz running through her to feel like someone maybe *wanted* to flirt with her, despite her having zero reciprocal feelings.

Ryan excused himself to go to the toilet just as the others arrived. Evan went straight to the bar whilst Amy and Daisy headed over to Millie. After initial greetings and settling into seats, Millie found her loosened tongue opening up to them.

"I know this sounds stupid and ridiculously self-indulgent, but I think Ryan was just flirting with me?" she whispered. Amy and Daisy traded a glance and then they both began to smirk. Amy leaned in slowly, causing Millie to do the same.

"I hate to break it to you Mils, because I know he's bloody gorgeous, but he wouldn't be interested in you if you were the last woman on earth." Millie's eyes widened – was she really *that* unattractive? But keeping her eyes locked with Amy's and then glancing at Daisy, the penny dropped, and she realised what she was referring to.

"You're extremely gay, aren't you Ry?" Amy yelled as he came back towards the table. "Millie here thought you might have had a crush on her." Instantly, Millie dipped her face into her hands in sheer embarrassment as he sat next to her laughing.

"He's more likely to have a crush on me," Evan responded, just appearing at that moment with a tray full of drinks and placing them down.

"What do you mean, "likely to"? I've got you earmarked for an illicit affair," Ryan answered cheekily, and everyone burst out laughing. Relieved, Millie joined in. Her serious misunderstanding seemed to have gone relatively unnoticed, despite Amy's big mouth. She must keep her own mouth shut in future, almost full bottle of wine or no almost full bottle of wine.

"Here's someone who clearly *does* have a crush on you," Daisy said and all eyes turned to the doorway of the pub, where Alfie had just entered. Millie's stomach flipped. What was that expression she'd heard before? How, when someone walks into a room, and it feels like the sun has just come out. That's what she felt like right now, completely against her will. Even better, he was walking towards their table and there was no Dana in tow – she wasn't certain what had happened there, but Millie was just relieved not to have to face her right now. She'd pissed her off once already from her drunken behaviour and again with the whole drama from the weekend before and, whilst she wanted to apologise to her, she didn't want to confront that right now, here in the pub.

She'd texted him earlier that day letting him know she had some super exciting news to tell him but hadn't given away any more clues, intending to tell him tonight. She'd get the initial conversation out the way and then pull him somewhere on his own to chat about her ideas. The excitement was palpable within her – whilst it wasn't *her* village, she felt so passionate about helping those whose it was, especially with a hobby they both shared an intense love for. He sat across from her and they locked eyes a little longer than usual, his small smile making her melt inside. He broke contact and pulled his phone out of his pocket, beginning to type.

"Now we're all here, I have some news to tell you," Daisy announced. Millie's phone buzzed and she briefly glanced down. "*Your hair looks really great.*" She peeped back up at him and he was looking at Daisy, but gave her a sneaky side-eye and a small smile. She went to smile back but then tried to focus instead on Daisy and what she was saying.

"You've probably not noticed because you're all *hideously* self-involved, but if you'd look at this table, what do you notice about the drinks?" Everyone searched the glasses on the table.

"I need a top up?" Amy said, indicating her near empty pint glass.

"Evan didn't get shots again because he's a tight ass?" Ryan added causing Evan to drain his glass and shake the remaining droplets over his head.

"I've almost consumed a bottle and starting to regret it already?" Millie added, realising she'd slurred at least two of those words and needed to slow down. Daisy rolled her eyes impatiently.

"No! I'm drinking lemonade," Daisy declared, holding up the half-pint glass and displaying it around like a prize on a gameshow from the nineties. Everyone stayed quiet until Amy's eyes widened.

"NO!" she declared in disbelief. Daisy and Evan looked at each other and nodded furiously, enormous smiles breaking out on their faces.

"YES! These two incredibly irresponsible adults are having a baby!" she yelled, making a *ta-da!* motion in the air. Immediately, the group broke out into rapturous applause, congratulations and excited embraces.

Millie, however, sat there feeling completely and utterly *numb*. All the excitement, happiness, joy and confidence drained within an instant, like a snake had aggressively latched onto her leg and was furiously sucking it all out. She felt her breathing quicken and all sounds around her muted. Through bleary eyes, she could make out everyone embracing and was very aware she was still sat on her stool, but nothing could make her move. Feeling bile rise in her throat, all of a sudden her body reacted and she was up on her feet and out the door of the pub. Cold air punched her in the face and it was only then she was aware of the tears coursing down her face and the fact she was bent over next to the sea wall, trying not to empty the contents of her stomach all over the pavement.

"Millie?" She recognised his voice instantly but couldn't bring herself to look at him. This could be the unravelling of all the careful steps she had taken to ensure that *no-one* down here knew about her past. She'd already revealed about her mum to Alfie – that had been a slip-up - but especially not *this* part of it. She knew from previous experiences back in London how people treated you when they found out you couldn't have children: all different ways. She'd had the people who sent her inspirational quotes about "life going on" and how strong a person she was, the other people who had spoken to her then cast her pitying glances like she was some injured puppy. Then others with children who had notably stopped inviting her to any event or gathering, presumably because they thought it might make her feel uncomfortable. In reality, she wasn't sure exactly how she wanted to be treated. But she knew she didn't want to be the elephant in the room during any situation – this is why retreating to Cornwall where nobody knew her had seemed the best choice. A chance for a fresh start. Except now, due to her own unhinged reactions and responses, her demons were coming back to bite her.

"I'm fine, go back inside," she called shakily, trying to steady her breathing. She straightened up slowly once she realised that, thankfully, the copious amount of wine in her stomach was staying put (for now).

"You don't seem fine?" he challenged, his voice closer now and she could feel his presence just behind her. Dabbing her mouth delicately to remove any rogue saliva that may have accumulated, she slowly turned and came face to his concerned face. Even with a furrowed brow and eyes dancing with apprehension, he was an incredibly handsome man. She managed a weak smile.

"Just too much *vin rouge*, that's all," she replied quietly. He still looked uneasy, so she peered past him into the pub. "You head on back," she said, desperately fighting to remove the tremor from her voice. "I think I'm going to head home before I make more of a fool of myself."

"Then I'm coming with you," he replied firmly and upon noticing her change of expression quickly added, "but only to your door. Just to make sure you make it OK?" She realised by the resolve in his words that he wouldn't budge so to avoid creating even more of a scene, she agreed, on the condition that he went back and apologised to the group. She couldn't bring herself to think how rude they must think she is. Her new friend Daisy, who was an incredibly lovely person and had opened her arms to her, had announced one of the most exciting things you could hope to announce, and, in response, she had dashed out without a word? Not to mention Evan sat next to Daisy, who had also welcomed her warmly to the group, despite the fact she was a complete stranger. No, it didn't look good at all. How on earth would she explain? Even if her fake story of feeling sick from the alcohol were true, it wouldn't have been an excuse to not return, even for a brief moment. What a mess.

But this was Millie's reality and had been for a long time. She so dreadfully wanted to feel happy for people who had, or were able to have, children. Even just feeling neutral would do. She didn't want to be jealous, for fear of ending up a bitter and twisted spinster, with only seventeen cats and a half dead houseplant for company (the future she had envisioned for herself many an early morning hour.) These thoughts spiralled in her head as they began the slow walk up the lane, back to her cottage. They walked side by side in silence, the sounds of the pub gradually replaced with the crunch of their shoes on the ground beneath them. Being out in the countryside, the streetlights were scarce and so above them lay an incredibly dark sky which tonight was cloudless, exposing hundreds upon thousands of glittering stars littered throughout. Just looking up and slowly counting them caused Millie's breathing to calm and her heart rate to return to a normal pattern.

Alfie glanced across at her and noticed her looking at the sky, mouth subtly moving as though counting. He gave a small smile and realised how endearing he found her in that moment. From the minute he'd walked into the pub that evening, he realised his eyes had been searching for her; only her. Isn't that meant to mean something? When you start entering a room and you look for "your person?" When he had clocked her, he noticed instantly she'd changed her hair and thought it looked incredible. Although he'd liked it before, it seemed chopping away a few inches of hair had uncovered her complete beauty. She'd never looked as confident and comfortable as she had in that moment, wine glass in hand and laughing with the rest of the group. Up until now, of course, where she looked vulnerable instead.

She noticed him looking at her and so to avoid her feeling embarrassed, he said:

"Did you know, there are more stars in the sky than grains of sand on every beach in the world?" He then scolded himself inwardly, realising how lame a statement it was, but thankfully she replied "I didn't. That's a very interesting fact." They walked a minute more when she added: "So how do they actually *know* that, though?" He paused for thought.

"I don't know. Maybe someone just has *way* too much time on their hands?" They both gave a small chuckle. The tension had broken slightly, which had been his intention. He couldn't help noticing she looked very cold despite her coat and thick tartan scarf wound around her neck. It took him all his resistance not to slip an arm around her shoulder and pull her close.

Within another minute, they reached her cottage door, and she pulled a key out of her coat pocket. They looked at each other and a moment passed.

"So…thanks for walking me back," Millie spoke softly, her eyes glistening in the dull glow of the streetlamp.

"No problem at all," Alfie began and then, taking in the

anxious look which remained on her face couldn't help adding, "…and you're sure you're OK?"

"I'm fine, honestly. Just too much to drink, that's all," she responded weakly. He hesitated.

"Are you sure? Nothing at all I can help with…?" he started to offer, but she cut him off.

"Seriously, Alfie. I'm fine. I just need to rest." The clipped tone of her voice was all the warning he needed that it was his cue to leave. After reassuring her he'd pass an apology onto the group – *especially* Daisy and Evan, he watched her go inside without so much as a hug goodnight. Waiting to hear the key turn in the lock and a light switch on inside, he walked back down the lane. So he'd only known her for a very short amount of time. He was certain there was something she wasn't telling him, yet knew it wasn't his business to go digging. Maybe not yet anyway.

Twenty

The last few days had been *rough*. Typically, the moment it felt as though things were straightening out and her life was settling, the usual curveball had to come and smack her square in the face. Despite sending grovelling messages to the rest of the gang and their apparent acceptance of her apology, she still felt like the worst person in the world and had turned down Amy's invitation of lunch at the pub, for fear of what she may ask her. The only elongated contact she'd had was with Alfie, who she'd texted instead to share the news of Lauren's offer and the ideas for the village hall. It didn't feel half as exciting telling him via text rather than in person and seeing his subsequent reaction. But with the way she'd snapped at him when he'd walked her home combined with the knowledge that Dana was back for the foreseeable and sleeping at his apartment, it had seemed the most sensible thing to do. Despite the informal nature of it all, they had agreed to hold a village meeting that weekend; it happened to be the 1st of December then and Millie planned to appeal to everyone's festive senses in a bid to win them over.

Alfie had whipped up some posters advertising the meeting and placed them around the village: one in Mr Slee's shop, another in the pub and one on the noticeboard on the wall of the village hall. Millie had also posted on the local Facebook group to bump up interest. They needed a full meeting and plenty of people on board if this was going to work.

Saturday morning arrived and along with it, the day of the meeting. Millie woke with a concoction of nerves and excitement twisting around her stomach. She'd been up almost the entirety of the night before writing out notes for the meeting – she'd thought of so many ideas of where they could take the classes; she just needed the people power to bring it to fruition.

She'd exchanged a couple of texts with Alfie but it was purely focused on the matter at hand. It was like they had taken a few steps forward but were now almost back where they started when she first arrived. For what felt like a fleeting moment, it seemed like something was going to happen - despite Millie having barely any time to process whether it was something she wanted or, indeed, could cope with. Looking back now at the night she stayed at Alfie's following her chaotic foray into amateur lifeguarding; it seemed like nothing but a fever dream. Like it had almost never happened – maybe that was for the best, she'd thought. Besides, he was with Dana still. Nothing could – or would – happen. They could work together in a professional capacity on these projects and that's where it would end.

However, once she entered the village hall early that morning, her feelings unwillingly came flooding back. He hadn't spotted her in the doorway, too focused on unstacking chairs. He had wireless earphones in and seemed in a complete world of his own. He was wearing black jeans and a black jumper, broken up with a plaid shirt style jacket and complimented by bright, white trainers. His dark hair was tousled, and he had to keep flicking it off his face in a motion he was clearly unaware of. It was only after half a minute or so that Millie realised she'd been gawping but thankfully he hadn't noticed.

As she walked across the scuffed wooden floor, each step echoing loudly around the hall, Alfie paused and turned towards her. He gave a shy smile and gently pulled his earbuds out, shoving them into his pocket.

"What're you listening to?" she asked, not sure what else to open with.

"*The 1975*," he replied. "I seem to have them on repeat at the moment."

"Great choice," Millie said, although she had only listened to a few of their songs.

"Stops my brain from ticking over too much, anyway," he continued before breaking eye contact and continuing to rearrange chairs. "I didn't go for a horseshoe shape – I didn't want it to feel too 'Alcoholics Anonymous' if you get what I mean," he explained, gesturing to the rows he'd set the chairs up in.

"Good plan," she replied, hovering around them, finding her mind wandering to her mum at the mention of alcoholics. She wondered what she would make of her new life down here. Would she be proud? Millie sure hoped so.

"I have a few notes I've made on how we could go about the meeting, if you want to see?"

By the time they'd shared ideas, it was five minutes to the meeting time and the nerves set in – no-one was here yet. What if nobody was going to turn up and Millie would have to contact Lauren telling her thank you, but she wasn't going to be needed after all? How mortifying that would be, after Millie's initial excitement.

They perched on two chairs at the front, waiting. Five minutes passed and the door opening made them both snap up to look. In came Ethel, Dennis trotting on companionably at her side.

"Ee's alright to come in too, ain't he?" she called, gesturing to the enormous pooch.

"Of course!" Alfie replied. "He's bumping up our numbers, at this rate," he said, casting a glance around the empty chairs dejectedly.

"They're coming m'boy. Just seen a load heading down the hill," she said, taking a seat at the side as Dennis sauntered over to Millie and shoved his giant head into her lap, waiting for a scratch.

True to her word, the door opened and a group of around ten people entered, waving to both Alfie and Millie. Moments later, Mr Slee entered with his wife and a couple of friends, calling a friendly hello to them both and then to the other people who had now congregated around the edges. Alfie and Millie shared a relieved glance at the sight of the hall now filling nicely and a buzz of excitement flashed through her. This could actually work?!

Amy entered next, followed by Ryan, Evan and Daisy. Millie smiled at them all and whilst Daisy smiled back, she could tell there was reluctance. They hadn't spoken properly since the night Millie had run out on her incredible news and an awkward air lingered. She felt like a truly terrible person – she would rectify it soon. She just wasn't sure yet what she would say to explain.

By half past ten, the hall was fit to bust, with people having to stand around the edges due to all the seats being taken. Whilst she hadn't been in the village long, Millie tended to know most people but there were several faces here she didn't recognise, suggesting that some had even come from further afield to join. She'd never experienced a sense of community like this. It felt a very special thing to be a part of. She glanced over at Alfie, and he gave her a knowing look. She nodded towards the gathered crowd, indicating they should make a start. With one swift move, he leapt down from the stage they had both been sat on and the noise caused a hush to wash over everyone there, as he began:

"I'm so glad you all decided to come today…"

"That was *amazing!*" Millie declared as they reached the top of the stairs leading to Alfie's apartment. "I can't believe the amount of people who have volunteered to run classes!"

"I know! And *great* call on posting in those local news groups on Facebook. Having a media presence there today is really going to highlight what's going on. Hopefully the council will see and have a rethink about the use of the hall," Alfie continued, heading straight for the kettle to make some warm drinks. Millie threw herself down onto his sofa and looked out at the beautiful view from the picture window. It was overcast, grey and gloomy but her mood felt anything but. This morning had completely overshadowed the ill-feelings she still had about the previous week at the pub. Plus, despite the initial awkwardness between them this morning, being around Alfie now felt more natural and relaxed than ever. As she continued to take in the view, comfy on his sofa, with the sound of him bustling around in the kitchen behind her she found herself thinking she could really get used to this…

"Where's Dana?" she found herself asking before she could reconsider, as he approached and placed an enormous mug on the coffee table in front of her. Alfie paused before answering.

"She's away with work again," he replied. "Up in Birmingham this time. Some launch event."

"I see," Millie nodded, then without deliberation, continued: "What's the deal with your guys' relationship anyhow?" Alfie squirmed slightly in his seat, pressing his palms together and fiddling his fingers; either in deep thought or trying to avoid the question.

"We…we have fun," he stated simply, not meeting her gaze.

"Is that it?" Millie responded, surprised at her brazen tone. He looked up now into her eyes and half-laughed.

"Is that not enough?" he asked.

"It could be. I just…I don't know…I get the impression you don't really get along? Not properly."

"And you get that impression, how?" he said, now taking his mug in his hands, leaning forwards on his thighs. Whilst his tone was full of question, he had an almost amused look on his face.

"Just the way you are around each other. Not so much the way she is around you…she seems to be all over you when you're out in public together." *Who can blame her* she thought. Alfie gave a cheeky smirk, not leaving her gaze.

"Are you *jealous*, Melissa Jones?" He'd never used her full name before. She wasn't even aware he knew her full name. She felt her cheeks flush and realised that the audacious attitude she'd been rolling with the last minute or so had disappeared completely. Alfie raised an eyebrow, and she had to break the moment by looking down and reaching for her mug, else she wasn't sure where it would lead. The air definitely felt charged.

"She's not here right now and she never seems to have

an intention of staying very long. Does that answer your question?" he said, matter-of-factly. Glancing up at him again, both eyebrows were now raised before he placed his mug down with a start and announced "Right! Let's get planning, shall we?!"

Millie climbed into bed that night completely exhausted. They'd spent the entirety of the afternoon and most of the evening planning out the next couple of weeks at the village hall. With just over three weeks until Christmas, they knew plans had to be made quickly if they were going to maximise this opportunity. After much discussion, drafting and "re-jigging" as Millie had called it, they had a schedule for up until Christmas, with a big New Years' Eve party planned for that well-celebrated night. They hadn't wanted to take any business away from the pub so, as it was just metres away from the village hall, they'd struck up a deal whereby all alcohol be provided by the pub and the celebrations be spread across both venues. A live band would play in the pub with a disco in the village hall, to suit all tastes and ages. As it was the 1st of December, the village was almost fully bedecked with decorations, the official "switch on" taking place the following day. It seemed like it would be the perfect beginning to a fabulously festive few weeks. She'd even contacted Lauren who, despite it being super last minute, had agreed to come and switch on the lights and give a brief speech about the coming weeks' events.

The most exciting and nerve-wracking thing of all was the class Millie had agreed to run – art for beginners. It was weird to think that little old she would be guiding others through the basics of art, but she'd realised she needed to start realising her ability. The way both Alfie and Lauren had reacted to her paintings had helped to raise her confidence levels. Despite this, there were still some echoing words from Sam in her head. He had always found a way to give a backhanded insult or make her feel art was pointless, nothing more than a meaningless hobby used by broken down creatives to pass the time.

Sam. He hadn't been in her head too much lately which had been such a blessing. The night of "babygate" at the pub, as she was now calling it, she'd gone to bed replaying several situations over in her mind that she'd rather forget - he had featured in the vast majority. It was only when her brain allowed her to look back that she realised quite what an asshole he'd really been. The way he'd spoken to her, the way he'd gaslighted her, confirmed why he had eventually done what he did and cheated on her. And yet, there was still a part of her that missed him. He was the first and only serious boyfriend she had ever had and the little life they created together had, at the time, been a dream. She'd never imagined having feelings for anyone else but him. Yet here she was, growing increasingly fond of another man who, she was sure, had feelings for her too. There had been no official discussion as such, yet comments from other people, their intensifying exchanges and a general sense of "something is going to happen" led Millie to believe something *was* going to happen. It was just an idea of "when" and not "if" …

Twenty-One

Despite another grey day dawning on Sunday, the mood in Sandyhaven was anything but dreary. The village Christmas lights were strung all around the square ready to be brought to life for the first time that year. Standing proudly in the centre was the village Christmas tree, which had been kindly donated from nearby Rockery Farm. Mr Slee's shop was packed full of culinary festive goodies including potent sherry and fruitful panettone. The pub was raring to go, with buttery mince pies and warming mulled wine on tap. A heady scent of cinnamon and firewood filled the air, the beach today home to a blazing bonfire which luckily had timed perfectly with the waning tide. A couple of market stalls had been erected outside the pub selling a range of beautiful, handmade decorations and gifts. Millie browsed them carefully as she walked by, stopping to chat to the owners who were clearly so talented.

She hadn't planned to purchase anything – having vowed not to do presents or major celebrations of any kind this year – but she simply couldn't resist a delicate, macramé Christmas tree decoration, expertly handmade from a gorgeous sage green cord. After thanking the seller and walking away, studying the intricacies of each knot as she moved, she felt a presence in-front of her and looked up into Alfie's beaming smile.

"Treating yourself? Or is this a gift you were supposed to keep secret from me?" She rolled her eyes with a smile, placing the stripy paper bag into her coat pocket carefully and continuing to stroll down towards the beach. Alfie kept step with her.

"No gifts. Not for anyone," she reiterated. "Well, except for my Godson. But he's the only exception," she explained, her heart doing a double beat at the thought of little Leo who she was yet to meet.

The beach came into view down the slope, with groups milling around, wrapped up warm in hats and scarves. The barrier around the bonfire was lined with people soaking up its warmth and at a safer distance, children and dogs ran and played, with their parents close by in groups, holding mulled wine in gloved hands. The sight of the beach and the water still made Millie shudder following her close call weeks ago, but she knew she had to move on. There would doubtless be multiple opportunities for her to get back in that water in the warmer months and she didn't want the memories and the "what ifs?" to ruin that. Strange how she was thinking of being here next summer…her subconscious was obviously sure that's what was going to happen. But would she be alone, or would she be with…

"So, what're your plans for Christmas then? I know you're totally against it and all that but surely you won't be spending it on your own?" Alfie asked. Millie wrinkled her nose at him.

"I really don't have any," she replied honestly, "and besides, I've got far too much to think about now with the next few weeks the way they are. There's so much to coordinate."

"Yeah, but you're only doing the one class, with me. That's two hours per day."

"And the rest! I've got a lot of preparation to do, you know." She ignored his eye roll, instead stopping to take in the hard crunch of the sand beneath her feet now they were on the beach. They stood companionably, the gentle crash and ebb of the waves providing a mesmerizing and hypnotic soundscape. "What are your plans?" she asked nonchalantly, not even turning to look at him. There was a long pause; so long she almost thought he'd walked away until he spoke.

"Dad's invited me up there," he said, referring to his father's home in London. "But I'm not keen. It's not that I don't *like* his new partner I just…" he trailed off, unsure how to finish his sentence without it becoming too deep. He glanced down to see Millie's beautiful brown eyes staring up at him gently. "I'm just not ready to spend Christmas in his house with anyone other than my mum," he finished, quietly. He focused hard on the waves, desperate not to let too much emotion show. He very rarely spoke about his mum and had no intentions of starting now. Seconds later, he felt Millie's arm gently thread through his own, linking them together and warmth rushed through his body.

"I get you," she whispered and, for the first time in his life, he felt like someone genuinely did. She had lost her mum too and, despite not knowing the circumstances, or the relationship she'd had with her, it was still a strong common ground they shared. Their family situations were actually very similar – both "only" children, both lost a parent, both living away from their families in a remote corner of the country.

"It's actually my first Christmas without mum," she continued. "We hadn't spent the last few together anyway, not properly. She was usually black out drunk and it wasn't the most pleasant company to be around." He reached up and squeezed her hand. He couldn't imagine how difficult it had been for her. Yes, he'd lost his mum but at least the time they'd spent together had been happy, secure and full of love. It sounded like their relationship had been incredibly strained.

It was as they stood there together on the beach, surrounded by happy, chattering people and the palpable magic of the season that he realised he really would like to be part of a family with her and show her the love she had so obviously missed in the past.

"I can't remember the last time I felt that relaxed. I wasn't snoring, was I?" Amy asked as the rest of the hall slowly packed up belongings. Millie tightly rolled up the yoga mat and chuckled.

"Could barely hear Maya over you, actually," she replied, and Amy pulled a face at her. The classes had been running for over a week now and the success had far exceeded anything she'd imagined. There was such a variety it had been hard to know which ones to choose to go to, alongside planning and preparing for her own sessions, which ran on Tuesday and Friday evenings. Yoga had attracted her though as it was something she'd always wanted to get into after trying a few tutorials online. A young girl called Maya who lived around fifteen minutes away in neighbouring Trewithen had just returned from a gap year in Bali where she'd earned her yoga instructor accreditations. Since returning, she'd started a few classes locally and had jumped at the opportunity to run one in Sandyhaven when the opportunity arose. Millie watched her at the front of the hall now collecting mats and blocks back in and thanking everyone with huge enthusiasm, her jet-black hair swishing as she did so.

"I may not be attracted to women, but *she* is stunning," Ryan mumbled in Millie's ear, yoga mat tucked under his arm. He had arrived in a flurry of Lycra and fluorescent headbands, making Millie and Amy hoot with laughter. It had transpired though that the gimmicky clothing had been a ruse because he was incredibly flexible and had moved from position to position with sheer elegance. Millie, on the other hand, had staggered between poses like a cat with a broken leg, puffing and straining as she went. Despite this, she'd really enjoyed herself.

The other classes had been a hit, too. Monday morning had been bookbinding with an elderly man from the village. The afternoon brought a soft play company with all their equipment and mums and babies from surrounding villages had come out in force, grateful to finally have somewhere to meet and sip tea whilst their children crashed around. Tuesday was paper craft run by two middle-aged sisters who had their own little business alongside their part-time office jobs. The Tuesday evening saw Millie's first art class, where she introduced painting as a skill, demonstrating the various affects you could achieve from using different sized brushes and building a mixture of strokes. The results had been so effective and despite barely breaking even after deducting the cost of materials, she hadn't minded. The sole aim for her was using the ordinary village hall and bringing it to life with all these different crafts and interests. And that had certainly happened.

Wednesday saw a change of pace with a vibrant and upbeat Zumba class, this week inspired by music from the 80s. Millie had popped to the pub that lunchtime to finalise some details around the New Year's Eve party and had been astounded to see fifteen *"Flashdance"* lookalikes taking up one whole end of the building. Black leotards, a rainbow of fluorescent tights, sweatbands; the full works! The afternoon calmed down with a wreath making workshop by Mrs Slee, the shopkeeper's wife – however, Millie had since heard the CD player from the morning's dance session had been left switched on standby, so the traditional Christmas carols, which had played at the beginning of the session, were soon replaced with the likes of *Funky Town* and *Holiday*, (now *that*, she would have paid to see). Children's Christmas crafts adorned the hall on Thursday morning, run by a group of parents who home educated their children. In the evening, there was a men's mental health group, an initiative set up in Truro but now trialling outreach sessions in more remote locations. Alfie had agreed to play host for this one, setting up a refreshments table and making himself available for whatever the guys needed. He recognised several faces from the village and whilst he hadn't intended to eavesdrop, he found himself listening intently to the stories being shared amongst the men. Some of the things these guys had been through were so incredibly sad, yet it made him feel more validated in his own struggles since he'd lost mum. He'd gone home that night vowing to call his dad soon. He'd pushed him away long enough.

Friday saw Millie's art class come around again and this time she would be sharing it with Alfie. They'd agreed to collaborate to bring not only extra knowledge but also different styles. They'd planned to take the class outside on the beach for the first hour, if the weather was kind, as they would just catch the sunset. After taking some photographs and some discussion around colours and possible techniques, they would head inside and watch as both Alfie and Millie live demonstrated their own styles. The final hour would allow the group to start their paintings, with a view to finishing them the next week.

It had been bitterly cold but bright and luckily they'd had a tremendous sunset, with pastel oranges and pinks streaking through the sky. Millie had surprised herself with how at ease she felt in-front of the canvas with people watching. Never had she been so exposed whilst creating but painting alongside Alfie made it seem so much less scary. Whilst hugely focused on her painting, she'd made several glances across at his, admiring his style and the way a paintbrush worked deftly in his large hands. His grip, she'd noticed, was loose and he bit his lip whilst he worked, accentuating the stubble stippled around his chin. Judging by the way all the other women in the room were gazing at him, she'd guess they'd noticed too. By the time she'd finished packing away she found herself continuing to admire him from across the hall, with her perched on the stage and him tidying the last few bits away, chairs and tables rearranged again ready for the second bookbinding session first thing the following Monday morning.

He must have felt her gaze boring into him as he glanced up and they locked eyes. She felt a buzz of electricity jolt through her, and he felt it too. "That went well," he spoke out loud, attempting to diffuse the intensity of the moment, although he questioned if he wanted it to go at all.

"Extremely," she replied, swinging her feet and leaning forwards slightly. "Your painting was great. You're incredibly talented." He smirked, wiping his hands down his paint splattered shirt.

"You of all people should know it's just making marks on canvas," he said, finishing the set up and standing back. "It's just putting them in the right order that counts."

"Don't be so defensive," she replied, frowning at him. "Just accept the compliment." He moved towards her slowly and her heart began to thump.

"And you can accept a compliment, can you?" he asked in an accusatory tone, knowing full well she couldn't. She hadn't been used to her artwork receiving praise for a long time, the snide comments from Sam resonating in her head always. He stood just a metre in-front of her now and she must've carried a dejected look on her face from the memories because Alfie closed the gap between them, gently taking her hand in his. Millie couldn't bring herself to look up, instead focusing on his hand and the splodge of yellow paint on one of his knuckles, cracked a little where it had dried. She ran her thumb over it, feeling the smoothness, then the bump.

"Millie." He spoke it throatily and with her heart pounding, she swallowed and slowly looked up. A mere few inches from her face was his, staring intently into her eyes.

"Yes?"

He paused, leaning down until his lips were brushing her ear.

"I think you're incredible." He moved his lips away and within the next second, they were on hers firmly.

"It's amazing that I've even been asked," Millie shouted from the sofa, her knees tucked up under her chin. The clattering in the kitchen indicated that Sam had no intention of stopping what he was doing to listen to her; this infuriated Millie. She had received a letter that morning from an art gallery in Shoreditch – she'd submitted one of her paintings into a competition to be featured in their latest exhibition and whilst she hadn't won, they'd written to her to say they were still very impressed and would love to invite her to a private showing. And also that she could bring a guest.

"SAM?!" she shouted again, impatient this time at his lack of response. Enthusiastic or not, it would be nice to simply be acknowledged. There was no response, so she huffily hoisted herself off the sofa and went through into the kitchen, where Sam was concocting one of his disgusting protein shakes. Clearly, he was off to the gym again. She stood for several seconds, staring straight at him, leaning one arm on the counter and the other hand placed on her hip. He paused mid-action, his kale-filled hand hovering over the blender.

"You OK?" he asked, eyebrows raised.

"I've been calling you and you've been ignoring me!" she shot back. His hand released a cluster of wiry, green vegetable and it dropped into the blender on top of a mound of beige looking powder.

"You were in the other room; you should've come in here.

You know, to have an actual conversation," he replied, pouring water on top and securing on the lid. She sighed, just wanting to address the matter at hand.

"Well, I've been invited to this gallery in Shoreditch for their latest exhibition opening and I was hoping you'd come with me. You know I hate doing things alone for the first time." She studied his face intently to gauge his response. His brow furrowed slightly, and he screwed up his mouth.

"Isn't this the same gallery who rejected *your artwork?" he asked, the emphasis on the word 'rejected' stinging Millie's pride further.*

"Yeah but making links with galleries is huge. It could be a valuable connection for the future," she continued. "Especially because the owner of this gallery is the one who…" A loud whirring and grinding echoed around the room and Millie took a moment to realise he'd completely cut her off by turning on the blender mid-sentence. She stared at him in disbelief, but he looked back at her innocently. After a few more seconds, he turned it off and silence returned, its loudness deafening.

"What?!" Sam spat, taking in Millie's expression.

"You just totally cut me off!" she said, exasperated.

"Oh, so it's fine to holler at me from another room but raising your voice over the blender is unacceptable?" She had no words, just felt completely and utterly shocked at his attitude today. He'd been like this for a few weeks now, making her feel the least priority in his life, showing even less interest in her artwork than usual. It was starting to really grate on her, but she wasn't sure what to do about it.

Upon no response, Sam screwed the lid tightly on the bottle and shook it vigorously, before adding it to his full gym bag.

"I'm heading to the gym and then I'm probably going out with some gym friends after for a drink or two. Don't wait up for me," he said, hauling the bag onto his shoulder. Millie shuffled a little.

"Which friends?" she asked, keeping her voice as light and airy as possible.

"Just the usual. Matt, Tristian, Scott, Amelia…" his voice tailed off as he checked his phone absent-mindedly. He glanced up at her, noticing her vulnerable expression. He smiled then and Millie's body rushed with warmth and tingly feelings; that smile being one of the first things that had attracted her to him, all those years ago. He moved towards her and pulled her closer, his arms looping around her waist. He placed a firm kiss on her lips, lingering enough for her to wish he'd carried on.

"Of course I'll go to your art thing with you," he murmured into her neck, leaving a kiss there before pulling away and walking straight out the door, a cursory "bye" called over his shoulder.

The door slammed shut and the silence enveloped her once again. He made her feel so many things with that kiss, so why was the feeling of pure rejection the one encompassing her the most?

Twenty-Two

"The plot thickens, eh?" Jenny spoke through the video call. From where she'd positioned the phone a metre or so away, Millie could see she was sat on the floor of her living room, baby Leo sprawled on his tummy on a mat. A horseshoe shaped cushion was wedged under his chest and his little head kept lifting in the air for a few moments before dropping back down.

"He's getting stronger! Look at him holding his head up!" Millie exclaimed, feeling a swell of love, pride and, to her disdain, envy course through her.

"He absolutely is BUT we're talking about you and your snogging escapades," Jenny countered, and Millie screwed up her nose.

"I *hate* that word," she replied. Jenny frowned.

"Escapades?"

"No! *Snogging*," she explained, miming gagging. "It's so

coarse."

"Well, coarse it may be, but you clearly don't mind doing it," Jenny said, putting down the rattling lion toy she had been holding and gently lifting Leo onto her shoulder.

Millie sighed – she knew she shouldn't have mentioned anything to Jenny. She'd always had a habit of clinging onto moments in Millie's life and making them out to be more than they were. When Millie wrongly received a detention, Jenny led a protest to the teacher. Millie was overcharged in a coffee shop, Jenny walked right back in and demanded to see the till receipts. Millie was cheated on by her boyfriend; Jenny threatened to kill him and dissolve his body in acid… the theme is a recurring one.

The truth was, Millie wasn't sure what the kiss had meant. It had happened what felt so suddenly and as soon as he'd pulled away, she had desperately wanted to lean in for more, but her mind was screaming at her not to. It was a shame that her mind hadn't been clearer as to the reason *why* it didn't want her to. Alfie had said nothing, simply smiled at her and gently lowered his hand from where it had been nestling behind her head. She'd made her excuses and left shortly after. They hadn't exchanged messages since; who knew when their next encounter would be?

"I guess it *was* nice, whilst it was happening," Millie pondered on Jenny's last comment. "I'm just not sure where I see it going." Jenny frowned.

"Why do you have to worry about that right now?" she asked, with a quizzical expression. "Just enjoy it for what it is. You spent far too long faffing around with Sam at the beginning and look where that got you. Stop thinking about the future." Harsh, Millie thought, but fair. Maybe she needed to think less about the future and live more in the now? Yet, it had started to click in her brain exactly why she felt reluctant to pursue anything with Alfie, or anyone else, for that matter.

"Mils?" Jenny questioned, a concerned look on her face. "You look weird."

"Cheers," Millie feigned insult. "Look, I'm going to have to go, Jen."

"No problem. I think Leo needs a nappy change, based on the sudden smell that has entered my nose. Vile," she replied, wrinkling her nose. "Before you go…what're your plans for Christmas?" Millie rolled her eyes.

"What is everyone's obsession with me and Christmas? I'm not celebrating it this year. I'll be spending it alone, probably inebriated, in my home. A-l-o-n-e," she spelled out. Jenny exhaled.

"Jeeeez. Ok?! I was just asking because Paul and I had been chatting and we'd love to invite you to come spend it with us this year. You know, if you want? We decided before Leo was even born that we'd see our respective families either side of Christmas and spend the actual day just us three. BUT, we both agreed we'd make an exception for Leo's Auntie Millbobs." Millie's eyes threatened tears but she sniffed them away quickly. She opened her mouth to speak but nothing came out.

"Look, don't worry about a reply now. I totally get it if you want to spend it alone or whatever. Just know, the invitation is there, and we'd love to have you." Millie nodded slowly and Jenny smiled weakly. "Just give me a few days' notice, so I can get the extra wine in, you know?" she added and they both burst out laughing.

The sunrise was just phenomenal that morning, the perfect start to an otherwise anxious Monday. Alfie had been out on the coast path before even the smallest ray of light had broken, stomping the crumbly ground, torch in hand. It wasn't something he was accustomed to doing but had woken up with an urge to get out of bed and shake off the night before in fresh air.

He'd been working on a commission when the phone had rung. It was the very early stages of the piece, which he'd been asked to complete by a woman called Trina who ran her own complementary therapies business. She had handed him a photograph of a commonly known landscape in Monument Valley, Utah and asked him if he could paint it. (She had visited there when travelling years ago and knew she wanted it hanging in her studio.) He'd agreed, keen to turn his hand to something other than coastline and water for a change and he'd been sketching out the base of the painting. It was surprising how much detail you could get into what was essentially a couple of enormous rocks.

Just as he was about to consider mixing up some paints and giving it a go, his mobile vibrated across the kitchen counter. Annoyed at the distraction, he felt his heart sink when he saw the name. *Dana.* He hadn't seen her properly for a couple of weeks now due to her being away for work and then on a week's holiday in Ibiza with friends. They'd had minimal contact, but he had looked up her Instagram account a few days ago through pure curiosity: it was full of posed pictures of her and her friends. On the plane wearing an enormous pair of sunglasses, her long hair curled perfectly down to her waist. Laying by the pool in a miniscule swimsuit, which surely would leave the most ridiculous tan line (though he knew she fake tanned anyway, so that would surely even it out). Out in a club in a tiny, black mini dress. She looked model gorgeous and judging by the number of men surrounding her in the pictures, it was clear others thought so too.

He'd often wondered exactly what *she* saw in *him.* He wasn't going to be self-deprecating as far as saying he was *ugly* or anything, but he certainly wasn't anything outstanding. Plus, he lived in a tiny village which would have been better placed thirty years in the past, with its minimal phone and internet signal, singular shop and one road in, one road out vibe. It didn't compliment Dana's party lifestyle one bit.

He'd met Dana on a night out in Truro around a year ago, just after an anniversary of his mum's passing and he was incredibly fragile and vulnerable. He and the gang had booked a budget hotel in the small city to come back to after a night of drinking and partying, to provide somewhat of a distraction to the monotony of grief he had been experiencing. Not his idea by any stretch but he'd gone along with it anyway. Whilst out in a particularly sticky, grubby bar he'd bumped into Dana, and she'd immediately made it clear she had no intention of letting him go back to his room alone that night. After spending the night together Alfie discovered, through pure coincidence (or fate, as Dana called it) that her parents lived in Cornwall too, causing the relationship to continue from there. He hadn't once agreed to anything official, and Dana had this constant on-again, off-again attitude which was both unpredictable and sincerely irritating. But for the majority of the time, she'd disappeared, and he was alone, quite happily so, with no desire to be with anyone else. And so, it hadn't mattered.

It hadn't really mattered until Millie came along.

He paused on the path, looking back over his shoulder, gazing wistfully at the incredible break in the sky; powder blues, soft pinks and hints of yellow permeated the horizon and he closed his eyes, inhaling deeply. He kept replaying the conversation in his head. Dana was handing him an ultimatum. She wanted him to move up to Manchester or they'd call it quits. He'd never heard her so defiant before and wondered what had changed. She insisted she wanted to be serious with him, and did he have a reason why not?

What he *should* have said was *"yes, and she's called Millie Jones."* But those words didn't come out of his mouth.

Instead, he explained he wanted to chat in person with her about it first – he owed her that much to break it off face to face. But somehow, she had taken that as a hard "yes, let's move in together" and squealed excitedly down the phone. Before hanging up, she'd said she would be back before Christmas and that they would travel up north and spend their first Christmas together in "their" new home. He hadn't yet rung the gang – who he'd planned to spend Christmas Day with – he hadn't rung anyone. He'd barely had time to contemplate what had happened.

And most importantly of all, he hadn't heard from Millie. The kiss they'd shared after their art class a few days prior hadn't been mentioned again, yet it was all he'd been able to think about since (well, until this phone call had invaded all his thought space). It had felt so incredibly… *right*. This girl who he'd known only for a few months, and even some of those had been strained because he couldn't function socially. She'd kissed him back and it had been the most emotionally lifting, gentle and deeply felt kiss he'd ever had. Kisses with Dana hadn't even come close. He wondered why him and Millie hadn't exchanged messages since, and he realised it was because he wasn't sure if the kiss was just a one-off or the gateway to something more. He knew he wanted it to be, but this situation now with Dana was causing complications beyond his reach. Damn. He needed to speak to Millie first, see where her feelings lay. And then he needed to speak to Dana. But he'd have to be quick because Dana was back at the end of that week.

It didn't give him much time to figure out what he was going to say. But this felt like the kick he'd needed, to force him into breaking it off, once and for all. It didn't matter whether they were serious or not, Dana deserved more than being with someone who was with someone else.

With a final long look at the beautiful scenery in front of him, he headed back.

Twenty-Three

"I really can't thank you enough for coming, Lauren," Millie gushed again, watching in awe as one of her favourite artists finished laying out paintbrushes on each easel. Lauren beamed and swung her hair up into a leopard print claw clip.

"You've already said thank you and honestly, it's no problem. It's my pleasure," she replied. Lauren had gone above and beyond for the class she was taking in place of Millie's – she had half expected her to turn up and just do a little talk about her artwork and offer some tips and that would have been more than appreciated. But instead, she'd arrived in a Transit van with her name and logo plastered on the side, barely squeezing down the lane and swinging into the solitary parking space outside the hall (which was more just a concrete standing, really). Inside, she'd brought enough artist easels and professional materials from her shop for all twelve people booked on to the course. With Millie's help, they'd unloaded the lot and set it up, so it almost transformed the ordinary village hall into an artist's workshop. She'd even brought a few spare easels to prop her artwork onto, adding vibrancy to each corner. One easel remained bare.

"I was wondering if you had a piece of your own work to put on this one?" Lauren indicated the empty easel. Millie's jaw almost dropped.

"Mine? Why?" Lauren looked confused.

"Well, this is technically your class, isn't it? I'm kind of just gate-crashing," she chuckled. Millie's heart swelled with pride – yes, this *was* her class. Which *she* had organised. Maybe there was a future for her in art, whether it was here or somewhere else. Perhaps she *was* good enough. If Lauren Shilton herself seemed to think so, then it must be a possibility.

She agreed to dash home and grab a piece to share. It would only take ten minutes tops due to her close proximity to the hall, but the start of the session was only fifteen minutes away – some people had even started to arrive already. Without hesitation, she flew out the hall and awkwardly half-ran, half-walked across the square and ascended up the lane. It had started to drizzle and so she pulled up her hood, nestling down into her scarf so only her eyes peeked through. It was the first time she had cursed the lane for being so long. And steep. Now she'd probably be sweaty for the session and that would make her feel stressed and…

BANG.

"Millie?!"

"Alfie?" It was the first time they had come face to face since their kiss and the air felt charged. Talk about an elephant in the room – try a *herd* of elephants.

"What're you doing up this end of the village?" she said, indicating up the lane. He shuffled, almost looking shy.

"Well…I was looking for you, actually. But you weren't in and then I remembered today is Lauren's session? Isn't it…?" He glanced down at his watch.

"Right now? Yeah! I'm just rushing back to grab some artwork, then I need to be back right away."

"I'll walk with you," he said, more of a statement than a question and followed her the hundred or so yards back up the hill to her cottage. He waited patiently as she flustered around, slotting a painting into a folder and then bumbling back out, striding back down the hill.

"So, there was a reason I wanted to find you," he started, raising his voice, as the rain was harder now, coming down in droves; he pulled his coat collar up around his face to offer some protection. He'd been hoping to track her down and have an honest, open conversation about what was going on in his life. He'd left it a few days but finally felt ready to talk, having made some huge decisions. This wasn't quite how he'd expected to have that conversation, though. She glanced sideways at him briefly, her pace not faltering.

"I don't want to be rude Alfie, but this isn't a great time. The session starts in about two minutes, and I really don't want to be late." He nodded, understanding but frustrated at his timing. Why hadn't he remembered the class was on now?

"I get it," he replied as they emerged into the square and the hall was just there. She wasn't stopping. "I just…I really need to talk to you." Whilst not his intention, the desperation in his voice was clear and this caused Millie to stop before heading inside. She looked up at him from under her hood, fat raindrops dripping noisily from its rim.

"Ok?" she replied, her voice loaded with question. "I'm so busy this week…can it wait until Friday? Maybe in the evening, after the final session and when the press has gone?" She was referring to the last session of the week, which also happened to be the final session of the December run. Lauren was returning to run the last session, and local press had been invited to cover it for maximum exposure, in the hope the council would reconsider their plans for the hall and adjoining clock tower. It was going to be an extremely busy end to a manic couple of weeks and he knew she'd want to have full focus. Although he felt bursting to tell her sooner, he nodded and offered a smile.

"Sure. Come to mine after. We can chat then," he said, and she offered a brief smile before darting inside, leaving him standing in the downpour, alone.

Drum and bass pulsated through the floor and up into Millie's body, vibrating down all her limbs and buzzing in her brain.

People jostled her either side and her shoes stuck to the floor, making her shudder. It wasn't her idea of a great night, that was for sure. But it had been Sam's idea and for once he'd asked her if she wanted to go out with him and his friends. She'd heard so much about "the gym lads" but had never actually met any of them. It was curiosity and intrigue which had driven her to go rather than an actual desire to go clubbing.

Whilst she wasn't "old" she certainly felt ancient in the club, surrounded by impossibly thin and effortlessly cool-looking eighteen-year-olds, fresh out of sixth form and thrown into university. It was clear she'd missed the fashion memo too – all these girls wore flat shoes and casual clothing complemented by faces full of contour and big brows; a stark contrast to what had been on trend when Millie used to venture out at university. She felt hideously out of place in her leather-look black leggings, vest top and heels, more what had been in style when she was a fresher. "Mutton dressed as lamb" kept flickering in her head.

She stood self-consciously at a tall table, alternating her weight between legs because her shoes were already hurting her and scanning the room regularly for Sam; he'd been gone for ages. He said he was popping to the bar to get a round of drinks because that's where his friends had just texted him from. He'd explained it was best she wait there and keep the table so here she was, alone and feeling it. Men walked past and scanned her up and down, raising her anxiety further. She had never been one to enjoy attention, however innocent it may have been (and this certainly wasn't). How she wished Jenny was here – she'd know how to handle it.

She jumped at the feeling of someone brushing up behind her and was ready to turn and run when she realised it was Sam back from the bar and a gaggle of men arrived with him. He placed a tray of shot glasses on the table, filled with various, fluorescent-coloured liquids. He threw an arm roughly around her shoulders, pulling her head to his chest and instantly she knew he was drunk. He'd only been gone for ten minutes max, but he was clearly under the influence of something. His whole demeanour was different. She smiled as widely as she could but felt uncomfortable in his hold. She placed a hand on the arm round her neck in an attempt to feel some control.

"So, this is Millie," he announced, slurring slightly on the s's and all the men nodded and smiled mischievously. She couldn't help but feel there was a hidden joke she was missing. She gave a little acknowledging wave.

"Does Millie do shots?" one of the guys asked and she made a face, indicating 'maybe' but that she clearly wasn't happy about it. They all laughed coarsely and started picking up the small glasses. Sam, his arm still around her shoulder, placed one in between her fingers and they began to knock them back, swallowing in one and making excited noises to each other. She couldn't help but stare, mostly in confusion, at the clear enjoyment they were getting from it. She peered down at the bright red liquid in the glass, bringing it to her lips and taking a sip before promptly spitting it back in. It was vile.

"BABE!" Sam yelled, noticing what she had done, placing it back on the tray. They all took another one, Sam draining her rejected one on top of the other two. They pumped the air with

their fists and Millie looked across at Sam and thought she had never been less attracted to him in the many years she'd known him. Who was this person? She didn't recognise him.

"What now? Shall we dance?" Before she could protest, Sam had dragged her to the dancefloor where it felt people were fighting more than dancing; she hadn't remembered people being so wild in the clubs she'd visited during her university years. People were visibly drunk, thrashing around. Despite Sam being pressed right up against her, men were reaching out to touch parts of her body, women were gyrating, and the atmosphere felt heady and antagonistic, like anything could kick off at any time. She started to feel panic rise in her chest and indicated to Sam she wanted to get out of the crowd.

They pushed through the rabble until they reached the edge, but the air didn't feel much clearer here. Sam moved over to the edge of the club, pressing Millie against the wall and slamming his mouth into hers. He tasted of alcopops and cigarettes (clearly that's where he'd been for so long earlier, whilst she waited alone) and his hands squirmed around her body. She pushed him off and he looked shocked.

"What's the problem?" he hollered over the sound of the thumping beat.

"I'm not comfortable. I want to go home," she shouted back, not wanting to discuss it in depth here, where they could barely hear one another. She hadn't been impressed with his attitude all night but talking about this whilst he was drunk wasn't a viable option.

"Why?!" she lip-read.

"I'm just…tired," she yelled, shrugging her shoulders. He rolled his eyes.

"Oh, come on Mils, live a little. It's not like we have responsibilities, or a child to wake up for in the morning or anything." She paused and blinked twice, unsure if she'd misread the words on his lips, or misheard over this ridiculously monotonous track. She detected the faintest hint of regret in his face and realised then he had said exactly those words. Shaking her head in slow anger, she pushed him in the chest and stormed through the crowd, shoving people out the way to get to the exit. She wasn't sure if he was following because she didn't look back, just continued to plough onwards. She barely managed to see the taxi rank through her blurry tears but felt relief wash over her as she slammed the door shut and the car sped away, avoiding contact with him. She sobbed so loudly but the taxi driver left her alone, used to having crying women on the back seat on a Saturday night.

She would never forgive him. Never. It had been mere months since she'd received that life-changing news and yet he goes and drops that bomb. Well, that was it. They were through. But of course, they weren't. The following morning he'd apologised profusely, blaming it on alcohol and grief. And she'd accepted it because the truth was, she had no idea what she'd do otherwise.

Twenty-Four

*F*riday rolled around and Millie couldn't believe how quickly the last few weeks had gone and the final day of classes – plus the important press visit – was upon her. She had truly felt a sense of purpose for the first time in ages, and she didn't just mean since moving to Cornwall. For, maybe, the first time ever. She'd made so many connections throughout the village and beyond and the fact everyone referred to her by name now meant she really felt a part of the local community. Maybe this could be somewhere to lay anchor for a while?

Speaking of an anchor, she needed to get a jiggle on and get herself down to The Sandy Anchor. Last night, she'd bitten the bullet and pinged off texts to both Amy and Daisy. Things still hadn't been fully resolved since the "babygate" incident and it had gone on too long. She'd asked to meet them both in the pub, on neutral ground, and explain herself. Despite it being the absolute last thing she had wanted to do, she knew she had to for the sake of the blossoming friendships.

As usual, she found the morning ran away with her and she ended up sinking still-hot tea and burning her tongue in an attempt to get a shot of caffeine before heading out. She felt she'd need all the energy she could muster today. Pulling on an oversized, light brown fleece jacket and a thick woolly hat on her head she locked the door and wandered down the lane. Pockets of ice were visible through the centre of the road, shiny sheens in the watery sunlight and she skirted down the sides to avoid them. The sun was attempting to peek through the cover of light grey cloud but failing and it seemed an apt metaphor for Millie's current feelings: wanting to be positive but just not quite making it. She took some deep breaths, reminding herself that the feelings were valid; she had never spoken about this to anyone but Sam, Jenny or the doctors and opening up would leave her feeling extremely vulnerable. Yet, she also clung to the minor hope that this may begin some sort of healing process for her. Having it out in the open wouldn't make it any more real. It was her reality and she needed to own that. This was the first step.

The pub came into view on the left, the square bustling with people going about their daily business. She waved to Mr Slee who was out the front of the shop, organising some potted flowers for sale. A quick glance at her phone confirmed she had five minutes until midday, when they'd agreed to meet, so she changed course and headed across.

"Mornin' maid! Ready for your big interview s'afternoon?" he asked jovially. She gave a pretend shudder.

"No interviews for me, thanks. That'll be all Lauren's job. I'll be doing my usual job of keeping a low profile," she explained, her eyes wandering over the plants. "Did these come in today?" He nodded, running his fingers lightly over the petals, causing them to spring around.

"Sure are. From Becky over at Carnglaze. We've got these yellow winter aconites, camellias, some winter honeysuckle and these happy lookin' little cyclamens," he explained, pointing to each as he went. "All rather hardy an' robust enough to get you through the winter months. I liken them to my wife," he spoke purposely loudly, directing it towards his wife who was behind the counter in the shop. She waved her tea towel at him and laughed. Millie smiled at their camaraderie.

"They're all beautiful. I think I'll take…some of the camellias," she pondered.

"Y'know the different colours of camellia mean different things? Pink means someone is longing for you. Red means romance," Mr Slee explained. She raised her eyebrows and chuckled. "Hmm, not quite the message I'm going for. I'll take two of the honeysuckle then please. What do they mean?"

"Not a clue. But they smell *lovely*," he replied, taking two of the potted flowers and placing them in a large, brown paper bag.

Out the corner of her eye, she spotted Daisy and Amy

heading into the pub, so handed Mr Slee the cash and made her way over. One final deep breath in and out and she pushed open the door. The lunchtime hustle and bustle engulfed her as she entered; distant clatters of plates preparing for the lunchtime meals, a low drone of chattering from the old fellas sat at the bar, the whooshing of the beer taps. She spotted the girls instantly and made her way over to the round table in the corner, next to the Christmas tree. She plonked the paper bag down on the table.

"Peace offerings." The girls looked at each other and then back at Millie with confused expressions.

"Are we…at war?" Amy asked.

"No, but to be perfectly honest I've been downright rude and twat-ish," she blurted out, much to the girls' surprise. It wasn't often they heard her swear, compared to Amy who was fluent in profanities. She shrugged casually.

"You have been a bit of a twat, to be fair," Amy concurred, and Daisy smacked her arm. "What?! It was the only the other day when we were with Evan that we said how distant she'd been…" Daisy placed her entire hand over Amy's mouth to halt her.

"Let's not. Look, Millie. It was weird when you just ran out on my baby announcement, yes. But I'm not *mad* with you. I was worried about you. I figured there was something up but knew you'd have said if you wanted to. So, I didn't want to push it." Millie's heart calmed at hearing that. So they didn't hate her. That much was a blessing.

"However," Amy continued, through Daisy's hand and

Daisy promptly removed it, "we are worried about you. What happened that night? Alfie came back and said you'd felt sick, but I know you can drink more than you did and feel fine. So what's the deal?"

"Ams! She might not want to say," Daisy chided, but Millie shook her head.

"No, I need to explain. It's been too long not saying anything, and I've realised bottling it up is doing me more harm than good. That's why I got you both here today, to explain." The girls' curiosity was piqued, and they leaned in further as Millie began to explain the whole situation.

Tears had been cried and numerous hugs given after Millie had finished telling her story.

"Does anyone else know about this? Apart from your dickhead of an ex," Amy added scathingly, having learned a little more about him and his attitudes following the news.

"Only my closest friend in London, Jenny. And the doctors, of course," Millie replied, wiping tears away.

"Wow. You're so brave Millie. And it goes without saying I completely understand your reaction the other week. I'm sorry I didn't know. I certainly wouldn't have announced it in the manner I did," Daisy said. Millie shook her head.

"Don't be silly. You weren't to know. And you deserve to announce it in any way you please, and celebrate it in any way you want to moving forwards. Please don't let any of this change that."

"So…does Alfie not know?" Amy asked and Millie noticed Daisy dig her in the ribs.

"No, why would he?" Millie asked.

"Well…I just thought you guys were quite close now, that's all," she replied, inquisitiveness to her voice. Millie sighed.

"I don't really know what we are. I'm meeting him tonight actually, after the press visit, because he said he wanted to talk. But I don't know. He's not going to be interested in me if he finds this out, is he?" The girls looked hurt for her.

"You know that's not true," Daisy said after too long a pause to be reassuring.

"I'm not so sure," Millie answered, and then glanced at her phone – she had to leave. After a few hugs and more kind words of encouragement, she rose to go.

"Don't forget your "cancel of war" presents," she called, as she made for the door. The girls peered into the bag and Amy's face screwed up.

"I thought it was booze," she complained, and Millie chuckled to herself as she heard Daisy chastise her.

Lauren's final session had gone incredibly well and the enthusiasm in the room was tangible. Just as well, seeing as local news cameras had been there for the entirety, filming clips of people painting, Lauren speaking and some interviews with a variety of attendees. It was going to be edited into a two-minute feature and shown during Saturday evening's local news programme. It would also feature on their online newspaper forum and all social media. The main message everyone had been briefed to convey was how badly they wanted to keep their village hall and Ethel gave a brief interview all about the adjoining clock tower and how sailors from many years gone past had used it as a vantage point for home when returning. Everyone's individual anecdotes had added local colour and emotion, which Millie knew would be swept up by the public. Whilst nothing was ever certain, she was sure the council would have to reconsider their plans, knowing how much uproar it could cause.

Although the few weeks of classes had come to an end, several were going to stay on and become regulars, including the yoga, the baby and toddler sessions, the men's mental health group and dance fitness. One of the producers from the news team had mentioned they might also be interested in hiring the space for his child's birthday in the New Year too, as its proximity to the beach would be ideal for outdoor games as well. It seemed the possibilities were endless, and the injection of money would allow for further renovations and updating of the décor and facilities, breathing new life into the building. The villagers were ecstatic and so was Millie. What a success. After tidying away this afternoon, there were a few days to go until Christmas and then it would be about preparing for the New Year's Eve party around a week after that.

Of course, in between all of this business, Millie had a decision to make about where she'd spend her Christmas and also have this "chat" with Alfie tonight. She'd barely seen him today because of how preoccupied she'd been with everything else. What did he want, she wondered?

Alfie had opened a bottle of wine, gone to pour it and then placed it back in the fridge, deciding it looked too formal. He would offer it as a drinks option when she arrived, instead. They'd agreed to meet at seven and it was now three minutes to. Nervously, he paced the apartment like a caged lion. The phone call with Dana had left him a wreck earlier that day as it was. Despite wanting to talk to her face to face, she had rung back again in an excited frenzy, talking about all things "moving in" and he realised he needed to put it a stop to it right there and then. It had been absolutely the hardest thing he'd done, but once he started, he just felt the words roll out. She had cried many tears at statement that things couldn't continue. She'd also said many swear words and called him *many* names. He'd been expecting that, and in a way, felt he deserved it after causing this to drag out for so long. He should've put the nail in the coffin *months* ago but realised he'd been subconsciously clinging on. It made him feel like an almost normal thirty-something male which he rarely felt, especially since his mum had died. In fact, he'd struggled to feel almost anything at all.

However, the most shocking thing had happened – after an hour of talking and Alfie really pouring his heart out and explaining how he'd felt, it ended up being the sincerest and composed he'd ever known her and their conversation had changed his mind about her in many ways, throwing a real curveball into the mix. They'd talked for well over two hours and had finished on an overall positive note. Now, he just had to discuss the outcome with Millie…

"You need *to hear me out, Mills," Sam pleaded, following her around the house as she paced from room to room, trying desperately to process what she had just witnessed.*

"I don't need *to do anything Sam. You, however, need to get out of this house right now." She meant it too. Never had she felt the rage inside of her she felt now, bubbling menacingly like a dormant volcano about to explode, flinging months of pent-up emotion and frustration all over the walls.* "Always trust your instincts" *Jenny had always said, adding how the female intuition is one of impeccable accuracy, and this confirmed it. For months, things had felt different, and Sam had continually pushed away her subtle questions, pushing it all onto the infertility news, claiming she was bound to be feeling "upside down" and "vulnerable." How* dare *he use that piece of information about her to cover up the fact he had been unfaithful! And how many times had it happened that she didn't know about? There were so many questions flying about her head which she couldn't bring herself to ask yet. Had it just been Amelia? How many times? Were there other women? Did he really think he could shit on his own doorstep, and she'd not find out?!*

"I totally understand why you're frustrated Millie and I deserve all of your anger, but I wish you'd just pause to listen to me." She stopped pacing and was stood still on the landing, just outside their bedroom. She hadn't gone back in it after pushing open the door around an hour ago and witnessing what she had. She was afraid of what she might see. Sam stared back at her; concern etched on his face. His hair was ruffled, bare chest rising and falling more quickly than usual due to his flustered state. Light grey tracksuit bottoms hung loosely from his hips, having been thrown on in a panic. He continued staring and she raised her eyebrows.

"Well? Go on then if you want to speak so badly." He ran a hand through his hair and lifted his shoulders in a slight shrug.

"It's just been so hard," he said quietly, and she motioned at him to explain further. "Everything that's happened since finding out…what we did. I haven't known how to act around you Millie. It feels like there's nothing I could have said to make you feel better when all I wanted to do was make it all go away." She furrowed her brow.

"OK, I'm struggling to understand how any of that links to you ending up in bed with someone else, OUR bed?!" He sighed exasperatedly.

"I get that. I don't really have an explanation you're going to want to hear. I've just felt…empty. And in need of some reassurance and connection. And I sure as hell wasn't going to ask you after everything you've been through so…" Her temper raged again inside of her.

"So you figured CHEATING on me would be…what exactly?

Doing me a FAVOUR?!" She spat the words like poison.

In a split second, the Sam she knew before the day they'd received the news whirled in her mind. He'd done all the chasing at uni, desperate for her number and to take her on a date. They'd slipped comfortably into one another's lives, and he'd never indicated he'd do anything like this. Yeah, so he hadn't always been crazily supportive of her artwork and there were quirks of his which drove her insane but, nobody's perfect. She'd always envisioned them buying a home and settling down with kids. I guess once that became an impossibility with her, he was thinking of searching elsewhere.

The rage dissipated and complete numbness took over.

"You need to leave," she spoke quietly. His eyes widened.

"I'm sorry?"

"You need to leave and not come back for a few weeks. I'm going to find somewhere else to live." She spoke scarily calmly, surprising even herself. He stepped towards her now with hands reaching out, but she jolted backwards, as though even the slightest brush of his skin would scar her. "You can't convince me otherwise, Sam. Grab some things and leave, now. I'm being serious." She met his gaze and fixed it, indicating she wasn't going to change her mind. He held it a few moments more until sadness overcame his face and he gently pushed open the bedroom door and went inside, closing it behind him.

Twenty-Five

Millie twiddled the stem of the wine glass between her thumb and forefinger – she hadn't intended on drinking tonight but the high she still felt from such a positive and productive few weeks spurred her to take a glass. However, that "glass" had turned into her about to sink her third glass, and she felt tipsy. One thing she'd realised since moving to Sandyhaven is how many times she'd drunk alcohol…whilst she could just give herself a break considering she'd just gone through a long-term relationship break up, a huge location move and a life-changing piece of news, she knew it was something she wanted to try to curb in the New Year, especially with her mum's history forever present in her mind.

She'd been at Alfie's for just over an hour and so far, they'd had a long talk about the last few weeks; its successes, its difficult moments but, ultimately, what a roaring success it had been. The news report would go out tomorrow and hopefully generate a lot of interest in their little community.

"Because you know it is *your* community too now, don't you?" Alfie had said, causing a warm glow to surge throughout her.

"I'm not just some outsider London girl anymore then?" she asked coyly, taking another sip of wine. He gave a small side smile, causing her stomach to somersault.

"I think you'll always be known as the London girl. But definitely not an outsider anymore," he replied. "Besides, you *look* more like a Cornish girl now." She pulled her brows together in a frown.

"How so?"

"You look so much more...relaxed. Carefree." She snorted into her wine glass and winced at her total inability to remain composed.

"If only that was how I felt." Alfie's face turned thoughtful, but he chose to leave that comment hanging; what he really wanted was to address the elephant in the room. The fact that he had actively asked her to come here tonight hung in the air.

He cleared his throat by way of changing the conversation and Millie shifted in her seat, aware too of the loaded atmosphere.

"So...I wanted to talk to you Millie..." Alfie began, desperately trying to push the tremble out of his voice. She leant forwards to place the wine glass – empty again – on the coffee table and sat back, feet tucked up underneath her and hands clasped in her lap. God, she looked so beautiful and the fact she was here, in his flat, on his sofa, sent all sorts of feelings through him. The main one right now, to his shame, was pure desire.

"Ok…" she began. He too placed his empty glass down next to him on the floor and leaned forwards on his knees.

"The truth is Millie…what I want to say…I mean, what I've *been meaning* to say is…" He met her gaze, and the warmth of her eyes encouraged him to just go for it. "I really like you." He died a little inside at how pathetic and juvenile it sounded out loud. It was like he was back in high school telling the popular girl he fancied her. So cringe. He ran both his hands through his hair in frustration. "I know that sounds really pitiful," he continued, not gauging anything from her lack of reaction, "but I don't really know how else to put it across. I know when we first met, I was anything but friendly and you'd have every right to tell me where to shove it right now." There was still no noticeable emotion on her face. Cautiously, he continued. "I know it may have been just a total one-off but our kiss the other night really got me thinking about…about us." He paused, praying she'd say something.

"I've thought about the kiss too," she replied quietly, and his heart raced. So she *had* been thinking about him? He swallowed.

"I spoke to Dana today…we had a good, quality talk through things. She said some things I'd never expected her to, and I really saw a side to her I'd never seen before. I wondered in that moment if maybe we *could* work. Despite what I'd said, she still seemed keen…" Millie's expression remained indifferent, but inside her heart was racing. Where was he going with this?

"But…I called it off. It's you I want Millie. Just you." His voice was shaking as he said it and he just knew that if he was to stand up now, his legs would likely give way.

Adrenaline coursed through Millie's body upon hearing his words. She'd had her suspicions – the increase in flirtatious comments, the consistent messaging and obviously the kiss had indicated towards something like this happening – but to actually hear him say it was more than surprising. It was shocking. And he'd spoken to Dana! She couldn't imagine her being as measured as Alfie had insinuated she had been. Did that mean Dana wasn't coming back? That she was truly happy for Alfie to move on with someone else. Her head began to spin. This was totally unexpected for sure. She sat up, placing her feet back on the floor.

"So…you're not with Dana anymore?" she questioned carefully. He shook his head.

"No. That's over, once and for all, and it should have happened a long, long time ago. We mutually agreed. Her parents are in the process of putting their home in Cornwall on the market and purchasing one further up country to be nearer to her, so there's nothing to bring her back here either. She's going to be just fine. You've met her, you know she could succeed anywhere. They don't make confidence like hers anymore." Millie processed the information, before moving onto the bigger piece at hand.

"I'm not really sure what to say," she said truthfully. Alfie's heart dipped a little. The fact she hadn't immediately said she liked him back didn't fill him with hope. "I mean, I'm extremely flattered," she continued, smiling softly. "And I can't lie. I've thought about you a *lot* since I met you." She paused. "Even when you were being an arsehole to me." Her cheeky smirk made him burst out laughing and the heady tension in the air dissipated. Their laughter subsided and she glanced downwards, looking shyly back up at him from under her eyelashes. "I'm just not sure where I'm at with anything remotely relationship wise. I've not long come out of a long-term relationship which ended badly," she explained, shuddering at the memories. "And I'm dealing with something personally which is just a huge barrier for me." Nerves rose in her body at the mere mention of it, regardless of the fact she'd given no actual details.

Alfie reached across the gap between sofas and gently took her hand.

"Hey, it's OK. You don't have to explain yourself," he said tenderly. His hand felt so natural in hers, she noticed, and she gave it a little squeeze. Several moments passed with silence and hand holding until Alfie said, "I was going to ask you to stay to spend Christmas with me and the guys but…" She shook her head gently.

"That's such a kind offer and I'm extremely grateful but I've decided I'm going back to London for Christmas," she said. She'd only made the decision that afternoon but had dropped Jenny a message to say she'd love to come and stay with them for the holidays. She knew she had to go back to London eventually, not solely so she could finally meet her Godson, but to face the demons she had left behind. She noticed Alfie's eyes had changed and knew he was probably wondering why she was going back to London. "I'm going to spend it with my best friend and my Godson. I've not met him yet," she explained quickly. He visibly relaxed and wrapped his other hand around hers.

"That sounds amazing," he said. "Just…promise me you'll think about what I've said? About us?" She nodded and he thought he could detect the slightest gloss of tears coating her eyes. He'd have to stay focused or else the same might happen to him too.

Just ten minutes later, they'd shared a warm, lingering hug at his front door, and he'd smoothed his thumb gently over her cheek, using every shred of restraint he had not to kiss her. She'd just left his apartment, insisting she wanted to walk home alone for some space, when he remembered he'd forgotten to give her something he had bought earlier that day. Hastily, he dashed back up the stairs, grabbed the gift off the table and ran barefoot back down the stairs and out the door, not bothering to close it behind him.

"Millie?!" he shouted, the frigid cold air smacking him in the face and seeping through the soles of his feet. He could just see her silhouette in the distance, beginning the ascent up the lane. She didn't turn around so, presuming she hadn't heard, he began to pound the pavement after her.

Once he was within a few paces she turned around and surprise registered on her face. He stopped, his breathing faster than normal due to the sprint and it was clearly visible in the freezing night air.

"Sorry I…I forgot to give you these." He handed a brown paper bag across to her and she received it, looking taken aback. He took in her face one last time and leaned in. For a split second, Millie thought he was going to kiss her but he diverted, whispering in her ear,

"Merry Christmas, Millie."

He turned and strode back down the lane, not once looking back. Under the dim streetlight, she carefully peered inside the bag. Her heart skipped a beat. She pulled the item out of the bag and held it with trembling hands.

Beautifully arranged, *pink* camellias. *"Pink means someone is longing for you."*

She bowed her head and sobbed.

Twenty-Six

*G*oing back to London had roused all manner of emotions in Millie. She'd decided to take the train back, mainly because she couldn't be bothered to deal with the intensity of Christmas holiday traffic but also because she wanted to have a couple of hours where she just didn't need to think about *anything*. Not even driving the car.

She'd been dropped to Truro train station by Amy, who had given her the biggest squeeze goodbye, promising they'd keep in touch regularly in the four days she would be away. They'd chatted on the journey to the station about Amy's plans for Christmas; she explained she had somewhat of a dysfunctional relationship with her family, so it wasn't all picture perfect over the holidays. She would be spending Christmas Day with Alfie and Ryan with Daisy and Evan joining for the afternoon/evening after visiting their respective families. Their plans were to eat hideous amounts of food, watch James Bond films and go for a Christmas Day dip in the evening. Millie had burst out laughing.

"I would *pay* to see that!" she chuckled, watching the now familiar landscape pass by.

"We'll send you a picture," Amy replied smiling, and then flicked her eyes across to Millie. "It's a shame you're not going to be there with us Mils." Millie took in a deep breath and exhaled through her nose.

"I know. It's a strange one this year because it's the first without mum. Not that we had wonderful days together either, but it still feels odd to not even be considering her. I'm so looking forward to meeting my Godson though. I've been putting it off and I can't do it anymore." Amy moved her hand up from the gearstick and briefly squeezed Millie's hand, indicating she knew why she had avoided it.

"You're the bravest person I know," she said softly, and Millie's heart warmed. Amy was mostly known for her brash and flamboyant nature but, deep down, she was a complete softie.

The fast train to London had taken just under four hours and her connections ran relatively smoothly the other end. Being back in the hustle and bustle of London, which once had been so familiar, felt obscure and uncomfortable. The screeching and scraping noises of the Underground had felt deafening, the packed in bodies on the tube too suffocating. The way people couldn't bear to make eye contact with you, instead burying their faces into their phone or a book felt outlandish after being used to waving hello now to everyone she passed. There was certainly no Christmas spirit being shared in this neck of the woods.

When she emerged from the overground train at Theobalds Grove station later that afternoon, the sun was fading fast and the air felt bitter. Thankfully, she was much further away from where she used to live and so she hadn't been faced with any direct flashbacks, but the familiarity of the area, having visited Jenny here more times than she could count, made her feel uneasy. It was like revisiting her past life and that had the potential to throw up a multitude of bad memories.

She felt drizzle begin to fall, splashing her face and leaving cold marks. They'd agreed to meet here at 5pm and Millie had even messaged Jenny to confirm she was on time. Glancing around, she couldn't see her, and it made her nervous. She knew the chances of seeing Sam were miniscule as there was nothing to bring him here, but she felt vulnerable. Being down in Sandyhaven, all those hours away, made her feel safe. It had taken leaving the village for her to realise just how safe she had felt.

"Millie!" Instantly, familiarity coursed through her brain, and she turned her head to see Jenny waving frantically at her from the car. She had pulled up in a space specifically marked as "No Loading" and was grinning from ear to ear. "Jump in, quick before he gets shirty," she yelled, indicating a stout looking station officer, eyeing her suspiciously. Millie grinned and dragged her case for the final time that day over to the car.

Hours later, she wiped the crumbs from her mouth and placed the plate down next to her on the sofa. A sense of contentment she hadn't expected washed over her – she'd been in Jenny and Paul's house for a couple of hours, and she felt so welcomed. Not that she'd ever really doubted she wouldn't, but she was gatecrashing their first Christmas together as a family of three after all. That didn't seem to matter to them though – she'd been cuddled so tight by Jenny for what felt like hours, followed by a shorter but equally as warm hug from Paul. She'd had a warm shower, eaten an Indian takeaway followed by not one but *three* mince pies, washed down now with a large glass of deliciously sweet wine. Curled up on the arm of the chair was their sleek black cat Pippa and snuggled into her feet the other side was their enormous ginger cat Muffin. With the fire roaring, the twinkling Christmas lights and *The Holiday* on the TV, it was the perfect festive scene.

She hadn't expected to experience what she had felt when she held Leo for the first time. He was bigger than she'd expected, now almost three and a half months. She'd expected to feel hideously unwanted stabs of jealousy but instead, she'd just been filled with a rush of love; both for him but also for her best friend, for whom she was wholly happy. She had a feeling some sadness would come once she'd had time to process everything but for now, she was happy to revel in the bliss the second half of this day had brought. And she fully intended to let those feelings continue throughout Christmas Eve tomorrow and up until the day after Boxing Day, when she'd return to Sandyhaven.

Back to a big decision which hadn't truly left her mind all day long.

"MERRY CHRISTMAS MOTHERF..." Amy's voice trailed off at quite an appropriate moment as she tore down the beach and flung herself headfirst into the murky, grey waves, joining Evan who had been in for a minute already.

"YEEEEEEAHHHHHH!" Ryan shrieked, having donned a pair of tiny, black Speedos and raced down after her. Alfie watched them both disappear under the water, before reappearing and squealing like piglets. They continued to push each other into the water, splashing ferociously.

"What's it like?" he called with amusement.

"Absolutely bloody *BALTIC!*" Amy called back, "but I *love* it!"

"Get your arse in here now!" Ryan shouted, ducking his shoulders back under. Alfie chuckled and began pulling off his shirt.

"You should be glad you're getting to miss out on this Dais," he said to Daisy, who was stood next to him wrapped up warm in an ankle length parka and thick bobble hat. She held a flask close to her body.

"You don't think I'm going to be pregnant and not use it to my advantage, do you?" she replied, smugly sipping her coffee. He smiled at her and began to remove his clothes, slowly at first, resisting the biting cold but then rapidly – the quicker the better. The quicker he was down to his swimming shorts, the quicker they could get back inside and warm up.

Without another thought, he barrelled down to the water, not pausing once he felt it pool icily around his feet, his calves, his knees and then wash alarmingly over his full body and head as he ducked under an incoming wave. Shock and numbness jolted through his body – it felt like being hit by a double decker bus. Yet, with a few deep, controlled breaths and the weight of Ryan jumping on his back cackling in his ear, he regained some composure and managed to almost enjoy the next minute or so in the water.

They emerged together in a gaggle of teeth-chattering giggles and shivers and grabbed the thick towels and robes they had laid out by the water's edge in preparation.

"Hang on!" Daisy called, placing her coffee down and rummaging around in her pocket for a phone. "Photo! Before you robe up." They all stood together, throwing arms around each other and posing.

"Hurry the fuck up Dais," Amy demanded through smiling gritted teeth.

"Got it," Daisy announced, and they all groaned in relief, throwing robes, hats and gloves on and heading back up to Alfie's apartment.

Back in the warm and stripping wet clothes down for the dryer, Alfie checked his phone for the fiftieth time that day. Still no message from Millie. Hesitantly, he clicked on her name and opened a new message…

They had just finished a game of Scrabble (along with the tub of Celebrations) when Millie's phone had pinged. Her heart leapt and then fell again when she saw it was Daisy. Feeling mean for being so ungrateful at her contact, she tapped open the message and laughed out loud. It was a photo of Amy, Evan, Ryan and Alfie on the beach at Sandyhaven with the message **Missing you! Merry Christmas x**. If their attire was anything to go by, they'd just come out of the water. Evan and Ryan stood in the middle, arms around one another's shoulders. Amy tagged on the end next to Ryan, her leg lifted and across Ryan's body, throwing the peace sign and a cheeky face. Millie's eyes swivelled over the screen to Alfie, stood on the end. He was wearing a pair of navy swim shorts, finishing halfway up his thigh and plastered to his legs. She involuntarily studied his broad chest, wide set shoulders and the lopsided smile which indicated he was more uncomfortable than he wanted to let on. She blinked twice and looked away, feeling like she was invading his privacy by staring so.

Seconds later, another text alert appeared at the top of her phone and this time her heart really did skip a beat. Swallowing hard, she opened it:

Merry Christmas, Millie. I hope you're having an amazing day.

> **It hasn't been quite the same
> here without you. See you
> soon. Alfie x**

She beamed, warmth and other lovely feelings spreading throughout her body. She startled at Jenny's voice.

"What's that *gurn* for?" she asked, indicating Millie's smiling face. She rolled her eyes and hastily locked her phone, shoving it in her pocket.

"Nothing," she replied, slouching back in her chair. Jenny eyed her suspiciously.

"I'd say any "nothing" that gives you a smile like that is worth becoming a "something"," she said, eyeing her knowingly and popping a mint chocolate in her mouth.

Millie pondered on her friend's words when she lay in the spare room bed later that night. A shaft of light from the streetlamp directly outside peeked its way through the blinds, no matter how much she'd fiddled with the cord, but it wasn't that keeping her awake. She knew that however lovely her visit had been, soon she would have to go back. It was a mixture of emotions: sadness at leaving her friend, her lovely husband and incredible Godson behind, but excitement to be heading back to her new home, keenness to get back to work on the New Year's Eve party and the important visit from the press – but overshadowing all of that was a deep anxious anticipation of seeing Alfie again. Her decision would obviously go one of two ways, but she had to decide if she wanted to follow her head or her heart – and she had to decide very soon.

Twenty-Seven

*L*eaving London as a place had been easy, but that's not to say she hadn't found going back a cathartic experience. Despite not revisiting her usual old haunts – they'd mainly stayed cosied up inside and only going for walks to the local park to ensure Leo had his fresh air – it had all felt too familiar. The fresh, clean air of Sandyhaven was calling her, along with her tiny cottage and new group of friends who she'd missed more than she'd thought.

Saying goodbye to Jenny though, hadn't been easy. Spending uninterrupted time with her best friend had been so good for her soul and watching her with Leo had been blissful. She was the most natural of mothers, not afraid to share her vulnerabilities and difficulties, and Millie admired the hell out of her for that. Watching Paul support her had filled her with joy, knowing her friend was truly loved and had the perfect little family here. Pangs of envy had threatened but she'd batted them away and felt proud of herself for it. They'd promised to continue the regular video calls and Jenny said they were thinking of coming down to the Southwest in the warmer months for a little holiday, so they'd definitely meet up then.

The train home took longer than before, stopping regularly at stations and Millie found herself becoming impatient. She'd have to call Amy soon and tell her she was about half an hour away, so she'd be ready to pick her up. All she wanted was to get back to her cottage, run a long bath and then go to Alfie's.

All the way back she'd thought of nothing else but him and replayed the last words he'd physically said to her in person. *"Just promise me you'll think about what I've said. About us?"* She knew that regardless of her decision she'd have to tell him about her life-changing situation – it was only fair to be upfront about something like that. But what she'd learned from being around Jenny and Paul the past few days was that, whilst having a baby seemed to be a wonderful thing for them, they were still just Jenny and Paul. He had shown such tenderness towards her, and she had reciprocated and seeing their relationship was wonderful. She realised not being able to have children was one part of her, but she still had so much to give someone. And if they were willing to be with her despite that, she shouldn't deny herself a relationship like theirs. Her feelings towards Alfie seemed to grow every day and once she realised it was him she was most looking forward to getting back to seeing, she'd answered his proposal a thousand times over. Now just to get back, freshen up, head to his apartment and tell him she absolutely wanted to be with him too. The excitement was brimming within her, making the slow train journey even more laborious.

Finally, she was in Amy's car heading back to Sandyhaven and it took all her efforts to keep a lid on her heightened anticipation. She didn't want Amy to notice or suspect anything. She'd only come to terms on the train home with her true feelings, so discussing it with anyone but Alfie was an absolute no-go. Thankfully, Amy was too busy chattering away about her Christmas and asking never-ending questions about Millie's to notice.

At Millie's request, Amy dropped her at the top of the village, insisting she could walk the few hundred metres down to her cottage. It was such a pain having to turn round down the bottom and Millie wanted to experience walking down the lane to her cottage. She'd looked forward to that moment for days now. Even the grey sky and drizzle wasn't even enough to put her off as she pulled her case behind her and her cottage came into view, set into the long row of other terraces, hers standing out as a pastel pink colour. She took in a deep breath: finally, she was home.

She went to unlock the door but frowned, realising it was already unlocked. Her heart began to pound; why was the door unlocked? She'd definitely locked it when she left four days ago. Had someone broken in?! Hands shaking, she cautiously pushed open the door, noticing dim lighting from her lamps flooding the tiny hallway. Someone was here. She *definitely* hadn't left *those* on?!

Grabbing a large umbrella from the bucket in the corner for protection, she took a large breath in and gradually pushed on the solid door through to the living room. Upon hearing no sound, she shoved it open and flew into the living room brandishing her umbrella. Sat on the sofa, looking outrageously handsome, was Alfie and she felt relief wash over her.

"Oh, jeeez Alfie, it's you. You scared the sh…" she began and then her eyes flickered over to another figure stood out in the small kitchen. She dropped the umbrella and felt her head spin, adrenaline pumping through her entire body.

"Oh fuck," she whispered.

It was Sam.

Sunlight poured in through the window, the type which bathed the room in a warm glow and accentuated all the miniscule pieces of dust floating in the air. It cast across the bottom of the bed, drenching their feet in temperate light. The thin sheet, which covered their bare skin from the room, crinkled as Millie shifted positions, draping an arm over Sam's chest. She nuzzled into him and felt him draw her in tighter, a soft kiss landing on her shoulder. Closing her eyes, she breathed deeply.

"You OK?" Sam asked quietly. Millie smiled.

"Never been better," she replied. "In fact, I don't think I've ever felt this content." He brushed her hair gently away

from her face and his touch made her feel mixed flurries of excitement and contentment.

She had met Sam a month ago and things had moved pretty fast, so much so she was now spending the vast majority of her time right here in this room, his studio flat. Practically like a glorified box room but situated in Camden; the partially open window let in the sounds of the hustle and bustle below, along with a gentle breeze which felt delicious in the intense August heat. Not that she'd had many boyfriends to compare to, certainly not "serious" ones but something about Sam had immediately been different. She normally went for guys with dark hair; his was a sandy blonde. She had always chosen guys with similar interests to her; Sam had already admitted he knew absolutely nothing about art. And she'd always been with guys a short amount of time before realising they weren't right for her (despite this, she'd still prolonged the inevitable break up because she didn't want to hurt anyone's feelings). Yet, with Sam she already felt like this could be a forever thing. He made her feel safe, he complimented her in ways no previous boyfriends ever had. He was financially independent, had his own goals, not to mention the fact she found him insanely attractive. Yes, they may only be one month in, but she knew he was her forever. If only she could pluck up the courage to tell him…

"What're you thinking?" he asked. She rolled over onto her front, her face only millimetres from his. He studied her face intently and Millie swooned inside with the intimacy of the moment.

"What makes you think I'm thinking things?" she said.

"Because you've gone quiet. You only really go quiet when

you're really thinking about things." She smiled and considered her response, staring up at the ceiling.

"I'm thinking about you. And how perfect this past month has been." Sam beamed at her before cradling a hand around her cheek and leaning in for a delicate kiss.

"Well, there's plenty more time for perfection," he said, and her heart leaped.

"How much longer?" she asked, teasing him for an answer. He waited a few moments before leaning in towards her ear and whispering:

"Forever."

Twenty-Eight

She wasn't sure if seconds had passed or minutes but, regardless, she couldn't fathom the scene in front of her. Sam was here, in her kitchen, in Sandyhaven? How did he even know where she lived? His height almost took up the whole of the kitchen doorway and he stooped under the doorframe as he moved towards her.

"You're back," he spoke and hearing his voice again felt jarring to her. A voice she had worked so hard to erase from her mind for the past few months. A voice she never thought she'd hear again.

She cast her eyes across to the sofa by the window where Alfie remained seated, his mouth set in a grim line. He met her eyes, but his expression gave nothing away. She looked back over to Sam who was now metres away and thankfully had stopped. Any closer and she may have been tempted to run.

"Yes I'm…back," she stuttered out before hastily continuing,

"Sam, what are you doing here?" His expression looked genuinely hurt but he composed himself before replying.

"I came to see you, Millie. I've thought about nothing else but you since what happened. I've missed you every single day. I wanted you to know that." Her mind was spinning, and it felt as though the room would give way beneath her. She'd played many, many scenarios over in her head since the day she'd walked out of their flat, but this had never been one of them. She wasn't mentally prepared for the enormity of the words he'd just said to her.

She opened and closed her mouth several times like a confused goldfish, rendered completely silent. In the corner, Alfie shifted in his seat, clearly wondering whether or not to get up and leave. He'd contemplated it many times in the past minute, but something was making him stay. There was an air around this Sam guy that made him feel uneasy.

As though reading his thoughts, Sam turned to him.

"You can go now, mate. But thanks for letting me in." Millie's confusion at the situation built even more.

"You let Sam in?" she questioned, looking between them both. Alfie looked uncomfortable.

"Yes, but not through choice," he replied, rubbing a hand across the back of his neck, before staring at Sam. "Can you just give us a minute?" Sam raised his eyebrows but walked over to the sofa and sat down, pulling his phone out of his pocket. *You won't get far with that* Alfie thought smugly, knowing how poor the signal was here. He gently took Millie's elbow and guided her so both their backs were to Sam. Muttering, he explained:

"I got a phone call from my dad. Said *he'd* received a phone call from a neighbour regarding an unknown man outside Rosemary Cottage and could he send *me* up to check on it. So, I came and…here we are." Millie's eyes widened. "I didn't know what to do for best Millie. What was I supposed to do? I had no idea what time you would be home, so I thought the middle ground would be to come and wait in here with him."

"And you didn't think to call me to ask?" she hissed under her breath. She took in his hurt expression and softened her features. "It's just a shock that's all. I'd probably have preferred to see him on neutral ground, I guess." *Or just never again* she thought. Alfie's face turned to one of genuine concern.

"Is there a reason you don't want to be around him in here…on your own?" he asked, mumbling even quieter now.

"No…not because of anything hugely sinister. I just… this is all just a total shock."

"Any chance I can come back into this conversation now?" Sam's voice spoke behind them, and they sprang apart, realising how close they had been. Although they weren't doing anything wrong, Alfie thought. Did this guy even know that he and Millie had kissed only a week or so ago? He decided probably not; considering Millie's absolute shock at him being here, he guessed she hadn't spoken to him for quite some time.

"Look, I have to go," Alfie spoke purposefully, patting his

pocket to check for his keys. "I'll see you later Millie?" he said, raising his eyebrows slightly at her, checking if she was OK with him going. She gave a small nod and an unconvincing smile and with one final glare at Sam, he left, the door latch clicking behind him. Millie watched Alfie stride past the window and out of sight as he headed down the lane.

Reluctantly, she turned back to face Sam who was casually leaning forwards now on his knees, giving her an intense look. She swallowed and prepared herself for whatever conversation was coming next.

Twenty-Nine

$\mathcal{S}$oap flicked into Alfie's eye, and he rubbed it furiously, ignoring the stinging. He plunged the squeegee back into the now tepid water and climbed back up the ladder. Despite the cold of the late December day, he'd stripped down to just a short-sleeved t-shirt. For the past two hours, he had been furiously cleaning the outside of the village hall. The New Year's Eve party was fast approaching and in just a few days' time, the local news crew would return for a follow-up feature on the hall and adjoining clock tower. It felt like the last-ditch attempt to prove to the council that the hall was a hub of the community and that by turning it into flats they'd be destroying a piece of local history. A list of jobs had been drawn up and messaged out in a group chat late the night before in preparation for the party and this morning he had chosen this one: not because he had a particular penchant for window cleaning but because it was the only job he could do alone. And he was doing anything he could right now to stay out of Millie's way.

Yesterday evening had been frustrating, bizarre, concerning…all the emotions rolled into one. He had been so eagerly anticipating Millie's return, praying that she had decided about them potentially giving things a go. They'd texted on and off during the Christmas break, mostly light conversation, but the connection had remained. Since yesterday evening, he'd felt ridiculously distant from her. He'd known there had been an ex-boyfriend but from the little she'd said about him thought he'd been a total dickhead, and they were completely over. Then without warning, this same dickhead guy is outside Rosemary Cottage, sat there like he owns the place saying he's looking for Millie because they have "unfinished business." To say it had been a total shock was an understatement.

The guy clearly couldn't be trusted. The way Millie's whole demeanour changed as soon as she saw him, the expression on her face; it all spoke a thousand words. Sure, most people wouldn't break into song and dance upon seeing their ex, but they wouldn't necessarily behave the way she had either. There was definitely more to their past relationship than Millie had let on. He had been so reluctant to leave last night, sensing her discomfort. An overwhelming urge to stay and protect her had washed over him and it had taken every ounce of strength for him to leave.

Navigating the wiper down the last stretch of window, he hooked it back into his tool-belt and paused at the top for a moment. It wasn't ridiculously high but when he turned his head back, he could survey the entire village square. It was a hive of activity, unusually so for this no-mans-land part of the year between Christmas and New Year. But the New Year's Eve party and the mission to protect their local buildings had breathed new life into the village community. He could see some people from the local craft group bringing some newly made decorations into the hall, ready to be hung on the day. The pub was bustling with people, all no doubt chattering excitedly about the party – just at that moment he heard a group of young girls going past discussing what they were going to wear. He smiled to himself. He wished that was his only concern right now. In truth, he wasn't even sure if he was going to go to the party.

"Oh my God, it's James Dean up a ladder!" He closed his eyes and grinned before looking down. Stood looking up at him was Daisy, hands on hips. Her hair in two plaits hanging down to the faintest hint of a bump beginning to grow.

"I wish," he called back, wiping his hands on his jeans and making his way back down the ladder. He reached the bottom and swept a hand through his hair, forehead glistening with sweat. Daisy surveyed him.

"Although I'm not so sure James Dean would've broken a sweat washing some windows?" she teased, eyebrows raised. He swiped her arm gently with his hand.

"In fairness, I don't think you'd have found him washing windows at all. It's not very "movie star" is it?" he replied, and they laughed. Out the corner of his eye, he spotted a familiar face coming across the square towards the pub. The man looked his way and raised his chin slightly in acknowledgement but then continued onwards towards the pub, disappearing inside. Alfie's jaw tensed. That man gave him a seriously bad feeling.

"Who was *that*?" Daisy asked inquisitively, peering after where Alfie was looking. He paused, wondering if it was his place to explain.

"That…was Millie's ex-boyfriend. Sam." A look of surprise registered on her face.

"Ah, so that's the mystery ex is it? Interesting…" Alfie looked at her, confused.

"Why is it interesting?"

"Well, I'd heard through the grapevine that he was here. Just hadn't seen him before and didn't really know what to expect." They stayed in silence for a moment before she spoke again.

"Right, I'd better be off. I've got a midwife appointment in Truro this afternoon."

"Everything OK?" Alfie asked, an edge of concern to his voice. Daisy smiled.

"Yes, everything's great. It's just a routine appointment," she explained, her hands instinctively smoothing over the raised area underneath her dungarees.

After they'd said their goodbyes, Alfie gathered up the window cleaning equipment and tucked it away inside the porch to the village hall, where Ray would collect it later. He was just about to step out of the porch and stride back across the square to his apartment when Millie caught his eye coming down the lane in the distance. He ducked immediately back into the porch, so he was out of sight but peered round the corner to see where she was going. She was alone, thick scarf wound several times around her neck, hiding the bottom half of her face. She was wearing her smart ankle boots with a long, padded coat for warmth and her hair was tied up in a messy bun. Alfie couldn't help but feel the ongoing attraction towards her more deeply, despite knowing that she very likely wasn't coming down to see him. Her head turned towards the hall as she neared and he tucked his head back in, before cursing himself. This was ridiculous. They were both grown adults. And in truth, he was desperate to talk to her: to find out how her break away had been, see if she was OK, find out what was really going on with this Sam guy who he didn't trust as far as he could throw him. He decided to stop being so silly and stepped out from his cover to go over to her, just as he saw her back disappearing into the pub. There was no guessing who she was going to meet. He'd missed his chance.

The reaction to Sam's arrival had been a mixed one. This was clear from the reception Millie had received when she'd entered the pub the following day. She could sense people talking about her as she made her way over to the occupied table next to the blazing fire. For a village like

Sandyhaven, this was *news*. Any new information travelled like wildfire, with it mostly being passed on multiple times and becoming warped all out of proportion or being totally stripped of its truth. Who knew what people were saying and whether it reflected reality.

In fairness, Millie wasn't even sure what was going on. Sam had only been in the cottage ten minutes after Alfie left before she'd asked him to leave. She felt completely suffocated, as though her entire face had been wrapped in cotton wool and then doused in water. The plan she'd so intricately mapped out in her head for how that evening would go had dissipated in a heartbeat and this new scenario was a completely unprecedented one. She couldn't stop envisioning Alfie in her mind either, the sheer distaste on his face when she'd entered the cottage yesterday evening.

She'd rung Jenny immediately after Sam had left to go back to his B&B (a small annexe of a local farmhouse around ten minutes away).

"I'll kill him," had been Jenny's initial response. "I really will. How *dare* he just show up unannounced like that?" Millie completely understood and agreed with her best friend's reaction but had talked her out of coming down here. She'd successfully talked her down once before, just after finding out he had cheated so she knew she could succeed again. Jenny just had a very hot head and was fiercely loyal to Millie.

Amy's response was a little different. Millie hadn't gone into huge details about Sam before – she'd told both her and Daisy about him in the sense that they had broken up because he'd been unfaithful, but she hadn't really elaborated. As with everything else in her past, she had wanted to keep things low key, but it was clear how difficult that was to do when you lived in such a small village. Especially when the past kept coming back to haunt her.

"So, he's actually here, in Sandyhaven?" she'd repeated, and Millie rolled her eyes in frustration.

"Yes. Well, he's staying up at Long Meadow Farmhouse but he's hanging around here. Obviously because he wants to talk to me."

"And are you going to?" Millie hesitated.

"Well, I have to," she replied. Amy snorted.

"No you don't. You can tell the dick to eff off if you want to. I'd say you're quite entitled."

Millie thought on that once Amy had rung off. There was a huge part of her that wanted to just tell him to leave, that didn't want to engage in any conversation. As far as she was concerned, they were over. He'd made that decision when he'd decided to jump into bed with Amelia the fitness instructor. She'd come here for a fresh start and in many ways, she'd felt like she had one.

Yet, there was a small part of her that was curious…what exactly did he have to say for himself? And why had he travelled all the way down from London to be here? She knew he hated being outside the capital, much preferring the comings and goings of a busy city, so he must *really* want to talk to her if he'd come here. That's why she'd agreed to meet him here in the pub today – neutral ground – and at least listen to what he had to say.

It felt like all eyes were on her as she sat down and self-consciously fiddled with her zip. Hushed murmurs rang around the pub as everyone cast glances their way. Maybe this wasn't such a good idea to meet in the pub after all.

Sam took a sip of his pint and it felt like the volume had almost returned to usual, the thrum of chatter and clashing of glasses.

"Feels a bit like being in *Hot Fuzz* in here, don't you think?" he said a little too loudly, eyes swivelling round the room.

"Don't say that," Millie scolded, feeling a protective wave towards her new local and the community who used it. "People here are just a lot friendlier than back in London."

"You can say that again. The couple who owns the accommodation I'm staying in wouldn't leave me alone when I was trying to go this morning. Asking me all sorts about my personal life! Damn nosiness if you ask me." Millie rolled her eyes.

"People are just genuinely polite and ask questions. They're not trying to catch you out, I promise," Millie replied, her voice tinged with sarcasm. Another glug of his pint.

"What made you choose this place, anyway?" he asked, picking up a beer mat and bending it between his thumb and index finger. Millie shuffled in her seat.

"It was a long, long way from you," she replied honestly, not wanting to go into the full details about the cottage ownership and quite how she was affording it. Sure,

Cornwall prices weren't as ridiculous as London ones, but she knew from a few late-night browses on Zoopla and Rightmove that you had to have a decent amount of money to buy a place here.

Sam paused as if contemplating her answer.

"OK, fair enough," he answered, now playing with the beer mat with both hands, elbows leaning on the table. "And do you still feel like you want to be far away from me? Even now I'm here?" She forced herself to look at his face properly, pretty much for the first time since she'd seen him again. His features were exactly the same as before, but she noticed that he looked even bulkier. He'd been a regular at the gym when they were together, but he must've upped his game or done something with his routine because his muscles were even more evident now through his thin jumper. His dark blonde hair was set in the same style as usual; casual but having clearly been styled. His brown eyes were as intriguing as before. There was no doubt Millie still felt physically attracted to him. After all, she hadn't fallen out of love with his looks.

Her cheeks burned pink when she realised she'd been staring too intently and that he'd clearly noticed too. The slight turn off with Sam had always been that he *knew* he was attractive. Millie never thought she was unattractive as such but had always felt slightly inferior to him in the "looks" department. She was just a plain, ordinary girl. She didn't live at the gym or drink healthy smoothies in fancy looking glasses or get her eyebrows and nails done like the majority of women in London do.

Like Amelia did.

Desperate to shift the sudden intensity of the atmosphere, Millie completely surprised herself with the straightforwardness of her next question.

"What's the deal, Sam? Why are you here?" He raised his eyebrows and slumped back in his chair.

"Jeez Mills. An arrow to the heart!" he mocked clutching his chest, but the smile wiped from his face when he realised she was being deadly serious. "I'm here because I came to see you," he said, as if it was obvious. Millie blinked a few times. Was he living in some alternate universe to her?

"We broke up. You *cheated* on me," she stated. She could've sworn a lull in conversation flew around the pub at that moment and scolded herself for being so loud. Sam leaned in closer.

"Millie, I know you're still upset. I understand why you are, don't get me wrong. I fucked up, big time. But we were *so good* together, you can't deny that?" He reached his hand across the table and clutched hers and Millie snatched it away immediately. Sam's face registered confusion and hurt.

"What is it?" She looked into his eyes and felt tears spring in her own. Suddenly, the noise seemed deafening, the air felt void of oxygen, and she needed to get out.

Scrabbling to collect her bag and phone as quickly as possible, she pushed back her chair causing the most hideous scraping sound on the stone floor that seemed to continue ringing in her ears as she exited. The cold air took her breath away as she raced outside and since they'd been inside, a thin drizzle had begun falling. She rubbed her eyes furiously; annoyed at the fact she'd started to cry. Thankfully, the square was now quiet.

She felt a hand touch her shoulder and then pull away and turned to see Sam in-front of her. Out here in the dim daylight, he looked less intense than he had in the claustrophobic setting of the pub. His features seemed… softer, somehow.

"I didn't mean to overstep the mark," he said quietly. "I just…I came all the way down from London to be here and see you and I was just *so* excited when I did see you and…I guess seeing you again looking so unbelievably gorgeous I just…I lost a bit of control." Millie's insides stirred a little at him calling her gorgeous. His smile reignited a spark which she had long stamped on and tried to forget. He stared deep into her eyes.

"I know you still feel it too Millie. I know you better than anyone." He slowly lifted his hand close to her face and paused, as if waiting for her to confirm it was OK this time. She gave a small smile back and he stroked her cheek with the back of his hand so delicately it almost made her shiver.

"Look, take a breather, yeah? Let's meet again later, say, for dinner? Only if you're comfortable with that?" Before she could fully consider her answer, she gave a small nod.

"There's no restaurant to eat at here apart from the pub," she replied.

"Then we'll go somewhere further afield. It'll be good to get

out of here for a bit anyway. Go somewhere it can just be us."
He smiled his heart-melting smile again and she returned it.

He turned to stride back towards the road which winds up
to the farm B&B and she stood and inhaled for a moment,
watching him go. She had no idea what had just happened,
or indeed what had happened in the last 24 hours. The
intensity of his company had left her feeling exhausted. She
felt like she needed a lie down in a dark room to recover,
especially as she'd be seeing him again tonight.

Before turning to head back up the lane towards her
cottage, habit made her glance upwards at Alfie's apartment
window. Her heart plummeted like a heavy brick when
she saw he was stood there, looking down at her and then
towards Sam who was almost out of sight. Tears pooled
again in her eyes, and she had to tear her gaze away and
leave, for fear of what might happen next.

"I shouldn't judge but I'm actually definitely going to – if
my ex came back and said he wanted to hang out with me
after he'd cheated on me, there's absolutely *no way* I would,"
Amy declared to the group the following lunchtime. She
was in the village hall with Ryan, Evan and Daisy, having
put their names down for cleaning the inside of the hall in
preparation for the party, much to everyone's disgust.

"I agree. The fact that he looks like a nineties Chad
Michael Murray absolutely would *not* swing it for me,"

Ryan responded, tongue in cheek and Amy swatted him with her dustpan and brush.

"Stop being such a slut," she replied jokingly and then sat back on her knees. "Are you actually sweeping towards me or are you just flicking it around anywhere?" she asked, referring to the large floor mop he was wielding aimlessly.

"Forgive me, but my heart isn't exactly in this whole cleaning malarkey," he moaned, and she rolled her eyes.

"Come on, I've only got two hours before my shift starts and I said we'd have this place spruced up."

"I've got to be honest Ames, I kind of have to agree with Mrs Mop here. You're not even going to see half these areas when all the decorations are up," Evan said, coming over to Ryan and flinging an arm round his shoulder. "That's only because you're practically allergic to housework of any kind," Daisy accosted him, continuing to wipe down all the tables and chairs vigorously. Evan mocked offence and she returned a sarcastic smirk.

The sound of the door opening echoed around the hall and all four faces turned to look at their visitor. It was Alfie. Everyone remained quiet – the whole situation with Millie and Sam hadn't been discussed in any way in front of Alfie and it was becoming a rather large elephant in the room – especially since they'd spent all yesterday evening together at the pub quiz clearly avoiding it. The fact that Millie wasn't there hadn't even been brought up and Amy especially was glad; she was certain she was the only one Millie had told she was going to dinner with Sam.

"Alf! I thought you'd ticked off your to-do for the party with your window cleaning?" Daisy asked, breaking the silence, much to the relief of everyone else in the room. He pulled off his plaid jacket and laid it across everyone else's coats, running a hand through his hair.

"Yeah, well. I had a spare hour so thought I'd pop across and see if there was anything else I could do to help?" he replied. "Is there?"

"To be honest," Amy replied, standing up and brushing down her legs. "We're pretty much done." He watched as they tied knots in bin bags and placed cleaning implements back into the cupboard, feeling like a spare part but relieved to not just be stuck in his flat. He'd spent the morning pacing around like a caged lion, constantly peeking down below to see if there was any activity from Millie or Sam. He hadn't seen them since yesterday lunchtime when they'd locked eyes and she'd scurried off, like she couldn't wait to be any further away. He'd also witnessed that slime of a man caressing her cheek,]=and it had made him want to race down there, wrench him away and threaten him never to come near her again.

But what right did he really have to do that? He and Millie weren't together, and they never had been. It killed him to admit it, but this Sam would know Millie better than he currently did. He had spent infinitely more time with her. He'd shared endless more memories with her. He'd know her in ways that Alfie could currently only dream about. Yet he felt so protective over her, and he knew that anyone who had the sheer insanity and gall to cheat on her did not deserve to be stood down there yesterday stroking her face. It made him rage just thinking about it.

The group gathered up their coats and said their respective goodbyes to Alfie, knowing they probably wouldn't see each other again until the night of the party. He still hadn't decided if he would be going to the party.

He waited around for Amy who was the last to leave. Just as she was about to leave, he caught her arm.

"Have you heard from her?" Amy glanced down at Alfie's hand on her arm and her expression softened into a sympathetic one. She covered his hand with hers and replied:

"Not today, Alf." He couldn't stand that she was feeling sorry for him, but he felt desperate.

"What about last night? What happened last night?" She paused, swallowing.

"They…they went out for something to eat. In Truro." He hesitated.

"And then…?"

"I'm not entirely sure." She shot him another sorrowful look and gently patted his hand before removing it from her arm.

"Talk to her Alf. It's the only way you're going to sort this out." She placed a small kiss on his forehead before throwing her bag over her shoulder and leaving him alone in the empty hall.

Thirty

The cottage door clicked shut behind her and Millie flopped down on the sofa. Her entire body ached with exhaustion and her throat felt raw from laughter. Now she was sat in a silent room, she finally had the chance to process everything that had happened that day and a whirlpool of emotions flooded through her.

She had just spent the entire day with Sam, touring around Cornwall. They'd left super early that morning, when the sun had barely risen and in the eight or so hours that followed, they'd visited several towns, villages and beaches around Cornwall, some even Millie hadn't been to yet. It had been his idea. Their dinner the night before had been more of a success than she'd ever thought would be possible. She'd been so close to cancelling, wondering why she'd even agreed to it in the first place. Yet, there was still a miniscule part of her which was genuinely interested in what he had to say for himself, how on earth he was going to defend what he'd done. It turned out, he *wasn't* going to defend himself. He admitted there was nothing he could say to explain himself or justify his behaviour but that he realised what a complete and utter *idiot* he had been. Having imagined the conversation happening many times before, she'd always thought she would be a strong, independent woman and tell him where to go, never succumbing to his pleading words. But she'd found herself listening intently, *believing* him. When he'd leaned across and took her hand on the table, she hadn't moved it away. When he threw his arm around her shoulder on the walk back to the car, she'd leaned into it. And when he'd kissed her after dropping her home, she'd kissed him back, the familiarity rushing back over her like they'd never been apart.

There was something about seeing Sam in a new setting as well; all she'd ever known of him was the sharp, fast-paced city boy who relished packed bars, bustling trains and high-rise buildings. Spending time with him away from all the expectations, the pressure, the need to impress had brought out a different side to him. He was listening to her, asking questions and showing a genuine interest in her new life here. He'd even asked her about her artwork which had *never* happened before. After the meal last night, she still sensed an element of confusion about how she felt but after spending the day together, she found her mind daring to wander to the thought of him moving down here and them beginning a whole new life together. Maybe starting over in a brand-new place could be the blank canvas they needed to move on from the dark memories, the fact he had cheated and the infertility news. Whilst it wouldn't change the fact, she'd never be able to conceive, maybe it wouldn't matter so much here? They could buy a farm full of animals, she could make jam to sell; they could live happily ever after…

Yet, of course, that would mean saying no to Alfie.

She had thought about Alfie on and off throughout the day, her mind more occupied with Sam; now that she was alone on her sofa, she found her mind wandering back to him. They hadn't had a proper conversation alone since before she'd left for Christmas. Since he'd given her the pink camellias – the message hadn't been lost on her. She glanced across at the table, where they sat in a stripy vase, looking a little sadder now than they had before. She leaned her head back on the sofa, closed her eyes and breathed deeply. There was no hiding the fact she still felt a huge attraction towards Alfie – all she'd thought about whilst she was away was him and she'd had every intention of coming back from London, heading straight there and telling him she wanted to give things a go. This had *seriously* thrown a spanner in the works. The thing was, did she cast caution to the wind, follow her heart and give things a go with a brand-new person, who, honestly, she still didn't know much about? Or did she place trust back in the person she knew the most in the world and try to recreate the good parts of what they had before?

Her brain fizzed and started to feel like it was overheating, and she suddenly felt like she really needed some air. Grabbing her scarf and coat from the hook, she pulled the door shut and made her way down to the beach.

"You've helped so much Alfie, we can't thank you enough." Alfie wiped his paint covered hands on his old jeans which were already splattered in various coloured streaks and smiled.

"It's honestly not a problem, Eric. I'm pleased to help." He'd answered a flustered call from Eric, the caretaker at the village hall, saying he'd received a call from a well-known travel magazine asking to do a feature on the village after seeing a local news report. It could really help their cause to keep the hall and the clock tower, but it was clear that if photos were to be taken for such a high-profile event, a facelift of the hall was needed – more than just the window washing and sweeping up that had already taken place. Eric had pleaded with Alfie to lend his painting talents and help him completely repaint the outside of the hall as soon as he possibly could. Alfie had explained he was in a lull of commissions (all of his Christmas ones had been and gone, and he didn't tend to open up to anything new until the end of January to allow himself some space to create without any pressure). So he could help paint the hall before the New Years' Eve party in two days' time. Eric had been so grateful, as he struggled to do more physical jobs since his hip replacement.

Alfie had been more grateful though, for the distraction.

He still hadn't spoken to Millie, not able to bring himself to message her after finding out she had gone to dinner with Sam the night before. If she'd wanted to talk, she would have messaged, he thought. And after not hearing from her all day today, he guessed she had been with him. He shoved his phone back into his pocket after checking it for the millionth time that day – nothing. If he didn't hear from her by tomorrow evening, he'd make the first move and contact her himself. The day after that would be the New Year's Eve party and he wanted to know where he stood before then, for fear she may turn up with *him* and make him look a total fool. He'd absolutely poured his heart out to her, and she'd suggested she would let him know where he stood when she returned from London. Yet here he was days later and nothing. It wasn't OK.

He flicked the lights off in the hall knowing Eric would be back later to lock up and stepped out into the twilight of the evening. Drizzle was in the air again. It was hard to remember a full day since she had left where it hadn't rained in some way and the darkness were starting to impact him. The dim, winter days affected his artistic creativity too – there was only so much inspiration he could suck from the same, dreary skies and shadowy corners of his apartment.

The pub, at least, glowed warm and, remembering he had no plans for that evening, he decided to head back to his flat, take a shower and pop in for an hour or so. None of the gang would be out tonight but there was always at least one local character he could sit at the bar with and chat to and it would pass the time. A strong whiskey wouldn't go amiss, either.

Taking the short walk back home, he glanced to the slope which headed down to the beach. The tide was out quite far, the murky waves and misty sky mixing like an inky concoction. A figure stood down by the shore and Alfie's heart leapt as he recognised it instantly; the enormous tartan scarf, visible even from the back, was undeniably hers. What should he do? Keep pacing past like he hadn't seen her and go for a drink, leaving the ball firmly in her court? Or go down and confront her, ask what the hell is going on and why hadn't she at least messaged him? He swallowed, glancing around as though someone was going to come out of nowhere and tell him what to do. But he knew no such person was going to do that and he needed to follow his head. With purpose, he started striding down towards the slope.

As he made his way down the beach towards her, he wished he'd at least grabbed a jacket from his apartment first. The dicey rain was freezing and was soaking his t-shirt quicker than he'd like. His bare arms and face bore the brunt of the cold, goose bumps erupting on his skin. She hadn't turned around – had she heard him? His feet crunched on the pebbles before landing on firm sand the further to the shore he walked. His heart beat in his chest. In reality, it had only been a few days since he'd seen her, but the distance had felt cavernous. He *had* to find out where he stood.

He reached her side and she turned, blinking in shock

at his appearance. Her hood was up covering most of her head and her scarf covered her chin, but the rest of her face was there, right in front of him and it was every bit as beautiful as he remembered. Her hair was down and exposed to the elements, a shade darker than usual thanks to the dampening from the rain. Her eyelashes glistened with the moisture from the air and her cheeks burned pink with cold. Slowly, she took her hands out her pockets and crossed them over her body.

"Hey," he said quietly, unsure if she was annoyed at seeing him.

"Hey," she replied, offering a small smile. A few moments of silence passed between them.

"Millie…" he began but was swiftly cut off.

"I'm sorry I haven't messaged you, Alfie. I had meant to, I promise. But things have been a little bit…different than I expected." She glanced downwards, not meeting his eyes and he studied her face. He couldn't work out if this difference had been a good or bad thing for her. She wasn't giving anything away.

"Yeah, I heard. I *saw*," he replied, referencing the moment he had witnessed her and Sam in the square below his apartment. Her cheeks pinked a little further and he suspected it wasn't due to the cold this time. She still didn't offer any other information, so he knew he'd have to pry if he wanted to know what was going on.

"So, Sam…?" he began and peered across at her to gauge her reaction. "How's that going?" She hesitated for a few moments before continuing.

"It's unexpected. Like, if someone had given me a list of scenarios for how the end to this year was going to play out, I never in a million years would have thought of this one." Alfie squeezed his eyes shut. She wasn't giving anything away. This was frustrating.

"Amy said you went to dinner with him?" he pressed further.

"Last night. And today we spent the day together." Ouch, that stung. In the fantasy turn of events he'd concocted in his head; they would have gone to dinner together last night and Millie would have realised he was still an absolute tool and told him it was over for good. Meeting up again today didn't confirm that dream. He wished he knew exactly what had gone on between them. If he knew that, he'd least have a strong case to make her see he wasn't good news for her. He had a feeling it involved him being unfaithful due to some cryptic comments overheard between Daisy and Amy. If that was true, he had no idea why she'd even be entertaining the thought of spending time with him, let alone actually doing it.

"I know what you're thinking," Millie continued. "That I'm absolutely crazy for seeing him again. I sort of think I'm crazy too," she admitted. She looked so vulnerable, stood there in the now almost total darkness, cold and damp. He wanted to wrap his arms around her, protect her, and reassure her that she deserved more than to be someone's afterthought.

"I mean, it might not be my place to say this but I'm

going to say it anyway. I know I don't know exactly the situation between you two, but I can tell you from just the few times I've met him – he's bad news for you Millie." She looked across at him, her brow creased. But he couldn't stop himself from continuing. "The way he acted when I let him into the cottage before you arrived home and the way he spoke to me. Simply the way he's striding around here like he owns the place. Like he owns *you*. He made that as clear as day to me when he arrived. I don't know if he saw me as a threat – I can't think how he'd know there was anything at all between us but it's like he was claiming you before you even had the chance to explain that." He watched her face register everything he said.

"He doesn't *own* me," she answered, disgust in her voice. "I don't know why you'd even suggest that?" Alfie paused, realising she'd taken his words and twisted them, accidentally.

"No, I don't mean that he *does* own you…"

"No-one owns me! And you're right; you don't have a clue what we went through. You don't know anything about him. I appreciate that you're feeling a certain way because I haven't replied to you and I'm sorry for that, but I've had a lot to deal with over the last few days…" She was babbling now, words pouring out like lava, unstoppable. Her arms had uncrossed, and Alfie gently took her hands, bringing them down to her side to calm her. She didn't resist so he kept hold of them. They were freezing.

"I didn't mean that, Millie. I mean…it's obvious from what I've heard that he was unfaithful to you. Do you really want to get involved again with someone like that? Who treats you like that? That's not what you deserve and deep down you know that." She snatched her hands back.

"You don't understand Alfie. Sam knows me better than anyone else. We've been through things together that I've haven't been through with anyone else. It's not something I've been able to easily forget!" She was raising her voice now, frustration spouting from every word. He had never seen her like this and the thought he'd upset her hurt but he had to keep going. Make her see that she was making a huge mistake.

"You deserve more than him, Millie! You deserve someone who won't cheat on you!" She flinched, as though the word "cheat" had slapped her. Darkness washed over her face.

"You don't understand Alfie. Again, I'm sorry I didn't get back to you but that's no excuse to come at me like this. You can't ambush me and tell me how stupid I am and then expect me to just fall into your arms and live happily ever after! It doesn't work that way." He closed his eyes and realised he'd lost her. This was a huge mistake. He shouldn't have stuck his nose in. If he wanted any chance of them being together, he should've left her alone and let her realise that for herself.

"You may be right. But I want to find that out for myself," she said, more quietly now, tears welling in her eyes. He held his hands up in surrender.

"You're right. I'll leave you alone, Millie. I never should have interfered. I'm sorry." He walked backwards a few paces, before turning and striding as fast as he could back up the beach. His legs felt frozen, his arms biting with the cold, but he had to keep going. That had been such a stupid, *careless* decision. He'd wanted to tell her what an amazing person she was and how Sam was certainly not the one to bring that out of her but instead he'd messed it up totally and pushed her away. Potentially forever.

He definitely still needed that drink, but it would be coming from his liquor cabinet to be drunk alone in darkness. He didn't want to see anyone. Not tonight. Not tomorrow. He would forget the party. Nothing seemed worth celebrating anymore. For the first time in ages, he found himself starting to cry, wishing his mum was still here. He'd do anything right now to have a chat and a cuddle from her, to reassure him that even though he'd seriously messed up, he was still a good person deep down. He was still her son, worthy of love.

Thirty-One

The sunlight was weak but bright enough to rouse her from sleep. Immediately, she felt the effects of a poor night's sleep: her head felt as though it were being constricted by a thick rubber band, her mouth felt as dry as the sand she stood on the day before and a general fogginess surrounded her. Insomnia had plagued her, thoughts of the day just passed resounding in her head. The conversation with Alfie had not gone as she'd have liked – she still hadn't decided conclusively what she wanted, and it was obvious in her mind that she still had feelings for him; feelings which were undoubtedly very strong. She couldn't get the thoughts out of her head she'd regularly had over Christmas; about the kiss they'd shared and how close they had grown in such a short space of time. She'd dared to dream of them becoming a couple, living together, spending long and lazy days painting side by side in his beautiful home…

And then she'd wondered if that could be her reality now she felt so…damaged. Aside from the harsh but true fact that she couldn't have children (and she knew that could be a game-changer in any new relationship), Sam was the only boyfriend who had lived with her through that period of time. He'd witnessed how it had made her feel and how she had attempted to deal with it afterwards – how could she open herself up to anyone else, explain how it made her feel? And who would be willing to be with her throughout all that? She had never felt more like a burden and the feeling overwhelmed her. She couldn't put that on Alfie. He was too kind, too loving and had too much of a future ahead of him. He needed to find a wonderful woman who could give him *everything* he wanted – including a child, if that was the path they chose together. She knew having children wasn't everything to everyone. But at least with someone else, he'd have a *choice*. After yesterday's argument, she wasn't sure Alfie even wanted to know her anymore. She hadn't exactly been kind to him.

She hauled herself out of bed – if it wasn't for the fact the party was the next day and she had put her name down to assist with the list today, she'd be flying straight back under the duvet. But instead, she shuffled down the narrow staircase and into the kitchen, heaping two large teaspoons of coffee into a mug and pouring on boiling water. She would need all the help she could get to make it through the day.

Her phone pinged as she drained the mug, instantly flicking the kettle on to make another cup. There were several unread messages, due to her leaving it downstairs overnight. The first was from Amy: **Haven't heard from you in a while... how is everything?** The next from Jenny checking in and sending a video of Leo laughing out loud for a minute straight at something funny on the TV. The innocent giggles warmed her heart. The final one was from Sam (had she secretly been hoping it was from Alfie?) He asked if he could pop over that morning and what were her plans for the day. She paused before answering – she had to do her jobs this morning for the party as she promised. She was looking forward to getting stuck into decorating the tables and designing the nametags for the buffet food, alone. It had felt like a long time since she'd been able to just sit and tackle a task alone. She hadn't painted for what felt like an age and she was raring to dive back into creating again, away from all the drama of this bizarre kind of love triangle she had found herself in.

Yet, she knew he would likely not take no for an answer. She had no idea what his plans were or how long he was going to be staying here – maybe she could ask him today. Maybe they needed to have a conversation about what was going on and what he envisioned in their future. She needed to know this to make a final decision about the direction of her life. She tapped back to Sam to come and meet her at the cottage in half an hour. Foregoing the second coffee, she dashed back upstairs, wanting to be showered and ready by the time he arrived.

"It's certainly different to our flat, I'll give you that," Sam said, stooping around the cottage, patting the exposed stone on one of the walls. She watched him carefully, sipping her coffee. He looked so out of place in here it was crazy.

"It's perfect for just me," she replied, feeling defensive over her little home. So it didn't follow a colour scheme, or wasn't full of all the latest technology but it was her little haven and she had grown to adore it here, the lack of central heating and all.

"Exactly," he said, slumping down into the armchair next to the lit fire. "But not enough room for both of us." She frowned.

"There's a "both of us"?" she questioned. He smiled at her.

"You don't think I've driven all the way down to the back-arse-of-nowhere, risked my life walking up and down that ridiculously steep lane every night, lived without decent phone signal for *days*…not to want to live with you again?" She rolled her eyes at his exaggerations, and he grinned, knowing he had amused her. "Seriously though, I don't wish to sound forceful but I'm not planning on leaving here without you." Her heart sank. His comment was loaded with an all too familiar forcefulness she had grown used to when being with him but now felt out of place and uncomfortable. He wanted her to go back with him. She didn't really know why this had come as such a surprise to her – it had been clear from the start he had no intention of living here. His life was back in London, and he wasn't going to give that up. She exhaled loudly, taking a seat opposite him, by the window.

"I don't know, Sam," she began, her voice wavering. She felt nervous suddenly. "I don't know if I want to leave Sandyhaven." He knitted his brows.

"You can't seriously want to stay *here*, Mils? There's nothing here! It's no comparison to London?" She ran her finger round the rim of her mug.

"It depends on what you're looking for in a place to live," she said, not meeting his eye. "London is great. But since living here I've felt…freer. The air is cleaner. I've felt more headspace to paint. It's simpler." His frown remained and she felt compelled to continue, to defend her newfound home and community. "The people here are lovely too. I've really felt accepted into the community." She continued to tell him again, in more depth, all about the new friends she had made (although she didn't mention Alfie's name purposely), about Mr Slee the shopkeeper, the village hall situation and the adventure she'd had meeting Lauren, her favourite artist. She told him about her artwork, the classes she'd held and how it had reignited her passion. He listened but his face remained unreadable, and she found her passion and excitement waning following every sentence that passed with no reaction. A familiar feeling washed over her – this is how he had made her feel many times before when she'd shown interest and excitement in something; not insulting her directly but just not mirroring her enthusiasm or providing any encouraging words. She tailed off and waited for his reaction.

"It sounds great, Millie. And it sounds like it's all been a great break for you. But it's time to come home now. What I haven't told you yet is that I've received a promotion at work. It includes a company car *and* a handsome raise. So we could maybe afford to move into the suburbs a little further out of the city centre. You'd like that, wouldn't you? That may suit your new preference for quieter places to live, like here."

She ignored how he said the word "here", as though it were offensive and processed what he'd said. She wouldn't necessarily compare a suburb of London to here in terms of what she would now be looking for in a home. Frustration began to rear its ugly head; he wasn't listening to her. He *never* listened to her.

All of a sudden, she stood up and headed to the kitchen to place her mug in the sink. She needed to get to the village hall, with or without Sam.

"I need to head out. I have some jobs to do," she announced, pulling on her coat.

"Where? Doing what? I didn't think you had a job right now?"

"It's not a *paid* job," she said, rolling her eyes whilst pulling her hat down over her head. "It's to help prep the hall for tomorrow's New Year's Eve party." He pulled a face.

"Gosh, yeah, it's New Year's Eve tomorrow. I was planning on being back up home for that. I've got tickets to a boat party on the Thames. A contact in work hooked me up. It's supposed to be one of the most sought-after parties of the night." Of course it was, Millie thought. He followed her out the door as she pulled it shut behind her.

"I've got *two* tickets, Millie. Why don't you come back and join me?" She hesitated, counting all the cracks in the road as she considered his offer. "I don't know, Sam. Coming back is a big decision…"

"You don't have to come back for good. Well, at least not tomorrow. But come back for New Years? All the lads are going, it'll be a laugh." She winced inwardly. Whilst she'd spent nights out with "the lads" many times previously and tolerated it, it wasn't exactly her idea of a great time. In fact, after spending so much time in the simplicity of Sandyhaven, the thought of being on some millionaire's boat, stuck in the middle of the dingy Thames, sucked into a far too tight dress, wearing uncomfortable shoes and sipping a bitter fizzy champagne substitute sounded like her idea of pure hell. She had been looking forward to the village hall party; the chance to eat some good picky food, drink whatever you wanted and have a dance and a laugh with friends. Plus, so much work had gone into it, including all the stuff with the news report. She *had* to be there.

She glimpsed the village square in the distance and the hall further beyond it and sighed, realising Sam wasn't going to take no as an easy answer.

"I don't know Sam. I've made a promise to be here," she explained, and he noticeably groaned.

"To who? Who have you got such an allegiance to?" She opened her mouth to answer but paused and his eyes widened. "It's him, isn't it? The Alfie guy? You've got a thing going with him, haven't you?" Not knowing how to reply, she said nothing, and he shook his head. "I knew it! I could tell he had a problem with me when he let me into the cottage that very first time." Sam had raised his voice by now and Millie felt a swathe of embarrassment. Hopefully no-one would hear him. She pushed open the door to the hall, ushering him inside so at least in there no-one would hear him. She pulled the door shut and braced herself for the conversation to come.

Alfie was in the kitchenette of the hall when he heard the door bang and immediately noticed raised voices. He was about to walk out to see what the problem was when he spotted the back of Sam and the front of Millie. Like a flash, he ducked back into the room, flicking off the light but leaving the shutters slightly ajar – he really didn't want to make himself known in that moment. Mainly because the curiosity had got the better of him – he wanted to know what this guy was like when no-one else was around and why he seemed to have sucked Millie in, once again. She hadn't struck him as the type of person who would fall for an idiot, especially not twice. He froze on the spot, praying they weren't heading into the kitchen. Thankfully, they stayed standing in the middle of the hall. He squinted to look through the gap; there was Millie, and his heart softened upon seeing her beautiful face. But the anxious expression on her face caused him to tense up. And there was Sam; there was something about his body language that immediately got Alfie's back up.

"Just say it, Millie. Say it's *him* who's keeping you here." The hairs on the back of Alfie's neck stood up – who were they talking about?

"It's nothing to do with Alfie!" she yelled back, and a shiver coursed over his body. They were arguing about *him*. How he wished he'd been witness to the first part of their conversation.

"Then why won't you come back. Back *home*. Leave this dump?" Sam indicated the hall around them and flung a hand towards the door, presumably referencing the village as a whole.

"Stop calling it a dump! It's the first place I've ever really felt is home," she counteracted, and Alfie felt a rush of pride that she was standing up for herself. This was the strongheaded Millie he had come to know. Sam scoffed.

"Oh please! So let's say you stay here then Millie, yeah? What are you going to do for work? There's no office block around here to do your little assistant jobs. I suppose you think your art is going to keep you sorted, do you?" Her face visibly fell, and Sam stared down on her, his whole demeanour menacing. "And who are you even going to live with?" he continued pressing. Alfie could vaguely make out Millie's expression – she looked wounded.

"I can live alone," she replied quietly.

"You don't like living alone!" he shouted. "That's why you chose to stay with your mum all that time before you met me, even when she was treating you like shit." Alfie started to feel a desire to rush out there and put him back in his box – he didn't like Sam's attitude. He was intimidating her, and he could sense that even from a different room. He watched as Sam took a step closer to Millie.

"You need to be with me, Mils," he said, his voice softer now. "I know you. I can take care of you. I'm the best person to do that. Think of what we've been through together." Sam reached his hand up to cup her face and Millie shied away.

"Don't bring that up now," she pleaded, her voice wobbling and Alfie's senses immediately spiked. Bring what up? What had happened?

"But it's reality Millie. You can't run away from it. It happened and I told you I'd accepted it. There aren't going to be many people that will." She shot him a look of disbelief and disgust.

"I'm sorry?! Don't throw that one on me!" she shouted, pushing him away. "Don't you dare make me feel unlovable? Like no-one else would ever want me?!

"Well, who would Millie?! Who would, when you can't give someone a *child*?!" he spat out and Alfie's heart thudded to the ground. So that was the "thing" that had been plaguing his mind – he just *knew* there was something she had been hiding. Something big. Suddenly, the reaction to Daisy's pregnancy announcement made complete sense. All the times she'd told him she was "dealing with something big" or "working through things" came into his head and everything fell into place. Poor Millie. His heart absolutely leapt out to her – he couldn't even begin to understand the enormity of what finding out something like that must have done to her – would *still* be doing to her. He felt complete sadness for her.

And then, anger exploded through his veins. A red mist descended over him and before he could talk some sense into himself, he burst through the door and strode across the hall. Both Millie and Sam's heads snapped towards him, registering shock. Millie's face was one of pure disbelief, tears streaming. Sam's now looked enraged, disgusted even, at the sight of Alfie there. He still didn't move back, and Alfie felt uncomfortable at how close he was to her.

"What are *you* doing here?" Sam spoke in an accusatory tone.

"I feel like I need to ask the same of you," Alfie replied, standing only a metre away from them. He immediately turned to Millie and placed a hand on her arm. He could feel her trembling.

"Are you OK?" he asked, and she looked down, with no response, which spoke volumes. Sam's hand pushed against his arm.

"Don't touch her?" he spat. "Who the fuck do you think you are?"

"I think I'm someone telling you that you need to walk out this hall right now, never come back and never harass Millie again," Alfie spoke firmly. Sam smirked, turning his body towards Alfie. Alfie squared himself, bracing for anything that may happen next. This guy was big, and he wasn't an enormous guy himself, and hell knows he'd never been in a fight. But he wasn't afraid to defend himself. Especially to a stuck up, entitled bully boy like him.

"I don't really think that's your choice, is it?" he replied. Alfie's eyes flicked to Millie, who now had mascara pooling around her bottom eyelids and a scared expression on her face. He couldn't begin to imagine how she was feeling, not only with the hideously hurtful things Sam had just said to her but also knowing that he had revealed it in front of him too. He desperately wanted to throw his arms around her and comfort her, tell her she didn't have to settle for this absolute dickhead.

"No. It's Millie's choice."

"And we know who Millie will choose." He grabbed her forearm a little too roughly for Alfie's liking and his whole body twitched. "She's going to choose the guy who has been with her through thick and thin. Who she's lived with, who has loved her for years, was there when her mum died and who sat next to her when she was told she couldn't have children. Can you top that?" Alfie narrowed his eyes. This guy's arrogance was really grating on him. And what was with that expression – could he *top* it? His whole personality was laid out in front of him – competitive, intimidating, wannabe alpha male. He just couldn't get out of his head how Millie could ever have been with a guy like this? Sam took a step closer, so they were almost touching.

"Sam, please…" Millie began.

"I don't think it's about 'topping' each other, Sam. I just

know that right now you are *seriously* overstepping the mark, and you need to be careful." Sam smiled slyly.

"Or what?"

"Sam, seriously. Just go," Millie begged, tears coursing down her face now.

"You're right, let's go," he said, grabbing Millie's hand but she immediately snatched it back. Sam's face registered total disbelief. "I mean it, Sam. Go! I'm not coming with you, but you need to leave. NOW. *Please.*" He stared at her for a few moments; clearly not knowing how to react. Alfie was poised and ready, adrenaline surging through his body. If he laid another hand on her, he knew he wouldn't be held accountable for his actions.

Sam scoffed, ran a hand through his hair and with one final, hard glare at Alfie, turned and strode out, his footsteps echoing ominously around the hall. Alfie waited for the door to slam shut before moving to comfort Millie, who fell full weight into his body. He gently shushed her in between her raw, guttural sobs and the feeling of her trembling body caused tears to threaten in his own eyes. It felt like her cries were letting out everything she had been holding in: all the emotions, the secrets, the past. He so desperately wanted to take it all away for her, erase that hideous man from her history and replace it only with love and care.

It felt like hours had passed, although it could only have been a few minutes, when Millie's head resurfaced from his chest and her cries had turned into deep, sorrowful gulps. He placed a hand on her cheek and gently wiped at the streaks of mascara, coursing down her face like inky streams. She looked so dreadfully sad that his heart broke.

"What do you need from me?" Alfie spoke softly. Millie could barely speak, her mouth set in a miserable line. "Would you like me to stay around?" he asked. Slowly, she nodded. "You're sure you don't want me to leave?" She shook her head, still hiccupping. He considered his next question carefully. He really didn't want it to come across the wrong way. "Do you want to go back to mine? Back to yours?"

"The first one," she spoke finally.

"OK," he whispered, bringing her close again and placing his lips on her forehead. "Let's go get you sorted."

"This has got to change, Sam. You can't keep doing this and expecting me to be OK with it!" Millie threw her coat on, rage coursing through her. They were due at their mutual friend's engagement party in half an hour, and it was at least forty minutes on the tube. She'd been ready for an hour but had spent the rest of the time waiting for Sam to get home. He'd been out with the lads watching rugby but had promised to be home by midday, insisting he wanted to come to the party. "It's a free bar after all," he'd exclaimed. Yet, he'd stumbled in clearly inebriated and very loud, antagonising Millie. There had been so many times now where he had promised he'd be ready for something or be available for something and he'd ended up being anything but.

"I went out for a drink Millie. To a pub round the corner. You act like I'm cheating on you or something." She paused packing her bag for a moment, thinking that was a strange comment to make but then continued.

"It's not the point of what you were doing, Sam. It's the fact you always promise me you're going to do something and then you end up doing the opposite."

"How is it the opposite?!" he protested, from his lying position on the sofa. *"I'm here, aren't I?"* She surveyed him, legs up and shoes off, not looking remotely ready for an engagement party. His slurred speech gave the same impression. She sighed heavily, grabbing her keys from the side.

"Are you coming or not?" He made a face, and she instantly knew what the reply would be.

"I don't fancy it any more Millie," he whined, and she groaned, although not surprised. He had a habit of letting her down, leaving her to awkwardly explain why he wasn't there. It was embarrassing. His face suddenly changed and he jumped up, striding purposefully over to her and grabbing her by the waist. She felt his lips crash into hers and then start to trace down her neck.

"Sam, I have to go…" she protested.

"Let's stay here," he said, in between kisses and she could sense the frantic need to his voice. She didn't want this right now. Not like this. She started to push him off.

"Sam, look, not now…"

"Why not? Come on Millie, we agreed last week we were moving on. It's not like this is the first time we'll have done it

since...?" She looked him directly in the face. She could smell alcohol on his breath, and it turned her stomach.

"Since what, Sam? Say it." He slumped his shoulders.

"I don't need to Millie. We had this conversation last week. I thought we agreed to move on?"

"We did. But that doesn't mean I'll just do it on command. It's not something I always want to do! It's still very much on my mind." He pulled her in closer and she felt herself relax a little. Perhaps he did understand.

"Come on Millie. I understand this must be so difficult for you," he spoke gently, rubbing her back. "But we have to try to look on the positive side, keep moving forwards. She tensed slightly.

"And what exactly positive is there about this?"

"Well, let's think about Simon and Maisy – they got pregnant when they didn't mean to and it's ruined their whole life," he said and she immediately stiffened, pulling away forcefully.

"You've got to be kidding me?" she stammered, and he registered surprise. "Are those supposed to be words of comfort?" He opened and closed his mouth like a goldfish. He clearly had no idea that what he just said was hugely disrespectful and upsetting to her. She shook her head and looked at him with disgust, storming out the house. It was getting more and more difficult to see how they could move past this, but clearer and clearer how much she didn't really want to be with him anymore.

Thirty-Two

She woke with a start and a scream, sweat racing down her back. She wasn't sure where she was and panic began to set in until the bedroom door opened, allowing a shard of light to spill across the floor and she felt Alfie's presence, arms tight around her.

"It's OK, I'm right here," he whispered softly, one hand on her head and the other around her body. It took a minute or two to regain some control to her breathing and realise where she was: she was in Alfie's bed, in his apartment. Faintly, she could hear the sea swooshing outside and it brought some immediate comfort. Glancing at the clock, it read two in the morning.

She sat up further and ran both hands back through her hair, wincing at the damp patches. It was no surprise she was having vivid dreams after the absolute rollercoaster of a day before. They'd left the village hall and headed straight to Alfie's apartment where he'd made her multiple cups of tea – some with a welcome tot of whiskey – and allowed her to just wallow on the sofa under a fluffy blanket. Some moments she'd spoken, a lot, about anything that was on her mind and others she remained silent, allowing the swirling of the sea to fill the silent gaps. By the early evening, after several measures of alcohol she'd started to drift off to sleep in the chair and when Alfie had offered her his bed for the night, she'd accepted without hesitation. He'd run her a bath and she'd changed into a pair of his shorts and a t-shirt, settling into his bed and falling asleep almost immediately. She hadn't even known where he was sleeping until just then; he'd clearly been on the sofa.

As completely emotionally wrecked as she felt, there was something ridiculously intimate about being here in Alfie's bed, in his clothes, not to mention him pressed against her. She felt her breathing return to normal as he softly stroked her hair.

"How do you feel?" he spoke, breaking the silence. She shifted slightly, leaning herself into him.

"I just had a bad dream, that's all," she replied. He leaned across to the bedside table and passed her the full glass of water, which she sipped appreciatively.

"Have you heard from him since…?" Alfie asked and she shook her head vehemently. She had checked her phone only once but there had been nothing from Sam. She had a strong feeling that she wouldn't be seeing him again. The thought brought her both great comfort and a sense of finality.

"I have to say something Millie…" he began, and she twitched, wondering what he was going to reveal. "I…I overheard what Sam said earlier. About…about you." She squeezed her eyes shut. She'd been afraid of that. The thing which she'd fought for so long to *not* define her was slowly seeping out to the world. It made her feel panicked and out of control. She sat up abruptly, shrugging out of his arms.

"I can't talk about it," she started but he placed a hand on her back causing her to calm the chattering thoughts in her brain.

"It's OK. I wouldn't expect you to be able to. Especially not to me." She turned back to look at him, for the first time properly since he'd entered the room. He was sat upright against the headboard, wearing just a pair of grey, flannelled tracksuit bottoms. His hair was unkempt, a shadow of stubble prevalent on his face. Her heart skipped.

"What do you mean, 'especially to you'?" she asked, frowning a little.

"Well…I'm sure there are other people you'd feel more comfortable talking to before you spoke to me about something so personal," he explained. She exhaled, managing a small smile.

"Then you don't really know just how much I trust you," she said. "I've told you many things I haven't told anyone else. Things about my past, about my painting, about my mum." Her throat felt like it may close over if she mentioned her mum again and she gave a little cough to clear it.

Alfie's heart swelled. For almost a week now, he'd been

adamant she was no longer interested in him, that she no longer wanted to foster a connection with him. Even her staying in his bed today hadn't really indicated anything – she was in emotional turmoil and staying here instead of going home alone had made sense. It didn't mean she was revealing a desire to be with him, he'd known that. So, to hear those words, that she had confided in him without him even knowing – it brought great relief. And in that moment, with her in his bed, in his clothes and in such close proximity, he wanted nothing more than to tell her he was so in love with her, that he had been for a while now but just didn't know how to say it. And of course, now was just not the right time to reveal that, what with the past few days she'd had.

Instead, he leant into her and gently kissed her temple.

"Well, I'm pleased to hear it. I'll always be here to listen to you if that's what you want." She turned her body to face him now and searched his eyes – his warm, friendly eyes. Why hadn't she seen them from the very beginning – even right at the start when she'd first moved here and he had pushed her away, his eyes had always been there. They'd been right there in front of her, all along. But she'd been clinging onto the past so much, allowing it to direct her future that she'd shut out all other possibilities and any chance that she could, in fact, be happy. Because that was all she wanted. To be truly *happy*.

Without another thought, she leaned across and pressed her lips to his, flashbacks of the time in the hall when they'd shared their first kiss racing through her head. He immediately responded, his lips keen and longing before pulling away only seconds later.

"Millie, I…I can't quite believe I'm saying this, but I don't think I can do this with you feeling, understandably, so emotional. I don't want you to regret this later, or think I was ever taking advantage of you?" She kissed him again, briefly this time, surprising herself with her forwardness.

"You're not taking advantage of me. I'm right here, wanting you," she replied, and he noticed him visibly swallow. Their faces were so close now, the space between them charged and she knew in this moment that things had changed forever, irrevocably. He stared directly in her eyes, and she held his gaze boldly. She watched his lip twitch, as though he was trying desperately not to jump on her right there and then. She could tell he was a gentleman, that he was considering his actions for fear of how the results would make her feel. Yet she knew that for once in her life she didn't want to stress about the future, and she certainly didn't want to dwell on the past. She wanted the right here and now and she had to make that happen.

Without another thought, she leaned forwards and kissed him, twisting her body to push him down further onto the mattress. Yes, this would change things forever. But maybe that's what was needed…

Thirty-Three

The waves crashing was the first sound he noticed upon waking; the cracks of light through the ajar door the second and finally, the gap in the bed next to him. This was the thing that made him sit bolt upright and run his hands vigorously across his face in an attempt to wake himself up.

The previous night had been incredible. Something he'd envisioned and dreamed about for so long had come true and it still felt like it surely wasn't possible. Of course, he'd wanted to join her in bed from the moment she got in last night but there was absolutely no way he'd suggest it – she was so vulnerable, and it would've been wholly inappropriate to even suggest it. When he'd heard her scream, he'd only intended to go in to comfort her and then leave straight away, retreating to the sofa and his makeshift bed, there if and when she needed him again. So, to leave the sofa and not return – that had never been on the agenda. But it had been *her* who had instigated everything, had suggested and started it. Sure, he hadn't taken much persuasion, but he truly felt like she'd wanted to and that had made it easier to agree.

All of these thoughts further spurred the confusion as to why the bed next to him was empty. She must be up and about already. He glanced at the clock on the wall – nine thirty. Jeez, he never slept in this late. Swinging his legs out of bed and pulling back on his bottoms, he squinted as he made his way into the living area, the huge picture window revealing another overcast day. He had expected to smell coffee, hear the TV mumbling or at least see Millie sat cross legged on the sofa, large mug in hand and admiring the view. He would join her, wrapping his arms around her waist from behind and bending his head into her neck, taking in her scent.

But there was no coffee, the TV was still off, and the sofa was empty. Where was she? She must have gone home. Glancing around the apartment, he tried not to let his thoughts run away with him when his eyes settled on a piece of paper resting on the kitchen countertop. Heart beating loudly in his ears, he made his way across the room and picked up the note carefully.

Albie. You are one of the most special people I have ever known. What we shared last night is something I will never forget. I've realised I need to stop living in my past and move forwards into my future. Thank you for helping me realise that. With all my love, Millie x

He read and re-read the note in pure disbelief and shock. Was it saying what he thought it was? Was this a *goodbye* note? He dropped the piece of paper to the floor and paced back and forth. Surely, she wouldn't just leave without saying goodbye. And had she just left to go home? Or left, *LEFT?* He had to find out what was going on. Within thirty seconds, he had pulled on a jumper, descended the stairs to the street and dialled his phone, all at the same time.

There had been several times in her life when Millie had been certain she'd made the right decision: when she'd dropped out of her psychology degree to pursue her art full time (so she'd ended up having to pick up an office job, she still never regretted it for a second); when she and Jenny snuck out of their houses at the age of fifteen and caught the train into London to watch Bloc Party (they were grounded for three months but again, never regretted it since). Even moving down to Cornwall – though it was hugely scary – had made so much sense to her once she'd jumped in the car and started driving. But right now, as she watched the "Welcome to Sandyhaven" sign disappear in her rear-view mirror, she wasn't sure in any way if it was the right decision.

The night before had been incredible. Ever since she had learned of her infertility, she had found intimacy incredibly difficult with Sam and his persistence and lack of understanding had further fuelled that. It had reached a point where she'd wondered if she would ever feel comfortable in a situation like that ever again. Last night had felt so wonderfully natural, like it was truly supposed to happen, and she didn't even have to think about it. In the hours following, snuggled in the warmth of Alfie's bed, listening to the rise and fall of his breath she'd dared to dream that this is what it could be like. That this could be her life moving forwards. But somewhere in the hours following *that,* her mind had started to spiral. She'd found herself having flashbacks to the early days with Sam, where they'd spend entire Sundays in bed, soaking in their own body heat, watching re-runs of *Frasier* and endlessly snacking. The simplicity of the time had gradually become overshadowed by the development of Sam's narcissistic, egotistical ways and it had been difficult to admit that was happening at the time because she had become so sucked in; the relationship with her mum had broken down, she had very few friends and Sam had become a central force in her life, driving her forwards. At the time, she thought she'd been in love, but it had taken that one night with Alfie to make her realise she hadn't been in love at all, not truly. She had been in love with the *idea* of being in love with Sam, but in reality, it was a matter of a convenient time and place and then something she just fell into. And then didn't know how to get out of.

She was sure that this feeling with Alfie was already different to what she'd felt with Sam – it was indescribable to anyone else, yet made so much sense in her own head. But how could she fall in love with someone when she couldn't offer them a future? Sure, Alfie may not want children right now, but he was bound to in the future – there was no way she wanted to be responsible for altering someone's life like that. The only way her jumbled mind had managed to deal with those thoughts this morning was to run – run away and not return. It would be much easier and kinder on both their hearts in the long run than having a drawn out, emotional conversation. Alfie would move on. He'd find someone else.

She realised now, having left the cottage only ten minutes ago that she hadn't truly thought it all through; she'd packed a small case but hadn't arranged any of her other possessions. She hadn't even told Alan she was leaving the cottage (that would be an awkward conversation, considering he was Alfie's dad). She hadn't mentioned anything to Amy, or the rest of the gang and she felt stabs of guilt at that – they had truly welcomed her into the fold since she'd arrived almost four months ago, and they'd been the tightest group of friends she'd had since school. She hadn't even mentioned it to Jenny because she knew she'd just get a lecture, or disapproving words and she couldn't deal with that this morning. Her immediate plan was to head back to London, hole up somewhere and decide what on Earth she was doing with her life.

Yes, she was just going to drive, away from Cornwall, and think about how all the loose ends were going to be tied up later. Distance was what she needed right now.

Damn. Voicemail again. He'd only left one message on Millie's answerphone, figuring that leaving multiples ones wasn't going to get her to listen any sooner. He knocked again at the door but there was no answer. He thought about the spare key to Rosemary Cottage hanging on the hook at home (he had it in case his dad needed him to get in due to an emergency or something. Like the other day with Sam – what a mistake that had been letting him in…) Should he grab it and let himself in? He wasn't sure he could bring himself to do it. If she was in, she would've answered. There was no sign of movement at the windows. She must have gone. The note she left insinuated she wasn't sticking around.

He pressed her name on the screen again and held the phone to his ear whilst looking agitatedly up and down the lane, as though expecting her to just materialise. Still voicemail. He groaned in frustration and squatted down, unable to hold himself up anymore. He hadn't dared to believe she had just done a runner, up until now. As each moment passed, things were becoming more and more bleak. The question he just kept asking himself was, *why?*

Realising he needed to change tack, he swiped back to the top of his call list and pressed the name of one of his oldest friends. If anyone could find out the truth behind something, it would be her. It rang only twice before she picked up.

"Amy? I need your help."

Thirty-Four

The sky was a brilliant, even blue and only a few delicate clouds scattered the view before her, a stark contrast to the grey initially after dawn broke –how ironic that the first spell of clear, sunny weather fell today when she couldn't be feeling greyer and more unclear if she tried. The lanes wound intricately as she made her way to a busier road – she hadn't come up this way since she'd arrived here back in September. She had a feeling that in her haste to leave, she'd taken a wrong turn meaning she had wound up on a road less travelled – barely one car could fit through here at points, let alone two. She had no idea what she would do if she came across another car.

Her phone had been lighting up constantly for the last fifteen minutes. A strong suspicion was that it was Alfie. She couldn't bring herself to answer him. The further she drove, the deeper the pit in her stomach grew, indicating that maybe bolting hadn't been the right thing to do after all, even though she'd thought it the best thing for Alfie when she woke this morning. Before she had the chance to muse further, she'd slammed on the brakes – a dead end and a chipped sign with *"You are Entering Private Property"* scrawled across it, like something from a horror movie before it all goes wrong. She swallowed, hoping it wasn't an omen and bashed the gearstick into reverse. Before she hit the accelerator, she noticed her phone flash up again. Curiosity got the better of her and picking it up saw Amy's name flash across the screen. She took a breath and answered.

"Hey."

"*Hey?!* Is that all you can say? Where the hell are you?" Millie closed her eyes – *obviously* Alfie would have rung her.

"My honest answer is that I'm not sure. I've hit a dead end somewhere." Millie wasn't sure if she meant literally or metaphorically.

"Ok, well let me rephrase then. Where are you going?!" Millie hesitated.

"I'm…I'm going back to London." She tried to sound confident in her statement, but the wavering voice may have blown her cover.

"What?! Why?! You do realise I've just had Alfie on the phone to me practically *crying* right?" she shouted down the phone and Millie's heart dropped. Practically crying? Amy took her silence as a response.

"Yeah, exactly. He told me what happened, Millie. Why would you do that?" She felt tears spring to her own eyes and switching off the ignition, she spent the next ten minutes explaining to Amy all about her feelings of self-doubt, all that had happened with Sam and how she just didn't want to hurt Alfie in any way.

"So I do want to see him at some point, even if just to say sorry," Millie wound up.

"OK, answer me this Millie. Do you love Alfie?"

"Amy…"

"No, just answer me the first word that comes into your head. Do you love him, yes or no?" She closed her eyes and spoke honestly.

"Yes. But…" She couldn't finish the sentence. But what? There was a silence so long she wondered if Amy had hung up on her.

"Fine," she spoke at last. "I get it. But Millie, *I'm* going to miss you too. I haven't had the chance to say goodbye to you. I know we've only known each other a few months but I feel we've struck up a lovely, genuine friendship. I know I can be a loudmouth and a bit nutty, but please come back so I can just give you a squeeze and say bye properly? And then, if you still want to go, you go." Millie's heart leaped out to her. She sounded so vulnerable – she was right, she was a loudmouth. But she had also supported Millie a lot in her own unique way the last few months. Without Amy, she wouldn't have met the rest of the group. She certainly wouldn't have had the memories she had now of Sandyhaven: the early morning dips in the sea, the chaotic nights in the pub and the general feeling of belonging to a group of friends. She owed her a goodbye, especially because she wasn't sure when she'd see her again.

"OK, you win," she replied. "I've taken a wrong turn, so I need to head back towards you anyway. I'm not coming into Sandyhaven though," she said.

"How about meeting you in Carnglaze? It's only ten minutes up from here and it'll get you closer to the main road," Amy offered. After thinking for a few moments, she accepted. A five-minute goodbye – and a thank you – and she'd be off.

"This could be the biggest decision we make together," Sam said seriously. Millie eyed him over her glass of wine. So this is why he'd brought her out tonight. It was rare he properly took her out on what she'd call a date. Their nights out usually involved spending time with his male friends and were less "romantic" and more "frantic." Maybe he'd thought bringing her to a posh restaurant and plying her with wine would convince her to up sticks and move abroad to Singapore for his new job opportunity.

He'd pushed it on her quite quickly, labelling it as the best thing that could ever happen to him. And whilst she'd been shocked at the revelation, of course she felt happy for him. He was so animated whilst he talked about it; in fact, she didn't think she'd ever seen him so excited. When she'd pressed for more details (where would they be living, how long was the job for?), he'd been a little sketchy, which had automatically raised her suspicions. But he'd insisted it was an incredible opportunity for them both – after all, Millie was just in a standard office job and "she could do her art anywhere" (his words).

Millie's immediate inner reaction had been a hard no though – she'd never been particularly interested about living abroad like some people were. Also, they were still fairly early into their relationship. And it wasn't that she didn't think they would last a change like this, but they had yet to discuss the deeper intricacies of their relationship, especially moving forwards. She knew she wanted to get married and have children – where would that fit into this new, exotic life?

Above everything else, Millie's had just learned of quite how bad her mum's addiction had become and it was uncertain where that was going to go. Despite their rocky relationship, she knew she didn't want to leave her.

How on earth she was going to explain this to Sam though, was a tricky one. She could tell he already had his heart set on it – he'd probably already agreed to it. She'd made a habit of going along with things to keep the peace so far in their relationship, but it had been over menial things like what colour they'd paint the flat, or what takeaway to get on the weekend. This was a whole different level.

She shifted uncomfortably in her seat and noted as his face dropped, his expression turning to a mixture of disappointment and irritation.

"I'm guessing the fact you haven't said 'yes' straight away means you're opposed to it then?"

"I wouldn't say 'opposed' exactly," she replied quickly, leaping to her own defence. *"But it's a huge thing to reveal to me. I need a bit of time to process it."* He frowned.

"You do realise what's on the table here, right? We'd be able to move out there and you wouldn't need to get a job? The salary is great and there are living expenses included too." He was right, it did sound great – for someone else. She studied his face as he watched hers back and couldn't help but wonder: if they'd met all over again now, would they still have got into a relationship? Would she still have been attracted to him?

"It sounds wonderful, Sam. And I'm really proud of you for getting it. They obviously think a great deal about you there," she said enthusiastically, hoping it would soften the blow of what she was going to say next. *"But I can't go with you."* His face dropped.

"Why not?" His voice was raised and Millie cast a brief glance around the restaurant to see if anyone had noticed. Thankfully, no-one seemed to be obviously looking their way.

"Because," she began, fiddling with her wine glass. *"There's too much going on here right now. And we haven't even had a conversation about…us."* He looked even more confused now.

"Us?"

"Yeah, you know…" She really didn't want to have this conversation here. *"Our future. What we want."*

"I'm telling you what I want. I want to move to Singapore. With you." She didn't like how he'd just tagged her on the end of that sentence. Like an afterthought.

"Exactly. That's what you *want. But what about what we*

want together?" He looked genuinely confused and she could tell this wasn't going to be an easy conversation. She'd suggested they talk about it back at home, in private and not within earshot of strangers. He hadn't been happy but agreed and they'd eaten their meal in awkward silence.

In the taxi on the way home, Sam broke the silence.

"I think the problem with you Millie is you don't just trust the process. You overthink." She remained silent. She partially agreed with him, but it still felt deeply personal to hear someone else say it. "You don't know how to just reach out and grab things." She stared out the rain-streaked window at the glimmering lights of London flashing by, knowing he was right. She had never been able to just trust the process.

Thirty-Five

On the headland, next to the village welcome sign. That's what Amy had said. Thankfully, Millie had managed to navigate herself here easier than her failed attempt at leaving earlier. The hedges either side opened out and she was on the coast road, the stunning peninsula laid out before her. She felt her heart sink – she had been so lucky to live here, even for just a short period of time. She wished she'd explored more whilst she was here, but her focus had simply been on survival for much of it and that had left little time for sightseeing.

Carnglaze showed as half a mile away on the road sign just passed and she braced herself for the emotional drain this meeting would likely be. The sign came into view in the distance, and she saw the lay-by just beyond it, where she'd pull in. Amy's red car was already there, waiting for her. She took a deep breath and indicated left. As she drew to a stop, she noticed again the incredible scenery surrounding her: the peninsula showing Trewithen to the left and villages scattered beyond, and then Sandyhaven to the right, nestled in a bay, then curving and disappearing into the distance. The broad expanse of sea lay out in front of her, seemingly endless and currently flat thanks to the calm weather. She felt blessed to be spending her final few minutes in Cornwall – and the final day of the year – here. Her heart dropped when she remembered tonight was the New Year's Eve party. All that hard work, all the commitment and dedication she put in – and she wouldn't get to see it.

She stepped out of the car and instantly felt a breeze on her face, highlighting the icy cold temperature. She pulled her coat further around her and snuggled into her scarf. She heard the car door behind her slam, and she turned away from the beautiful view to face Amy.

Except it wasn't Amy's face she was met with. It was Alfie's.

She gasped at the sight of his face, a face she definitely wasn't expecting to see again so soon, if ever? He gave her a small smile, but his eyes were full of sorrow and his expression was one of pure hurt and she felt her heart break into a thousand tiny pieces. *She* had been the one to do that to him. And she suddenly hated herself for it.

"Hey," he spoke, still the other side of the car.

"Hi," she replied, not taking her eyes from his face.

"I know I'm not Amy but thanks for coming," he said. "I really appreciate it." She gave a small shrug.

"You shouldn't be thanking me for anything. I haven't

exactly done a nice thing today." He exhaled slightly and glanced downwards, his hand resting on the open car door.

"I'm not going to disagree with you," he said, and she felt an enormous pang of guilt. "But, if I'm honest, I was more just…confused?" He closed the car door and started walking around to her side.

"Confused?" she asked, as he came within a couple of metres. He leant against the other car door, facing her, hands in his front pockets. He was wearing the same tracksuit bottoms he'd worn the night before and her heart flipped at the memory of him taking them off.

"Yeah. Millie, last night was one of the most incredible I've ever had. I know I can't presume it was the same for you but the fact that you instigated it made me think…maybe wrongly…that it was something you wanted too?" She could detect an edge of anger and frustration to his voice. She glanced downwards, not able to meet his gaze. She couldn't blame him. It really wasn't her finest moment, but she'd felt absolutely no choice. She had to make him see that.

"Alfie…I never meant to hurt you. I know that probably sounds ridiculous to you right now, but I truly mean it. Last night was incredible for me too. It's the most comfortable I've felt in *that* situation for an amazingly long time. Maybe *ever.* And what we've shared over the past few months has been truly magical. But I realised after last night, when I woke up this morning, that…I can't give you what you really want. Maybe not what you want right now but…" He stepped forward, taking both her hands in his.

"If this is referring to what I found out about you the other night then that doesn't matter to me," he said earnestly, deep consideration on his face. She gave a small laugh, feeling tears form in her eyes.

"You can say it, Alfie. What it is. It's my reality and I'm learning to live with it. I can't have children. But I don't just mean I can't give you a baby. I'm sure you don't want that yet, anyway. What I really mean is that I can't give you the *choice*. The prospect of a family. The transition from man to father. The first steps, the first words. Day trips to the beach, watching little ones build sandcastles and run in and out of the water, squealing. The birthdays, the bedtime stories, watching them grow. And then the grandchildren…" She realised she'd been quoting everything she'd prematurely reminisced about since she'd found out and warm tears were dribbling down her cheeks. Alfie gazed at her intently.

"You're so brave," he said quietly, his own eyes glistening with threatening tears and squeezing her hands. "And I can see why you might be thinking about all of that. But I mean it *truly* when I say that whilst all that sounds amazing, it's honestly not a deal breaker for me. I'm a huge believer in living in the *now*. Grabbing the moment. Seizing the opportunity. I realised after last night, I'd fallen in love with *you*, Millie. Not any possible future. But *you*. And any future with you in it is better to me than a future without you in it. Do you believe me?" She couldn't bring herself to look at him. He gently lifted her chin to meet his gaze and held the side of her face delicately. "You've been open and honest with me, Millie. It's my turn to do the same to you. You deserve someone who loves you endlessly, regardless of anything else you have going on. I want to be with *you. You* are enough."

She sobbed: those were the words she had longed to hear from Sam when they were together. Just the reassurance that she was not defined by her infertility – she was an individual person and entity outside of that, who was just as loveable, desirable and worthy as anyone else who didn't have that. He'd alluded to it a few times but only when prompted by her. The way Alfie had spoken to her made her heart swell and a relieving warmth flooded through her, filling her with comfort and – dare she dream it – happiness. *Acceptance.*

She realised they'd been staring at each other intensely for at least half a minute without speaking and they both started laughing at the same time; a release of emotion and pent-up pressure from the past few days came rolling out for both of them and they embraced tightly, Alfie's hands around her waist and hers bear hugging his neck. He squeezed her gently, so her tip toes brushed the ground, before setting her back down and pulling away.

"You need to know now that the emotion I showed just then should not set your daily expectations of me," he said with a joking tone to his voice. She cocked her head to one side and raised an eyebrow.

"I'm going to be seeing you daily, am I?" she teased, and his cheeks shone a pink hue.

"Well that all depends on whether or not you're going to

continue on your Magical Mystery Tour out of Cornwall – or whether you even manage to get out the county that is." She lightly pushed his shoulder as he chuckled at her; Amy must have spilled the beans about her failed attempt to do a runner.

"Amy told me that you were planning on leaving," he said, as though reading her thoughts. "I knew right away I had to get to you. She leant me her car," he explained, gesturing behind him to the little Ford, which was now bathed in a glorious winter sunlight glow. The bitter wind continued to rip around them and Millie pulled her scarf around her, giving a shiver. Noticing this, Alfie spoke.

"Look, I'm sure there's more things we want to talk about…how about we do it back at my place with a warm cup of tea and the heating on?" She stared into his eyes and suddenly her earlier attempt at escaping following an incredible night with this beautiful man in-front of her seemed so abhorrently *stupid*, she knew there was only one choice for her now. Him.

He awaited her answer with bated breath.

"Let's do it," she replied, not able to stop the smile spreading across her face. He returned it and leaned in to kiss her sweetly, with the sound of the crashing waves below resounding around them and her tartan scarf flapping joyfully in the wind.

Six months later

The lane was immersed in a glorious, balmy sunshine as Millie locked up Rosemary Cottage, balancing her phone between her shoulder and ear, and headed down to the village square. Although it was almost half past eight, the impending summer solstice meant the sky was still a wonderful blue and the evening stretched on before her. Her frayed denim shorts and thin strapped white vest indicated the raised temperature, a constant for the last two weeks as a heatwave had blessed Cornwall and beyond.

"It's been just lush to speak to you and hear you sounding so contented, Mils. I literally can't wait to squeeze you so tight tomorrow you can't breathe," Jenny exclaimed. Millie burst out laughing.

"Sounds brutal! But I can't wait to see you all too. It's going to be so lovely showing you round," she replied warmly. Her best friend's first visit to Sandyhaven was only a day away and she was bringing her lovely husband and gorgeous Godson too – it was going to be a new kind of special.

After she hung up and made her way down the lane, past the now ever so familiar rows of quaint cottages either side (some adorned with polka dot bunting and most with pretty flower boxes outside), she could smell the faint traces of barbeque smoke dancing on the gentle breeze, and she knew it would be coming from the beach. The Sandy Anchor held barbeques out on the beach every Saturday evening throughout the summer months and she had made it down most weeks, as had many other villagers. The sense of community in the village was stronger than ever and it was down to the success of their campaign at the end of last year. The New Years' Eve party had been a total triumph: the news crew had turned up all guns blazing as planned and their report had gone viral across social media. Following a few more liaisons with the council, it was announced that the site in question would *not* be knocked down and turned into flats. Instead, they would use a large patch of wasteland two miles up the coast, where they wouldn't be blocking anyone's view or destroying pieces of history. They were even going to employ multiple local people to work on the flats creating job opportunities for many in need. It had been everything everyone had been hoping for and more.

It had also been a magical night for Millie personally too; her first social gathering with Alfie as an official couple. Not that they'd made a huge announcement or anything but naturally, living in Sandyhaven, word wasn't going to stay hidden for long! Many congratulated them heavily, much to their embarrassment, but lots of others were certain they knew it was going to happen all along, and so didn't see it as much of a surprise. Millie hadn't understood that, as to her it had been the *ultimate* surprise, but she guessed the intuition of those around her was strong.

She smiled as the clock tower came into view, standing steadfast against the bold blue of the sky, exactly where it ought to be. The square was buzzing with people moving back and forth from the beach into the pub to get another round of drinks and then back to the barbeque. She exchanged "hellos" with almost everyone she saw, feeling warmth at being a part of this wonderful community, basking in the sense of belonging. It was more than she'd ever dreamed possible.

Down on the beach she spotted Amy, attracting attention in a flowery summer dress, her skin glowing brown having spent every second not at work over the last fortnight improving her tan. She was speaking to two guys at the same time and clearly loving every second. Millie had never been that confident and if she hadn't been so contented herself, she might even envy her. With their backs to that conversation, were Evan and Daisy. Poor Daisy, she was so uncomfortable now: she was past her due date by two days and whilst she advocated all along that due dates were "a load of miscalculated nonsense", she'd give anything right now for them to be true. But good for her still being out of the house and socialising, Millie thought. If she was in her position, she'd be horizontal at any given opportunity.

It shocked her to realise that having a thought like that no longer brought her immense sadness – whilst she knew that would never be her, she had slowly started to come to terms with it, guided by those around her, and actually being able to feel happiness for Daisy had been filling her with such joy and gratitude. She watched Evan as he eyed Daisy carefully – he had been so on edge the last two weeks anticipating the impending labour. She wouldn't be surprised if he had her bags for labour stashed behind the bar at the pub, ready to be hoisted out at a moment's notice and whisked off to the hospital.

She saw Ryan talking animatedly to the pub landlord Arthur, who was now running the barbeque and they both burst out laughing at something he must have said. And Millie's heart flipped when she looked to the other side of Ryan and saw Alfie standing there – he must've been the most handsome man in the entire world, and he was *her boyfriend.* She watched as he took a sip of his drink and then they locked eyes. His tanned complexion looked so different to the one she had met when she'd arrived last year, yet she'd never seen someone so familiar in her life. He gave her a huge smile and waved her over and she picked up the pace to reach him.

"Hey," he said warmly, wrapping his arm around her shoulder and giving her a squeeze. "How was the cottage?"

"It was fine. Jean left at three this afternoon, but I just wanted to double check everything over before Jenny arrives tomorrow morning." Rosemary Cottage still belonged to Alan, but now that Millie lived with Alfie in his flat, it was being rented out as a holiday let. She had initially worried what the villager's reaction would be; knowing that they didn't want Sandyhaven becoming a hub of second homes, but as Alan seemed to be held in such high esteem here, it hadn't really been a problem. He'd agreed to split the earnings with Millie and Alfie fifty-fifty if they ran the booking system and checked in on it, alongside their cleaner Jean, and it had turned into quite a profitable little side project for them both.

At first, Millie had wondered if Alfie might want to move back into the cottage; after all, he'd expressed many times how many memories he held there of his mum. But he'd declined, saying his flat was their home now and he wanted to keep Rosemary's memory alive by allowing other families to come and make their own wonderful memories together. The picture of him and his Mum was tucked into the guestbook in the porch with a short description of who she was and her connection to the cottage, so anyone who came to stay could learn of her story. It felt like the most wonderful dedication to a woman Alfie clearly loved so dearly.

"Amazing. Thanks so much for checking in. I'll do it next time."

"It's OK, I like doing it. I like giving it a little "Millie touch"" she explained, and he leaned down to her ear.

"I think I'm the one who likes the Millie touch." She groaned jokingly and he burst out laughing.

"You are so cringe," she teased, pretending to bat him away. "Seriously though, you're busy enough." Alfie had been inspired by the art classes he and Millie had run back in December, and they had continued as another income for him, alongside his usual commissions which were steady and secure. It meant he got to spend all day doing exactly what he loved: painting. And that made him incredibly happy.

Millie also had managed to finally secure a job linked to her true love of creating. Following the successful campaign of the village hall classes and opening the first one, Lauren Shilton had been back in touch with her and asked her to come and meet for a chat. Millie had gone, widely anticipating what it could be about. It turned out Lauren wanted to open another shop in Perryn Bay, which was only half an hour from Sandyhaven. She wanted Millie to help her run it, as creative input but also on an assistant managerial role. Of course, Millie had immediately said yes and had dived headfirst into the incredible opportunity. She now worked thirty hours per week at the shop and ran mini online tutorials around various art forms on their social media pages. It meant she was able to be creative and use her skills to help others *and* be paid for it at the same time. For once in her life, she felt like everything had fallen into place with her career.

And of course, her relationship had fallen into place too. Despite only being an official couple for two months, Millie and Alfie had thrown caution to the wind and moved in together that Valentine's Day, and it had been the most wonderful four months of her entire life since. Waking up to that stunning vista from the enormous window in the living room every morning had been an absolute dream come true – even better that she got to wake up to it next to Alfie.

There had been no more heavy discussions about their future together or what it might hold – it hadn't really felt like it was needed. Ultimately, they were both incredibly happy being together as they were – Millie was finally ready to accept that whatever was going to happen, would happen and she knew she'd get through it with an incredible man by her side.

Standing on the beach bathed in warm sun, surrounded by a wonderfully supportive community, a fantastic group of welcoming new friends, eagerly awaiting the arrival of her oldest and best friend and with the arm of the most incredible man around her shoulder, Millie had truly never felt more complete in her life.

ACKNOWLEDGEMENTS

I wrote "Secrets and Surprises at Sandyhaven Bay" over a 14-year period: the opening paragraphs came at the age of 18 when I wasn't really sure where I wanted the book to go. I had a few ideas of generic "will they/won't" they storylines but knew I wanted something with a little more substance. The book was shelved and then picked back up again multiple times over the next ten years, and it was then my own experiences with fertility struggles that inspired what is now a core storyline in the book. An extremely sensitive, yet sadly very relatable experience for many people, I wanted to give it the exposure it so often doesn't get. Because whilst it's devastating, it's real life for so many and it felt important to me that their stories are also heard. This is just one of them.

My debut novel would not have been possible without the help and support of so many people and I have to thank them here now.

Firstly, to my daughter Esther. I won't lie, whilst you generally make regular writing sessions an impossibility, I found my drive to complete the novel returned after you had been born. Having you arrive in our lives after previous devastating events and years of emotional turmoil was a true blessing and I realised I needed to grab life a bit more.

I hope one day you'll read this and realise you inspired it more than you know.

To my husband, Mark. A self-confessed non-reader, you've still supported me endlessly through the big push to finish the book. From the weeks on end I'd disappear into my office after Esther went to bed and not emerge until midnight, the many times listening to my ramblings on what should happen next, to bringing me endless drinks and snacks. Thank you x

To my mum, dad and brother Jack: thank you for always supporting my ventures and showing an interest in the things I want to achieve.

To my Uncle Chris, the true writer of the family! Thank you for proof reading and making edits on this book, despite it not being your usual genre of choice. I hope the "thank you" wine went down a treat and know you did such a great job, I shall be calling on you in the future. When I grow up, I want to be a writer just like you!

To the people who read small excerpts, chapters or the full unedited manuscript to give me their thoughts, ideas and opinions: thank you. It's nerve wracking having anyone read your writing so to have you lovely people do it was exactly what I needed.

To the Romantic Novelist Association for their New Writer's Scheme. The feedback I received on my manuscript was incredible and simply the most wonderful confidence boost. It's a great scheme and I'm looking forward to rejoining as a full member once this is published!

To Molly Phipps of "We Got You Covered" book design. She is solely responsible for the absolute stunner of a front cover on this book which has received so many compliments. For also the formatting and help getting everything up and running: thank you, thank you!

To my ex-work colleague who gave me the initial "shove" to get going again after all my writing inspiration had dissipated and for buying me the infamous "writer's block." I never would have opened this document back up if it hadn't been for you.

To my wonderful friends who have listened to me harp on about this and nothing else for a very long time, your support is never taken for granted and I love you all dearly.

To my favourite authors who inspired me to even start a writing journey: Heidi Swain, Phillipa Ashley, Kiley Dubar, Sue Moorcroft, Jessica Redland, Katie Fforde and Giovanna Fletcher to name but a few.

To my beautiful county of Cornwall, particularly "The Forgotten Corner" of the Rame Peninsula. You have inspired the village of Sandyhaven Bay and the colourful characters within it and I hope to do you proud with the description our lovely home.

And finally, I can't express how truly grateful I am to you, the person reading this book. The difference between my thoughts sitting on my laptop and them being released into the world is you and your decision to read this book. I really hope you enjoy it and fall in love with the location, characters and storyline as much as I did when writing it.

ABOUT THE AUTHOR

Kate lives in Cornwall with her husband Mark, young daughter Esther and flat coated retriever Lola. Having lived in Cornwall for the majority of her life, she's taken great inspiration from the beautiful county she's called home. When she's not writing or reasoning with her toddler, she can be found running her tutoring business, reading, eating copious amounts of chocolate and wondering how to stretch 25 hours out of a day.

www.ingramcontent.com/pod-product-compliance
Ingram Content Group UK Ltd.
Pitfield, Milton Keynes, MK11 3LW, UK
UKHW040727210725
6983UKWH00039B/646